THE SILENT AND THE DEAD

by

Stephen Wheeler

Text © Stephen Wheeler

Cover photograph © Philip Moore

By the same author:

Brother Walter Mysteries:

        UNHOLY INNOCENCE
        BLOOD MOON
        DEVIL'S ACRE

Epilogue
Friday 31st October, 1986

NO-ONE saw death enter the hall. No-one heard its footfall or felt its chill breath as it passed. With every manner of malefaction already here who would notice one more?

In the middle two ancient hags cackled excitedly together, their grotesque faces hideously illuminated by the glow of ultraviolet lamps. Nearby a third witch stood seemingly in some kind of a trance. She was Winifred Jonah, and when she heard her name she turned towards the speaker shielding her eyes and squinting into the darkness.

'Who's there?' she asked. 'Who calls my name?'

They were the last words she spoke. A moment later Winifred Jonah's body lay on the ground her head having disintegrated in the full blast of a shotgun fired an inch from her face.

PART ONE

ONE

THE newspapers called her *The Caisterbury Witch*. It made a catchy headline but hardly an accurate one. Winifred Jonah wasn't a real witch any more than the gathering in the church hall was a real Sabbat despite what some of the papers tried to make out. It was an innocent Halloween party, nothing more. But they could be forgiven for exaggerating. Even the police were at a loss to describe the horror they found in the little bungalow at the end of Ethel Smyth Close. It was the reason she had to die. Her executioner used a twelve-bore shotgun although in a less scientific age she might well have been burned at the stake for what she did. Well then, perhaps *witch* wasn't such an inappropriate sobriquet after all.

She certainly didn't look much like a witch. At fifty-six Winifred Jonah was short and plump with a jolly round face and a bright welcoming smile. Her ankles were a little thin for her bulk, but they could carry her for miles without tiring – the legacy of a childhood spent on her uncle's farm. The bungalow where Winifred and her husband, Albert, lived had been their home for just four years. It was an old people's bungalow really and they were lucky to have it, according to the council, considering their age. Albert was two years younger than Winifred but it was his disability that had got them the bungalow. A year before their marriage a motorbike accident had partially crippled Albert and left him disfigured. Most specifically he was unable to father children.

Despite this the union seemed happy enough. Albert got a job in the local wood-yard and the Jonahs settled down to married life. But thirty-two years later further tragedy struck when Albert contracted spinal paralysis which left him without the use of both legs. They had to leave their flat in the middle of Caisterbury and move to the new council estate on the outskirts of town. All the streets were named after famous women and each was a cul-de-sac off Lady Astor Crescent. The names ran alphabetically the last four being Emmeline Pankhurst, Catherine Parr, Edith Sitwell and finally, furthest away, Ethel Smyth. Seventeen old people's bungalows ran round Ethel Smyth Close and Albert and Winifred moved into number nine.

Like all the bungalows in Ethel Smyth Close the Jonahs' was equipped with a sloping pathway, strategically-placed handrails and an emergency alarm button in the hall that simultaneously flashed an alert beacon on the outside of the building and sounded a buzzer in the warden's office at the entrance to the close.

Winifred was delighted with her new home. Having grown up on a farm she missed the open spaces of her youth. This wasn't the same but the open countryside was within easy reach, just across the garden fence in fact. She quickly made friends with the farmer and bought from him fresh milk and eggs and vegetables in season. For the rest, Winifred would happily trudge the three-quarters of a mile into town and lug back heavy bags of shopping, then potter about her postage-stamp garden pausing to look out across shimmering fields of wheat and barley and constantly move Albert's wheelchair from bedroom to garden to bathroom to bedroom. The bungalow was all that Winifred could have hoped for and she was quite content.

For Albert it was a prison. He hated the isolation and longed for the bustle of the town. Now completely housebound, he didn't even have the occasional passing bus to watch over the fence. His one pleasure now was his pipe which filled the bungalow with acrid yellow smoke that discoloured the wallpaper and the curtains. It was the only means he had left to impress his personality on Winifred and it was never out of his mouth.

Albert's bitterness was understandable. He was in constant pain and as the years dragged by he grew increasingly rancorous and took it out on the only person he could: Winifred. Nothing satisfied him. His wheelchair was uncomfortable, the garden too cold. He often took to his bed for days on end filling the room with pipe-smoke and refusing to open the window. His fits of temper, physical abuse and increasingly humiliating demands on Winifred made her life unbearable. In the end he would not allow her to visit her friends and he timed her shopping trips into town tipping his tea over her if she was back late.

It wasn't his fault. Winifred made allowances. But slowly the last glimmer of love she had for the man died.

Her only respite from all this was the monthly visit from her nephew. Drew was really Albert's nephew but Winifred had always treated him like the son she never had. To Albert it was yet one more reminder of his failings as a husband and he resented their close relationship refusing to come out of his room when Drew was around.

Drew and Winifred drank tea at her small kitchen table and ate the chocolates he brought her while Albert lay in his smoke-filled bedroom with the door aggressively shut.

'Why don't you leave him, Aunt Win?'

'Leave him? Oh no, I couldn't do that. Who'd look after him? How would he manage? Oh no. I couldn't leave him.'

They sat in silence munching orange creams a few feet from the bedroom door.

'Well,' said Drew getting up to leave. 'If you ever change your mind remember there's a spare room with Susan and me in Norwich.'

It was Drew who showed Winifred the advertisement from Lifeplan Assurance. It had come unsolicited with the Saturday post and he had thrown it into the rubbish bin where all the junk mail went, but on second thoughts he had retrieved it and taken it with him to Caisterbury the following Tuesday.

It seemed a good idea, almost too good to be true. Life assurance for £10 a month – they could afford that. Albert didn't even have to know about it if Winifred thought he would object. And the insurance company wasn't too bothered about medical histories. How could they lose? It would provide a nice little nest-egg after ten years. And if, God forbid, either of them should die in the meantime there would be a cash payment of nearly five thousand pounds. Not much, but what could you expect at their age?

Winifred wasn't sure. She kept the leaflet and application form in her shopping bag for three days not daring to show it to Albert. Then on the Friday she made up her mind, filled out the form and posted it on her shopping trip into Caisterbury.

A few days later the cover note arrived and Winifred quickly secreted it in among the photo albums in the kitchen drawer where she knew Albert would never find it. It would be easy to save the £2.50 a week out of her house-keeping money and Albert would be none the wiser. Wouldn't he be surprised in ten years' time when the policy matured and they'd have money in the bank for the first time in their lives? How much did Drew say they'd get? Five thousand pounds. It seemed a fortune.

Drew never thought she'd actually do it. He was both surprised and pleased the next time he visited his aunt when she silently eased open the drawer, mindfully watching the closed bedroom door, and produced the documents. She was afraid to leave them out in the open for too long in case Albert should catch her, just long enough to prove to Drew that she had done the deed. Then she whisked them away again between the yellowing folds of wedding and seaside snaps.

Drew congratulated her. It was the sensible thing to do. No-one should be without protection in this day and age. They celebrated with another pot of tea and a hazelnut cluster. Albert need never find out.

But Albert did find out. He kept a closer eye on the weekly budget than Winifred realised and he'd noticed her of late at the kitchen drawer rather too frequently and too furtively. When daily life is full of empty tedium it is the little things that attract attention. He said nothing to his wife but when she returned from the shops he was waiting for her in the kitchen billowing smoke and holding the insurance policy triumphantly in his hand.

Winifred dropped the heavy bags on the floor and drew the two halves of her coat together in despair. It was exactly the response Albert had wanted. He smiled his satisfaction, withdrew his pipe from his lips and blew a long trail of smoke towards her.

'Thought I wouldn't notice, did you? Thought I couldn't see? You can't wait for me to die, can you? You and that bloody nephew of mine. How much am I worth, eh? Well, it's not going to be that easy. I'll make you suffer the way I've had to. You won't get a penny out of me alive or dead.'

As Winifred cowered before him, Albert tore the insurance policy slowly and deliberately into pieces and threw them in Winifred's face. Then gripping his pipe between his teeth, he propelled himself out through the kitchen door.

Winifred looked at the torn fragments of the insurance policy on the floor and the walls of the kitchen seemed to close in around her. Before she knew what she was doing she had grabbed the handles of Albert's wheelchair and with a tremendous cry she heaved sending the wheelchair and its occupant careering across the hall.

It stopped abruptly against the wainscoting and Albert was flung forwards and backwards in the chair. In horrified fascination Winifred watched the back of Albert's head rising and falling convulsively, his hands silently groping at his neck.

In a stride she went to him her face contorting with fear as Albert turned his pleading eyes up at her. The impact of the wheelchair hitting the wall had sent him crashing forwards and the stem of his pipe had been rammed down his throat. Only the bowl of the pipe remained outside while around it a pool of blood welled up into his mouth and trickled down his chin. Every spasm of choking sent another spray of the hot sticky liquid over the wall in front of him.

Winifred instinctively made to remove the pipe but it was too slippery, she couldn't get a purchase. She stepped back in panic not knowing what to do as Albert continued to splutter blood. She tried again, but it was no good, the pipe was stuck fast. Winifred watched with mounting horror as the wheelchair rattled backwards and forwards and Albert's hands flayed impotently in the air. She looked desperately about her. He seemed to be reaching for something - but for what?

Then she saw it: the alarm switch. The little red button on the wall which, once depressed, would instantly sound a buzzer in the warden's office and bring her rushing to the rescue. Winifred reached out a finger to flick the button and -

Something distracted her. The sound of a child's laughter. Winifred blinked and glanced out of the window. In the sunshine a little girl was riding her tricycle up and down the pavement. She seemed so happy and carefree. Beyond her stood the bungalows on the opposite side of the street. Behind them a row of poplar trees, and beyond them were green fields. Winifred's finger continued to hover.

Then a miracle: the wheelchair was starting to move. Those useless legs that had remained immobile for so many years were slowly, almost imperceptibly, inching the chair towards the button. Another moment and Albert will reach it. Winifred blinked and looked out of the window once more. Delicately, almost without thinking, she stretched out one toe to the wheelchair and clicked on the brake. Albert thrashed wildly about trying to release it again but Winifred kept her foot firmly on the lever and her eyes tightly shut. The sound of thrashing grew ever more frantic as the wheelchair rocked under her foot. But gradually it slowed; the spluttering eased and finally it stopped altogether. When she opened her eyes again Albert's lifeless eyes stared accusingly back at her.

Realising what she had done she drew back in horror. She couldn't scream. From somewhere a memory came to her and she turned just able to push the red button before collapsing unconscious to the floor.

TWO

THE Coroner's verdict was Accidental Death. The police did have their suspicions when they found the torn fragments of the insurance policy on the floor of the kitchen, but Albert's own nephew and the warden of Ethel Smyth Close both testified to Albert's sudden and ferocious outbursts of rage. No evidence could be found to contradict Winifred's account of Albert's anger at discovering the insurance policy and hurling himself out of the kitchen in a fit of temper. The file on Albert Jonah was closed almost before it was opened.

'What will you do now, Aunt Win?' asked Drew when they returned to the empty bungalow. 'There's still that spare room in Norwich if you want it.' He didn't like to mention it so soon after the funeral but now that Albert was gone it seemed likely that the council would want to take back the bungalow. Winifred was anything but an invalid.

'You're a good boy, Drew, and don't think I'm not grateful for the offer. But Susan won't want an old hen like me clucking round her. Not with two small children to look after. Besides, I couldn't leave this bungalow, not now. It has too many memories. I'll be all right here. I'm sure I'll get used to being on my own eventually.'

She got used to it very quickly. Not giving a thought to the council she was out every day visiting the friends with whom she had lost touch over the years, walking in her beloved countryside or window shopping in the town centre. With no Albert watching her every move she could go where she pleased and stay out for as long as she liked. For the first time in her life Winifred was truly happy.

In the weeks following Albert's death there seemed no end of well-wishers calling to offer their condolences: friends of Albert's from his days in the timber-yard, none of whom had visited him once during his years as an invalid, and neighbours would pop in for coffee to hear the gruesome details of poor Albert's last moments on earth. Winifred didn't mind. She quite enjoyed the attention. There had even been a piece in the local free newspaper which included a photo of Winifred standing on her front lawn next to Albert's empty wheelchair and holding his pipe. So when she returned home one afternoon to find the warden and an unknown man with a briefcase standing on her doorstep she wasn't unduly alarmed.

'You see, Mrs Jonah, we have no option but to repossess.'

The man with the briefcase, who turned out to be from the council, was very nice, very understanding. He had waited some time before coming to see Winifred not wishing to intrude on private grief. But painful as it was he had his duty to other, more appropriate tenants. Nice euphemism that, *appropriate*. He meant another cripple, or at least a geriatric.

Winifred was devastated. 'But this is my home. I can't leave it.'

The warden tapped the table impatiently. 'Now come along, Winnie, don't be selfish. Think of all those people worse off than you. It wouldn't be fair on them for you to keep the bungalow, now would it? It's not as if you're going to be homeless. The gentleman is offering you a flat in Caisterbury. A nice modern flat just two minutes from the shops. Think of that! No more trudging up that hill with heavy shopping.'

'No more garden you mean,' she pouted. 'And a lot more noise and filth. Boys doing things up against your door at night. I know what goes on. I seen 'em.'

The man from the council glanced at his watch. He'd spent enough time on this already. 'What you have to understand, Mrs Jonah, is that these bungalows were built for the elderly infirm – pensioners - people who can't look after themselves and need the help of people like Mrs Willet here. Not sprightly youngsters like yourself.'

'I'm a pensioner,' sulked Winifred. 'I got my Albert's pension.'

'That's not the same thing, is it Winnie?' interrupted the warden shortly.

Winifred eyed the warden coldly. She would have liked to break her jaw.

'So what you're saying,' she said laboriously, 'is if I was old or crippled I could stay?'

'That's it precisely!' affirmed the man from the council relieved that the message had finally got through, and by the look of Winifred she wasn't likely to be either inside a decade.

The meeting amicably concluded, the man from the council left to discuss with the warden who the next deserving couple should be whom he could remove from his burgeoning list of applicants.

Overnight Winifred's hair turned white. She affected a slight stoop and her knees developed early signs of osteo-arthritis.

To be fair, such a sudden deterioration in the health of the newly-bereaved is not uncommon. It's psychosomatic. Winifred was blaming herself for her husband's death, irrational though that might be, and her illness was her way of punishing herself. That, at least, was the opinion of her GP who arranged for Winifred a walking-stick, home help twice a week, and a course of physiotherapy treatment at Caisterbury's cottage hospital.

The next time the man from the council came he thought the door had been opened by Winifred's mother. She looked twenty years older and much frailer than when he'd last seen her. She moved slowly with the aid of a stick, and her voice had grown weak and pathetic. As a final touch Winifred had acquired a cat, a large fluffy white thing, which she cradled in her arms as if it were the last friend she had in the world. Its very colour seemed to mirror Winifred's own rapidly advancing decrepitude.

The man from the council sighed philosophically. Under the circumstances perhaps it would be best if things remained as they were - for the time being at least. Inwardly he groaned at the thought of having to explain to the elderly couple he had spoken to that morning why they would not now be getting the bungalow in Ethel Smyth Close.

Once she had closed the street door Winifred straightened up, propped her walking-stick against the wall and carried the cat into the kitchen for a well-deserved saucer of milk.

The cheque from Lifeplan Assurance arrived pretty quickly, all things considered. A copy of Albert's death certificate and a transcript of the Coroner's report had been sent off and payment arrived by post at the end of February. Drew opened an account for his aunt at the Caisterbury branch of his own bank and showed her how to write out cheques.

'I'll be able to come and visit you now,' she chuckled. 'On the bus, when the weather's fine.'

Drew wasn't so sure. 'You take it easy, Aunt Win. We don't want you falling down on the bus with your bad knees.'

'Oh, don't you worry about that. I put it on a bit for the warden's sake. My old knees aren't so bad.'

Drew had to laugh at that. He didn't blame Winifred for "laying on the agony" as she called it. Her secret was safe with him. Besides, she wasn't getting any younger and she might genuinely need the bungalow soon.

Winifred became serious for a moment. 'Drew, I want you to have some of the money.'

He was shocked. 'Oh no, Aunt Win. I couldn't possibly do that. It's your money.'

'I know, but I want you to. You have the little one to consider now. It'll do you far more good than it will me. I don't need it all, just enough to do this place up a bit. Goodness, five thousand pounds! It's a fortune! Besides, you deserve it. I wouldn't have it at all if it wasn't for you.'

Drew protested as any dutiful nephew would, but in the end he saw the logic of what she was saying. Truth to tell, he could do with the money what with the new baby and Susan having to give up work. And he might now be able to put the down-payment on that new van he'd been hoping to buy for work. Yes, a couple of thousand could make all the difference in the world. A loan, then, just until he got on his feet. And in the meantime if Winifred should need it back for any reason, any reason at all, she had only to say.

That settled it. Winifred sat down at the kitchen table to write her very first cheque made out to *Andrew Cattermole Esq*, for the sum of *Two thousand pounds*, and signed at the bottom *Winifred Jonah (Mrs)*.

'Things will get better for you now, Aunt Win, I know they will,' said Drew folding the cheque and putting it in his pocket. He sat down opposite her and took her hand in his. 'It's terrible what happened to Uncle Albert, something you wouldn't wish on your worst enemy. But he did lead you a dog's life towards the end.'

'He was in a lot of pain, Drew, that's what you have to remember. And being stuck in that wheelchair all day long, he was a prisoner in his own home. It can't have been easy for him.'

'I know he was my uncle, but you were the one who was the prisoner, Aunt Win.'

'Well, that's all over now,' said Winifred with a wan smile.

March was as bright and warm as February had been bleak and cold. The clocks went forward bringing closer by one hour the moment when Winifred's world would explode. But she couldn't know that, of course. If she had she might well have taken Albert's old shotgun from its place on the sitting-room wall and broken it into pieces, or at least hidden it away. As it was, she did take down the gun, along with the framed pictures and the willow-pattern plates, just long enough for the decorators to cover the old nicotine stains with a bright flowery wallpaper. When she put the pictures back she hung one, of a little boy with a tear in his eye, over the red alarm button in the hall. She didn't really need the alarm and it was an unpleasant reminder. In the sitting-room the shotgun was replaced on the two hooks from where it had been removed and Winifred turned her attention to the curtains.

Decorating the bungalow at the top of Ethel Smyth Close was another mistake of Winifred's, along with replacing the shotgun on the wall and hiding the alarm button that would later contribute to tragedy. Not content with new wallpaper and new curtains Winifred bought another suite of furniture, albeit second-hand, and had the exterior woodwork, doors and windows, also re-painted. This last was an unnecessary extravagance. The council would have gotten round to redecorating the outside of the bungalow eventually. But Winifred had the money, now diminishing rapidly, and she wanted a fresh start. Mrs Willet wasn't very pleased, though. Tenants were not supposed to touch the outside paintwork, and now the bright red door and gleaming white window sills of number nine contrasted severely with the peeling greens and creams of the other sixteen bungalows in Ethel Smyth Close. By the end of April the decorating was finished and the workmen gone. Winifred was delighted with the result and settled contentedly into her new life.

Being an invalid was not without its drawbacks, however. She had to be careful not to give the game away. No more popping into town on the spur of the moment for some forgotten item. Shopping trips had to be carefully planned making extensive use of the local taxi service, the cost of which was an irritating but necessary extravagance. And no more strolls in the countryside - at least, not until she was well out of sight of the ever-watchful Mrs Willet. And when she did go out she had to remember to take her walking-stick with her. But once inside the bungalow there was no need to pretend. Behind the thick net curtains she was invisible to prying eyes. There she would sing and dance a little jig holding out her skirts and tippy-toeing across the sitting-room floor until she collapsed exhausted and laughing beside the cat on her new sofa.

But there were benefits, too. She quite enjoyed her weekly visits to the hospital and soon made new friends among the other patients at the physiotherapy clinic. Mrs Goffe, the home help, collected her pension and did her shopping on Tuesdays and Thursdays and was supposed to clean the bungalow for her. What Mrs Goffe actually did from nine-thirty to ten o'clock was to make Winifred's bed and run the vacuum cleaner sparingly over the floor. To Winifred this was a complete waste of time and she set about her own domestic routine as soon as Mrs Goffe was out the door. But it did give her something to moan about to Brian, the ambulance driver, when he came to collect her for her regular Thursday appointment:

'She flew in, flew round, and flew out,' guffawed Winifred horsily.

Brian wasn't interested. He had his own schedule to keep to and was relieved that he didn't have to wait for the home help to finish before he could bundle Winifred onto the ambulance. He stood in the sitting-room holding Winifred's grey overcoat for her while she laboriously eased her arms into the sleeves.

'She flew in, flew round, and flew out,' repeated Winifred more gravely.

'Did she?' Brian laughed not wanting to be delayed by chatter, but added, 'It all looks very nice in here.'

That was what Winifred wanted to hear and she accepted the proffered walking-stick and allowed herself to be gently coaxed into the hall. She paused by the tray of cat litter near the kitchen door. 'You haven't let my cat out, have you?' Her voice was as laboured as her gait.

'No,' said Brian with the practised patience of his profession. 'I haven't let your cat out.' Brian didn't like cats. They made him sneeze, especially big furry ones like Winifred's. He also wanted to tell her that it made the bungalow smell. Instead, he puckered up his nose behind Winifred's back and grimaced silently to himself.

Outside in the fresh spring air Winifred stopped again as she fumbled in her coat pocket to pull out the clean, man-sized handkerchief that had been Albert's and which she had knotted through the front door key. Brian took the key and quickly turned to lock and test the door noisily as Winfred inched her way along the path towards the ambulance. Brian opened the back doors to a chorus of welcoming voices.

'Good morning, Winnie,' articulated Martha Hodge carefully from the seat nearest the doors.

'Dear-oh-dear-oh-dear,' chuckled George Smith, an elderly Scotsman with a deerstalker hat.

'I'm not the first, then?' beamed Winifred to no-one in particular as she took Brian's arm and heaved her bulk up the steps. Brian in his dark blue uniform and peeked cap helped Winifred to her seat then he handed her back her front door key.

'Ooh!' screamed Sadie Collins, a cockney Jewish woman with a wart on the very tip of her nose. 'We didn't get that treatment when we got on. What've you got that we 'aven't?' She elbowed George Smith in the ribs and cackled.

'Dear-oh-dear,' murmured George Smith painfully holding his side.

'I thought I'd be the first,' grinned Winifred as Martha Hodge shuffled up to give her some room.

Brian just smiled in the general direction of nobody in particular, closed the back doors and drove the ambulance slowly out of Ethel Smyth Close towards the hospital. It was the beginning of a journey that would end six months later with four violent deaths and spread the name of Winifred Jonah across the front pages of every newspaper in the land.

THREE

THE offices of Lifeplan Assurance (UK) Ltd were three rooms above a pedestrian precinct in an inner suburb of Norwich. It was one of those concrete developments artfully textured to resemble timber but fooled nobody. It had walkways above street level, a car park below, and corridors of shopping arcades cunningly orientated so as to funnel every piece of waste paper along them in a force seven gale that never ceased blowing even on the calmest days.

Lifeplan was a minor subsidiary of a giant American Corporation registered, for tax purposes, in the Cayman Islands. All the office staff were English. There were three of these: Giles Slaker, the middle-aged and suave managing director who was never in his office; Paul Kerney, the young and athletic sales director who was never out of his. And Marcia.

Marcia – that's Mar-*see*-ah, not Mar-*sha* – Pike was blonde, blushing and bosomy. She had never really got to grips with the finer tuning of Women's Lib, but then at eighteen Marcia had not yet had to. She enjoyed the saucy attentiveness of Giles Slaker and disdained the curt officiousness of Mr Kerney. She blended impeccably with the decor of the outer office which was also the reception area and her demesne. The carpet was cream shag-pile, the curtains cream Hessian, the wallpaper was cream anaglypta, and the visitors' chairs cream mock-leather.

There hadn't been too many of these, visitors that is, in the three months that Marcia had been Lifeplan's receptionist-cum-secretary. In fact, there hadn't been any unless you counted Lifeplan's own sales reps, which Marcia didn't. Most of these were male and middle-aged and Marcia had seen them all at one time or another passing through her office on their way to Mr Kerney's. They'd all, more or less, tried to flirt with her, not that Marcia took any notice. Most didn't stay long enough for Marcia to get to know them except over the telephone. One, maybe two, visits to the office and she'd never see them again.

That was a pity in Marcia's view because she liked the Company and she enjoyed her job. There wasn't much to her job. She oversaw three filing cabinets but she wasn't entrusted with the keys to any of these and only vaguely understood that they contained the files on Lifeplan's clients. Her day consisted chiefly of making coffee, opening the mail, typing letters and answering the telephone. Nearly all the calls were from Lifeplan's sales reps who generally rang from telephone boxes dispersed around East Anglia. Much of the time the message on the little pink sticker stuck to the front of her cream telephone was superfluous: *Does your voice SMILE?* Not to sales reps it doesn't!

The telephone warbled and Marcia swivelled her chair, put down her compact and lifted the handset.

'Good morning-Lifeplan Assurance-how may I help you?'

She dropped the pencil that was poised in her cherry-tipped fingers and slumped bosom-first on to the desk.

'Oh, it's you. And don't call me *Marsh;* I'm not a blooming duck-pond.'

She glanced across at Paul Kerney's door.

'Yes he is in, but if I were you I wouldn't want speak to him *just* at the moment. He's not in a very good mood *and* he's been on about sales figures again. So unless you've got some *good* news for him...?'

She smiled knowingly at the reply.

'Thought not. Well, you'll just have to try a little bit harder won't you, Pet. Byeeee.'

Marcia replaced the receiver and went back to contemplating her eyebrows.

The caller had been Colin Brearney. Of all the Lifeplan reps Colin had stuck it the longest, more than a year now. As such he had been in to the Norwich office half a dozen times since Marcia started working there, and although he had "tried it on" as she contemptuously dismissed his approaches, she hadn't entirely discouraged him. She'd even been out with him – once, never to be repeated. Her idea of a Saturday night out didn't include having her tits groped on a crowded disco floor no matter how low-cut her dress or how provocatively they bounced, unrestrained by underwear, a few inches from his nose. At least, not until he had been home to tea with her mum and dad at least twice. Colin had taken liberties and she was punishing him for it.

In spite of this, she still had a soft spot for Colin. Unlike most of the other reps he was only slightly older than she was and not bad looking in an immature-sort-of way. For all his bravado there was something vulnerable about Colin. He made her think of little furry creatures with big, mournful eyes. Maybe that was what appealed about him. It brought out the maternal instinct in Marcia and made her want to - well, *cuddle* him.

All the time he had been speaking to Marcia Colin had been bobbing around inside the callbox. Or rather, he bobbed when he was doing the speaking. It was a curious mannerism and comical to observe: right hand clutching receiver and left hand in trouser pocket, his knees flexed with every word. In his creased and ill-fitting suit he was a fair-ground puppet that had lost its strings.

Despite his awkward appearance, Colin did have one surmounting asset – or rather, two. Twenty-one years earlier at his birth, the midwife had been the first to notice that he possessed the most beautiful and arresting eyes. Between bouts of crying they would open and instantly draw her to him. Perfectly-formed almonds, clear and the deepest brown, their magnetism was irresistible.

Colin never had any doubts about their effect. Even as a small boy he had been able to get away with things that would have sent his older sister, Helen, to her room without her supper. But Colin only had to fix his mother with his doleful stare and she would forgive him anything. Young or old, male or female, no-one was immune to the spell. Lifting the seven-year-old Colin in her arms one day, his aunt had gazed into the liquid brown pools and declared to his mother: 'Those eyes are going to break some hearts, Muriel.' And on another occasion: 'One day someone's going to kill for those eyes.' It was what attracted Marcia to him and what would once again ingratiate him with Paul Kerney the next time he visited the office. But on the telephone he was sightless, so he had declined to speak to his boss just as Marcia guessed he would, and replaced the handset.

It was one of those curious twists of fate that Winifred Jonah's ambulance should be turning into the hospital just as Colin was stepping out of the callbox. They had not yet met and were not to do so for another two months, so Colin stopped at the edge of the pavement and waited for the ambulance to pass before crossing the road and entering the café on the opposite side.

Over a frothy coffee and cheese roll Colin contemplated his next move. He was by now thoroughly disillusioned with his job. Being that much younger than the majority of Lifeplan reps, he had only gradually woken up to the confidence trick that had been played on him. The recruitment drive had been brilliantly orchestrated. Twenty of them had been put up for three days in a hotel with all expenses paid. The course had been intensive with daily lectures, films and slide shows, study groups, projects, seminars, all directed by the energetic Paul Kerney and designed to whip up the latent energy and drive that the American parent company knew would propel Lifeplan into the very vanguard of Britain's insurance broking community. The stuffy old-school-tie image of established British insurance houses was to be brushed aside, the cobwebs blown away and a new entrepreneurial dynamism instilled. And the shock-troops of this aggressive new assault were to be Lifeplan's sales-force. Only those with the conviction and will to succeed would still be with the Company in ten years time, only the best. Many would be called but few would be chosen.

It had worked. Colin was hooked. He knew he would be one of The Chosen Few. 'In order to succeed in this business you will have to eat, drink, breathe and sleep Lifeplan!' extolled Paul Kerney, the very epitome of the young, successful businessman, and Colin set about imitating him in style and fervour.

That's a bit difficult riding around country towns and villages on the back of a motor-scooter. It's not so much the image – scooters were very much in vogue with certain sections of the youth generation. But how many high-flying executives conclude world-shattering business deals then don a crash helmet and ride off astride a Lambretta Li125? Colin was always careful to park his scooter some distance from the house he was to visit so that his intended customers didn't see it. But even so, he could not help getting his suit crumpled or wind-swept or muddy or greasy or wet, and that did not create the right image at all. Whether this was the reason he was less than successful at selling life insurance than he had hoped it certainly didn't help. He had intended buying a car with his first few months pay-cheques, but somehow he'd never earned the promised bonanza so enticingly detailed on the training course. In fact, he'd never even got close.

'A good Lifeplan salesman,' Paul Kerney had told them, 'could earn as much as £30,000 a year', and that when the average wage was less than half that amount. And what did he have to do to achieve that exalted figure? Sign just one new customer per month aged twenty-seven or under, at two percent commission plus a ten percent bonus if twelve are sold in the same year and - Bingo! Gross earnings of £28,748. Colin had worked it out on his cigarette packet and smiled wryly as he glanced around at the other nineteen candidates in the hotel conference room. One of them, an old hack named O'Donnelly, had leaned across to Colin and whispered, 'Nothing succeeds like a budgie without a beak,' and grinned. Colin had thought about that, caught the sardonic nuance but wasn't sure he entirely understood it.

Anyway, for whatever reason, he never achieved the twelve new commissions in his first year. He could only manage nine which meant he lost the bonus straight away. Worse, the average age of his new clients was closer to fifty-seven than twenty-seven which slashed his commission rate and reduced his gross earnings for the financial year to a paltry £2,600. And for that he'd had to work seven days a week for up to twelve hours a day.

Colin was appalled. He simply could not understand why people in the prime of life were not interested in buying life insurance. How could they be so short-sighted? Even so, he did better than many of his colleagues most of whom left within a few months to be replaced by a fresh batch of hopefuls. And he could forget about buying that new car, he was already behind on the hire-purchase repayments for the Lambretta. He'd even borrowed the money for the deposit from

Lifeplan themselves, on an interest-free basis, which was steadily being deducted from his wages each week. Some weeks he seemed to be earning five pounds in order to pay back ten. It was a vicious money merry-go-round that was spiralling out of control.

It had to stop. But how? He couldn't afford to carry on working for Lifeplan but until his loan was paid off he couldn't leave either. Some other drastic solution had to be found, and as he parted and re-parted the froth on his coffee so a plan began to form behind his deep, seductive eyes.

Insurance fraud is a crime which, because it is regarded as largely victimless, few people have qualms about committing. Who hasn't been tempted to accidentally drop a dicky television set on the floor and claim for a replacement; or throw an extra bucket of water over the carpet when the hot water tank leaks? However seemingly innocuous, it is still a cost to the insurance companies who spend a great deal of time and effort trying to combat it. In this Lifeplan was no exception. In fact, an entire afternoon of Colin's training course had been devoted to the subject. And not just fraud perpetrated by clients: cheating by Lifeplan's own employees was just as big a nuisance for the company. In this, sales reps were undoubtedly the worst offenders - a fact of which Lifeplan were well aware. Indeed, they seemed almost to expect it. But Paul Kerney's message to the trainees was loud and clear: 'Try it at your peril because you will get caught, and when you are you will feel the full weight of the law come down heavily upon your head because fraud is theft, and Lifeplan *always* prosecutes thieves'.

But did they? Despite his insistence that Lifeplan always pursued dishonest sales reps, Paul Kerney hadn't been able to give a single instance where they had done so even when pressed by the sceptical O'Donnelly. Clients, yes - Kerney was more than happy to give examples of successful convictions of clients. But not staff. And why not? Because, said O'Donnelly with a triumphant smirk, the publicity would destroy them. What, he asked, his Irish brogue giving a mocking edge to the rhetorical question, was an insurance company's single most important asset? He glanced around the room expectantly but answer came there none. So he answered the question himself: Why, *Trust* of course. Without Trust no insurance business was worth a tinker's cuss. Prosecuting their own staff would be tantamount to Lifeplan admitting they employed crooks and no-one would trust them ever again. No, no, no, he insisted, the worst a dishonest sales rep could expect was to be quietly sacked with the least fuss possible. Lifeplan wouldn't dare risk the publicity of a court case. Thus spake the worldly-wise O'Donnelly, and from the almost apoplectic expression on Paul Kerney's face Colin had no doubt that O'Donnelly was right.

He was a clever bastard that O'Donnelly. After the session Colin sought him out and quizzed him further on the pretext of wanting to learn the pitfalls of the job. But O'Donnelly was no more fooled by Colin's pretence at guile than he had by Paul Kerney's.

'Got a scam of your own now, is it?' he grinned.

Colin's blushes answered that question. O'Donnelly had laughed, then lowered his voice.

'The key word, lad, is *greed*. If you're going to filch do it in moderation. That's where them there great train robbers went wrong.'

'That wasn't an insurance swindle,' Colin objected.

'Same principle. They pushed their luck. Upset too many people. Now all but one of 'em is behind bars. And all because of greed.'

Over the following months Colin found himself having cause to think more and more about O'Donnelly's words. Sales reps came and went - O'Donnelly among them, Colin was sad to see. But there was never any mention of criminal prosecution. They were simply there one day and gone the next, just as O'Donnelly had foretold. Naturally it would be a different matter if millions of pounds were involved. But Colin didn't want millions, just enough to pay off his debts, plus maybe a little bit left over. For O'Donnelly had been right about one other thing: Colin did indeed have a scam of his own.

Colin was no newcomer to deceit. In fact, in practically every job he'd had since leaving school he'd been on to one dodge or another. His first had been a Saturday job as a sales assistant in his local Woolworths. Here he quickly learnt how to fiddle the tills. It wasn't difficult. Practically everyone was at it – on the wages they paid it was difficult not to be. It even had an official name: shrinkage, although among sales staff it was better known as The Game. Naturally, all the supervisors knew it went on since they had once been sales assistants themselves. The risk was worth taking because a sales assistant could double his wage over the week. So long as the losses never went above two percent of sales the manager never bothered to investigate, and the police were rarely involved. Anyone caught would simply be sacked, not this time for fear of losing trust with their customers but simply because the sums involved were so petty it wasn't worth the manager's while – and because he and the chief clerk were running a bigger scam of their own out the back door.

But this new dodge was a little more adventurous. An idea that had occurred to him fairly early on in his career with Lifeplan and one that, as far as he could see, was completely foolproof. And if it worked, Lifeplan wouldn't even know the money was missing. In a sense it was only what Lifeplan owed him. After all, hadn't they perpetrated a sort of fraud of their own on him, luring him into working for them with false promises if riches and then putting him in hock to them so that it was impossible for him to leave? No, O'Donnelly needn't have worried. Colin wasn't being greedy. He just wanted what was his due. He wasn't sure he'd have the nerve to go through with it, but there was no harm in daydreaming. And at night he lay awake unable to sleep for thinking about it.

Just supposing he did do it? He would have to disappear afterwards, for even if he didn't think the police would get involved he wasn't prepared to take the risk. He'd always fancied going to London. It was easy to get lost there. And once Lifeplan realised he'd disappeared they'd be only too happy to leave him that way. As O'Donnelly said, there'd be no advantage in courting adverse publicity, certainly not over the miniscule amounts of money he was thinking of. Then when the fuss had died down set himself up and start a new life in the capital.

His mother would have to be told. She'd kick up quite a fuss if he were to suddenly disappear with no explanation. Not the truth, of course. He'd spin her some yarn about being offered a better job somewhere, a big promotion, something like that. She'd believe it. Muriel would believe anything he told her.

Then there was Marcia. She was a bit trickier. She couldn't know the truth either, but without her help the whole game wasn't going to get off the starting line. She might even refuse to help him in which case that would be that, it wouldn't be his fault. At the least he would have tried. Yes, Marcia was his first problem. If he was going to do it, that is. But it wouldn't hurt to plan and see how far he could get.

Having come to a decision he was at last able to relax. The illuminated clock face next to his bed told him it was nearly four o'clock in the morning. His eyes began to swim and as they finally closed the letters of Marcia's name burst like extinguishing light-bulbs before them.

FOUR

HE waylaid Marcia on her way home from work the following evening.

'Oh Colin, you made me jump!' she said spreading five cherry-topped fingers across her ample bosom. 'What are you doing hiding in that doorway?'

Colin glanced up the street towards the Lifeplan offices and tugged Marcia gently but firmly into the shadows.

'What are you up to?' she said trying to pull away. 'No, Colin, stop it!'

'It's all right', he said letting her go. 'Don't panic. I just thought you might fancy a drink, that's all. An after-work drink. You know – *after work?* It is Friday night, for God's sake.'

'Funny way of asking,' she said pulling her coat together. 'Anyway, I can't. If I'm home late my mum worries. Besides, it's fish-and-chip night. She'll have it ready for me.'

Colin was nervously fumbling the change in his trouser pocket. 'I thought you might like to try somewhere new that's just opened. It's a café-wine bar just opened up the road.'

Marcia curled up her nose in distaste. 'What's that?'

'It's very trendy. They serve food and wine. But we don't have to eat anything,' he added hastily.' Unless you want. Of course. I thought we'd just have a drink, see what it's like. We don't have to stay long.'

'Huh! I know what you're like, Colin Brearney. One drink and you're an animal.'

Colin put up an apologetic hand. 'I promise I'll behave.'

She eyed him suspiciously and looked up the road for hr bus. 'I don't know. I really ought to get home.'

'Just have the one. If you don't like it we can leave and I'll even walk you to your bus-stop. Can't say fairer than that, can I?'

Marcia demurred. 'Just one, then.'

Just one it was - a bottle, but still expensive in the pine-and-potted cellar of the former Grapes public house.

'Cold in here,' said Marcia shivering in her fox-fur.

'You can't be cold with that dead animal round your neck,' said Colin putting two glasses and a bottle of rosé down on the wooden table and pouring.

Marcia picked thoughtfully at a buttonhole. 'It's not real. I couldn't. Not as good, though.'

It was still early evening. The place was empty apart from a party of four sitting at the next table and eating something pale and steamy that Marcia couldn't put a name to. The sound of chatter was mixed with the scraping of cutlery against porcelain. At the bar a slim, young, handsome, Spanish-looking waiter stood reading a newspaper. She blinked her long eyelashes at him. He didn't seem to notice.

'Marcia -' Colin began thoughtfully.

'No,' said Marcia firmly, and sipped her wine.

Colin looked up. 'What do you mean, "No"? I haven't asked you yet.'

'Whatever it is you want, the answer's no.'

'How do you know I want anything?'

Marcia smiled. 'I know you reps. This is what you do with your clients, isn't it? Take them out for a meal, ply them with cheap drink, then try to sell them a policy.'

'*Cheap?*' Colin nearly choked on his wine. 'Have you seen the prices in here?'

But Marcia would not be deterred. 'It won't work, Colin. I don't need any life insurance. You're wasting your time.' She opened the small, grey, snake-skin clutch-bag she had brought with her, took out a compact mirror and started to fiddle with the mascara on one of her eye-lashes.

Marcia was enjoying herself. It wasn't often one of the Lifeplan reps wanted something from her, other than what men usually wanted from her. Whatever it was Colin wanted he wasn't going to get it, but she may as well get what she could out of him until he realised the fact. She held out her glass for a refill.

'I'm not trying to sell you life insurance, you silly cow,' he said pouring from the bottle.

She looked at him sharply. 'If you're going to get insulting -' She dropped the mirror back in the bag and snapped it shut with a resolute *click!*

'Sorry. Sorry. Don't go yet.'

Marcia blinked, looked into those deep brown pools of his. Images of puppy dogs came into her mind.

'Idiot!'

She slapped his arm and looked again for the Spanish waiter. Now he was standing with his back to her drying some glasses on a tea-towel. Marcia sighed wistfully.

'No, but seriously,' said Colin trying again and moving the glass bowl with the candle in it out of the way. 'There is something you can get for me.'

'Oh? What?'

'Nothing difficult. A few names and addresses, that's all.'

She stared hard at him for several long moments then burst into peals of laughter holding her hand over her mouth. The people on the table next to them momentarily stopped their scraping and turned to look.

'What's so funny?' said Colin looking around in dismay.

'You are! You really want me to steal for you?'

'Not *steal*,' frowned Colin, irritably. 'Just - *borrow*, that's all.'

'Oh?' she mocked. 'And how exactly do I *borrow* names?' She clucked at the balding, ginger young man sitting behind her who blushed and lowered his head.

'Keep your voice down,' said Colin. He glanced at the waiter who was back at the bar reading his newspaper again.

Undeterred, Marcia opened her clutch bag again and withdrew a packet of menthol cigarettes one of which she delicately plucked with her blood-red fingernails and sat blinking heavily at Colin with it poised between them. Colin grabbed at the glass candle-holder and held it out for Marcia to place the tip of the cigarette into the flame. She inhaled deeply and blew a long stream of smoke high into the air, then rather ruined the effect by having a coughing fit.

'You must think I was born yesterday,' she spluttered inspecting the end of the cigarette critically. 'Do you really think I'm going to *steal* Lifeplan clients from other reps to give to you? I should cocoa!'

He lowered his voice. 'I told you, it's not *stealing*. These are *ex*-Lifeplan clients. Clients that have already had their payouts. Financially, they're finished with. The other reps don't need them any more.'

'Then why don't you use your own?'

'I haven't got enough. Like I said, I need about a dozen. It's business - you wouldn't understand,' he said pouring himself another glass of wine.

'Sounds like *fishy* business to me. Colin Brearney, I'm surprised at you. Some of the other reps, yes, but not you.' She narrowed her eyes at him and puffed expressively on her cigarette. 'I bet Paul Kerney wouldn't approve of your *business*.'

'He won't know about it. Not if you get the names while he's out of the office.'

'Well that settles that, then,' said Marcia decisively. 'Kerney never leaves his office.'

'Of course he does. Even he has to go to the bog sometimes,' said Colin with exasperation. 'Unless he's God Almighty.'

'He certainly thinks he is,' snorted Marcia tapping the end of her cigarette into the ash-tray. 'Anyway, it's not just that. I don't have a key to the filing cabinets.'

Colin frowned, fiddled with the candle-holder then said quietly, 'There's a spare set in

Slaker's office, top right-hand drawer of his desk.'

Marcia's jaw dropped and her eyes widened. 'How do you know that?' She looked about her nervously, then frowned. 'Have you been into Giles's office?'

Colin waved his hand, 'Of course I haven't. I just know that's all.'

Actually it was O'Donnelly told him abut the spare keys, but he wasn't going to tell Marcia that. Better she thought he was the clever one.

'Look, will you help me or not? I need to know, because if you won't I'll have to do it myself.'

'Don't you dare!' she warned sitting back. 'I mean it, Colin.'

'Then help me. Look, you won't have to do anything. Just give me the nod when Kerney and Slaker are both out of the office.'

She grimaced. 'I don't know. They'll know it's me.'

'Not if you're out of the office as well. Go and powder your nose or something.'

Marcia said in a whining voice, 'Oh Colin, please don't. It's far too dangerous. They're bound to find out and then they'll question me. I'm no good at lying. You know what Kerney's like. He can get blood out of a stone.'

He sat back with his arm over the back of his seat. 'All right. I'll do it while you're there. And then if I get caught they'll definitely know it's you helped me.'

'You wouldn't.'

'Try me.'

'I'll tell.'

'And I'll tell about our little *tête-à-tête* here tonight and say we planned it together.'

'Christ, you're a shit, Colin Brearney!' She turned away from him, stubbed out her cigarette and immediately lit another puffing an enormous cloud of smoke over everything.

So engrossed had they been in their discussion that neither of them had noticed the party on the next table whose disapproving glances had been increasing in frequency and insistence in the past ten minutes. Not that they had been eaves-dropping. No, it wasn't the subject of Colin and Marcia's conversation that made the rather large, middle-aged woman in the flowery dress choose that moment to turn round in her seat and glare pointedly at the silly over-made-up girl with the cheap fur coat, lurid red nail-varnish and far too much thigh.

'Do you mind?' she boomed.

Marcia jumped as the woman entered the little world of her mind and waved away the smoke. She tried to focus on the woman's face. 'Pardon?'

The woman boomed again: 'My friends and I are eating.'

Marcia couldn't argue with that, she could see they were eating. She gave a little cross-eyed smile.

'Take no notice,' said Colin.

'Would you mind your own business?' bellowed the woman, laboriously turning in her seat to face him. Her companions, two men and a woman, looked down at their plates trying to hide among the debris of their meal.

'We are minding our business,' said Colin growing angry. 'Why don't you mind yours?'

'There is nothing we'd like better, as soon as your friend has put that filthy thing out!'

Marcia sat bewildered by the exchange and looked cross-eyed at the stumpy freckled finger that was pointing straight at her nose. She understood, roughly, that she was the centre of a controversy and that Colin was defending her – as he should, being the man. But she still hadn't grasped what the problem was. So she removed the cigarette from her lips and puffed out yet another stream of the offending smoke, this time straight at the plump woman.

It seemed to ignite her. Her jaw set and she looked with incredulity at her companions. Then muttering something about giving the little tart a taste of her own medicine, the woman heaved back her chair, rose to her feet and moved menacingly toward Marcia. What happened next Marcia could scarcely believe. The woman turned around, bent over and farted noisily into Marcia's face.

Marcia screamed, jumped up and fled up the stairs not stopping until she got to the street. Colin joined her a few moments later rather suddenly and rather forcefully ejected by the Spanish waiter. Colin made a move as if to try to get back in again but stopped at the threshold glaring at the waiter who made a Latinate gesture with his hand and let the glass door slam shut.

'Moron!' shouted Colin angrily and gave the door a sharp kick. He turned to Marcia who was cowering against the wall.

'Come on!' he barked, and strode off down the street.

Marcia followed a few paces behind trying to keep up with her quick little steps. She was still confused over what had just happened.

'What did I do?' she whispered.

'Nothing!'

'Well I must have done something. That woman looked as though she could kill me.'

'I could have killed *her*,' snarled Colin.

They marched on round the corner eventually Marcia managing to catch him up. She grabbed his arm and spun him round.

'*Colin!* What did you do that made that waiter throw you out?'

He hung his head. 'I pissed on her food,' he muttered.

'You what?' Marcia held her hand over her mouth. 'Colin! You never did!'

'Well, she did that to you.'

Marcia thought about it then started to giggle, the wine and the cold air at last having their effect. 'Probably improved the flavour,' she managed. 'All that steamy putty stuff.'

That made Colin giggle, too. 'You should have seen her face! She couldn't believe what was happening.'

'Oh Colin, we'll never be allowed in that place again.'

'Their loss, not ours,' said Colin waving his arm. 'Lot of toffee-nosed tossers. Did you see that balding ginger burke with her?'

Marcia nodded enthusiastically. '*And* that waiter was queer,' she said collapsing onto his arm.

43

They staggered down towards the bus-stop still holding each other up. Suddenly they were no longer adults but children again and they had played a great game.

They were still laughing when Marcia's bus arrived. Colin stood on the pavement as she carefully mounted the platform. She looked along the bus at the two rows of blank commuter faces and started giggling again. The conductor dinged the bell twice and the bus slowly started to move off.

'What do you think?' Colin called out after it.

She knew what he meant. She took another look at the passengers then pulled a face for only Colin to see. 'Ring me tomorrow at the office.'

Colin blew her a kiss and waited on the pavement until the bus had turned the corner, then Colin screwed his neck into his collar and punched the air.

'Yes!'

A light compulsive breeze lifted and propelled him down the hill to where he had parked his scooter.

FIVE

WINIFRED woke early most mornings. It was a habit she'd started fifty years earlier when it had been her job to help with the first milking of the day on her uncle's farm. Old habits die hard. It wasn't uncommon even now for her to wake some mornings before it was light ready to tumble out of bed and pull on trousers, layers of cardigans, rubber boots, and stagger bleary-eyed out into the yard to find buckets and cloths. On mornings like that she'd realise after the initial impulse that it was just a trick of the mind and she would lie back in the darkened bedroom for another ten minutes, blinking at the ceiling, and then get up.

    This morning, however, it wasn't the cows that wakened her - it was Albert. In those minutes of half-consciousness between sleeping and waking she could feel him lying next to her and began to stir herself for the familiar ritual of making the tea, sitting him up, washing him and then putting him in his wheelchair. She would do all that in a short while. Just a few more minutes to luxuriate in the warmth of the bed. But before those minutes had elapsed she'd remembered that Albert wasn't there anymore. As if the prove it to herself, she put out her hand to feel the cold, flat sheets where he used to lie. Winifred still found that she could sleep only on her side of the bed – another habit, formed this time over thirty-six years of married life, that wasn't going to fade after three months.

Three months. Was that all it had been since Albert's death? She counted them in her head and with the fingers of one hand tapping lightly on the mattress starting with the month he had died: February, then March, April and now May. Three months and four days. For three months and four days Albert had lain, not in this bed next to her, but in his grave in Caisterbury cemetery. In all that while Winifred had hardly had time to think about him. She certainly hadn't dreamt about him before. So why today, she wondered? But then, that was how it had been the first time, hadn't it? When the dreams had first begun. Could it have been as much as three months that time? The doctors had told her that the dreams would fade after a while and that she should try not to remember them. They had indeed faded just as the doctors said they would. But never completely. Even now, four decades on, they returned when she least expected them.

Her uncle's farm had been a small one, barely forty acres put mostly to corn with a few milking cows. It had always been a poor farm, too small to attract the kind of grants that the Government were handing out to boost food production after the War. So it was stuck in the old ways relying on draught animals for the heavy work and human labour for everything else. Life was hard but young Winifred accepted her lot with alacrity, as young people will, since she knew nothing else. The farm being so isolated, Winifred knew very few people other than her aunt and uncle, but she never felt lonely - there was always too much to do: milking cows, scaring birds, making butter, winnowing, threshing, hoeing. It was only when she was old enough to go to school did she begin to mix with other children, and even then she was constantly being kept back on the farm to help with the harvest, or at calving time. Consequently, her education was minimal. It had never occurred to her to ask about her parents and why she didn't have any. She had just accepted that as a fact like she accepted everything else. It was only when the other children started taunting her about it she became curious and decided to ask her aunt and uncle.

Most adults when asked difficult questions by children are able to find ways to evade them. So it was with Winifred's aunt and uncle. But children aren't fools. They know when they are being lied to. Besides, Winifred's school-friends weren't so circumspect. They teased her with the casual cruelty of children everywhere. Most of what they said was the garbled regurgitation of things they'd heard their parents say, but eventually one girl passed a remark that even Winifred could not ignore. She had to nearly twist the girl's arm off before she got the full story, but get it she did and that night she confronted her uncle with it.

She did not anticipate the violence of his reaction. He flew into a rage and forbade her to mention the subject again threatening to take her away from school permanently if she did. That was the time she threw the cleaver at him and he knocked her over breaking her nose on the hearth. But she refused to let the matter drop even though by now her schoolmates had. She nagged and nagged until at last, his patience exhausted,

Winifred's uncle blurted out the stark fact of her existence, that her parents were dead and let that be an end to the matter. But Winifred could tell from the way he said it that they weren't dead. She could tell other things, too, from what he said or the way he said them. For instance, that her uncle wasn't really her uncle at all but her brother. This confused her because her uncle was nearly twenty years older than she was. But she knew it must be true because her aunt hadn't denied it. Or rather, she had denied it but in such a way that Winifred knew she was lying. Winifred hated her uncle after that. She hated her aunt, too. Her sense of betrayal grew for three more years until she was fourteen.

The fire hadn't been her idea at all. Two youths from the next village had been setting haystacks alight in the area for several weeks. When they were finally caught they were naturally blamed for the fire that killed Winifred's aunt and uncle although they denied it. Winifred had seen one haystack go up when she was out one evening walking in the lanes. It had been an old-fashioned stack built up into the shape of a little house with a pitched roof. That was what made her think of it, really. Next to her uncle's farmhouse stood a similar stack. Winifred had set that ablaze first and then the house. Like everyone else, the police had assumed that the house had caught fire from the haystack but only Winifred knew that wasn't what actually happened. They never discovered why the front and back doors were both locked at eight o'clock at night even though Winifred was still out. Lucky she was or she would almost certainly have suffered the same fate as her uncle and aunt.

It was after that, some little while after, that the dreams had begun. It was always the same dream: Her uncle's face and her aunt's face at the bedroom window both screaming at Winifred to help them while Winifred stood in the yard and watched while the flames grew taller. It was a very realistic dream. But then, that was exactly how it had been.

Winifred heaved her legs over the edge of the bed and stood up. Things never look quite so bad viewed from a vertical position. She couldn't really complain. She had her home and the freedom, now that Albert had gone, to enjoy it. No point in dwelling on the past. Winifred couldn't change it and she didn't believe the saying about the past catching up with you. Her past hadn't caught up with her. None of it. She preferred the other saying, the one about the dead burying the dead. Maybe the dead were happy to leave the living in peace to get on with life. The only price Winifred paid were the occasional sleepless nights, and she could live with them.

All the same, it would be nice if she could make peace with her Albert. To tell him that she was sorry for what had happened and to ask his forgiveness, wherever he was now. He would know by now that what she had done hadn't been out of malice but out of necessity. Almost a mercy, really. As she had said to Drew, Albert's life had been miserable especially towards the end. The accident was really a blessing in disguise. Winifred really did believe that. Yes, she would like to be able to tell Albert that what she had done had been out of love. She might rest more easily in her bed if she could achieve that much.

Winifred took her time getting washed and dressed. She ate two pieces of toast and jam and drank three cups of tea. She fed the cat and emptied its litter tray. She turned out a cupboard, dusted the sitting room and hand-washed three pairs of stockings. It was still only half-past eight.

Standing at the back door of the bungalow, Winifred looked out over the garden fence at the sea of waving golden wheat. The sky was unusually blue for May with thin wispy strips of cloud high and white and fading to a purplish haze over the distant horizon. A single mature horse-chestnut tree, left by the developers when the estate was first built, lollipopped behind the furthest bungalow with its candles of red and white flowers pushing their way between the dark green foliage. It was the time of year when Winifred ached to get out into the countryside, to walk the country lanes and pick the wild flowers that grew by the wayside. When Albert had been alive she'd never been allowed to, and now he was dead she still couldn't, not and keep up her pretence of being a cripple.

Winifred slammed the door in her frustration. There must be some way she could get out of the house, just for a couple of hours. On a glorious day like today. There mightn't be many more opportunities before the end of the summer. But how? She beat a tattoo on the sideboard with her fingers. Drew was a good boy, but he was too far away to ask for a lift, and in any case he'd be working. She could get a bus she supposed, but she wasn't too sure of timetables. In the end she decided on a taxi. She could phone for a minicab although she thought they were probably expensive. But she needn't go very far, just a couple of miles out of town, and then she could lose herself along some deserted country lane. Yes, that was what she would do.

It took her a while to find a taxi company in the telephone book – who would have thought of looking under *Nitenday*? Half an hour later a big brown car turned up outside Winifred's front door and sounded its horn, but Winifred had been ready and waiting in the hall since before she even phoned and had the front door open as the cab drew up. It was only when she got within a few feet that the driver finally got out and held the door open for her.

'How kind,' said Winifred entirely without irony.

As Winifred settled into the passenger seat she could see the warden come bustling up the road toward her.

'How do I lock this?' said Winifred fiddling with the door.

The driver leaned across and depressed the little button beneath the window just as Mrs Willet placed her hand on the handle. Thwarted, the warden was reduced to yelling through the window: 'Going out are you, Winnie?'

'Yes, thank you,' nodded Winifred, all smiles and waving like royalty. 'Off we go, driver. Soon as you like.'

'Don't you want to speak to her?' he asked, amused.

'No, I don't think so.'

51

The warden tried the door again. 'Any idea how long you'll be?' she asked, frustrated.

Winifred cupped her hand to her ear. 'Sorry,' she yelled making a gesture of hopelessness at not being able to get the window down. 'I can't hear you. Come along, driver. I haven't got all day.'

'Which way?' he grinned, putting the car into gear.

'That way,' replied Winifred and gestured vaguely towards open country. She gave a final wave to the warden.

As the car started to move Mrs Willet had one last shot. 'You know, you really should tell me when you're going out, Winnie. Supposing I'd called and got no answer. I might have thought you'd had an accident.' But her efforts were in vain. The cab was already gathering speed. Winifred watched with satisfaction as the warden decreased in size through the back window and disappeared round the bend of Lady Astor Crescent.

They drove for twenty minutes across Norfolk's wide and undulating plains passing through several villages. At each one the cabbie slowed expecting Winifred to tell him to stop. He still had no idea where they were supposed to be going but Winifred seemed content just to sit and watch the passing countryside. He was beginning to think he might be on a fool's errand. Soon at every isolated barn and road junction he was glancing at Winifred for the slightest sign of recognition but saw none. At last he could stand the suspense no longer.

'We'll be half way to London soon. Are you sure you know where you're going?'

'Don't worry,' said Winifred without taking her eyes from the road. 'You'll be paid for your trouble.'

'So long as I am,' he muttered under his breath passing another sign-post to yet another village centre.

At last Winifred nodded. 'This will do nicely.'

The cabbie was taken so much by surprise that he pulled up sharply. They had stopped on an isolated part of the open road that looked exactly like every other stretch of road they had been on. There was nothing to indicate they had arrived anywhere.

'Are you sure this is where you wanted to go?'

'Quite sure, thank you,' said Winifred.

They were at the top of a small rise of land on the edge of a shallow river valley. Falling off to the right the land buckled and folded and looked as though it had been fashioned by a giant cook wielding a giant rolling-pin. Fields of waving barley dipped and rose and flowed away like an ebbing sea of gold. But what had caught Winifred's eye was a wide scar of bright vermillion poppies gleaming in the sunlight that slashed across one corner of the golden field like a stain of blood.

Winifred opened the car door and got out. 'I won't be long,' she said and headed off down a track that led into the field.

The cabbie watched until Winifred disappeared below the edge of the road. He was tempted to leave her and drive straight back to Caisterbury even though she hadn't paid him yet, but they really were in the middle of nowhere and he couldn't leave her. She was, after all, an old lady. He sighed with resignation and switched off the engine.

Half an hour later Winifred was tapping on the window.

'Good God woman!' said the cabbie startled out of his nap. 'You've brought back half the field!'

'I've really enjoyed myself,' Winifred beamed at him breathlessly.

She was standing on the road, her arms filled with huge bunches of poppies. The cabbie squinted at the corn field half expecting to see it stripped bare. He was amazed at her agility. Even he would have had difficulty clambering down that bank and he was relatively fit and active.

'You really want to take that lot home with you?'

'If you wouldn't mind,' she said amiably.

'It would have been cheaper to have phoned *Interflora*.' He reluctantly put them in the boot of the cab and slammed down the lid. 'Where to now?'

'Back to Caisterbury.'

Instead of driving back to Ethel Smyth Close, Winifred asked the cabbie to make a diversion to the cemetery.

'This will have to be it, I'm afraid. I've another fare to pick up in ten minutes.' He had nothing of the kind, but he'd had enough of Winifred's whims by now. He could be ferrying her around for the rest of the day.

'That's all right. I can get the bus home from here. How much to I owe you?'

'On the clock, eleven pound twenty-five. Call it a round eleven quid.' He held out his hand.

'Eleven -' Winifred pressed her lips together hard. She knew cabs were expensive but had no idea how expensive. But she paid the man who, not bothering to wait for a tip, drove off smartly before Winifred could change her mind.

Now that she was back in town she had to remember to use her stick. She was a little tired after her poppy-gathering expedition. Weeds, her farming uncle would have called them, and no doubt the farmer who owned that field would say the same. But how could anybody describe such beautiful blooms as weeds? Never mind, she had a huge armful and she knew exactly what she was going to do with them. She hobbled into the cemetery past the little Victorian brick chapel and along the well-tended gravel path. This was the first opportunity she'd had to fully act the part of a cripple as opposed to putting in an occasional appearance in the garden of Ethel Smyth Close. She thought her performance was quite convincing. She hobbled slowly across to the north-east corner of the cemetery to where Albert's grave stood with its simple black marble stone. Winifred had chosen the stone herself and it had not been cheap. She hadn't begrudged him that. And in a way it had been Albert who had paid for it. The stone, like the service and the plot, had all come out of the insurance money. Winifred had also chosen the inscription. Something simple and appropriate:

ALBERT JONAH
BELOVED HUSBAND AND UNCLE
ONLY SLEEPING

Winifred would have liked to get down on her hands and knees and remove the little colony of weeds that was already beginning to sprout on the otherwise naked mound of earth, but she had to forbear. Perhaps she could come back after dark one evening when nobody was about and tidy up a bit. She dribbled the poppies against the headstone and stepped back to admire them.

In her thoughts she conjured a picture of Albert's face as she had known it when they were first married and wondered where he was now. Could he see her? Would he even recognise her now all white and bent over? And if he could, would he understand? She didn't think he would mind. He would see that things had turned out for the best. He was probably better off wherever he was, free at last from his crippling disease and pain. He might even be thanking her for releasing him. She hoped so very much that he should. He would also know by now the truth about her aunt and uncle, she supposed, but she was sure that he would understand that, too. She spoke to Albert in her thoughts, unburdening her guilt and asking for his forgiveness for she had done and for his blessing on her new life.

A young courting couple, the girl in a short skirt and the boy in jeans, had been wandering round the graveyard arm in arm laughing at the inscriptions on some of the headstones. But when they came across Winifred and saw the pathos etched in her tearful face they passed quietly out of respect of this intimate communion. Winifred hadn't even noticed them. Her mind was filled with fire and blood and pain, all of it caused by her. The tear was for her.

For a while longer Winifred stood gazing down at Albert's grave. Then, with a resolute twist of her body, she turned and slowly edged her way back along the gravel path and out of the cemetery. As she passed the young courting couple the girl placed a sympathetic hand on Winifred's arm, smiled and kissed her damp cheek.

SIX

RING me at the office tomorrow, Marcia said. Well, it was tomorrow, Thursday morning to be precise. Colin should be setting off for work – he had a few client appointments for that day but having spent another fitful night tossing on his bed he was too exhausted to do any proper work even if he'd wanted to. Not that he did want to. He planned to see Marcia some time in the middle of the day when the office, hopefully, would be quiet. In the meantime, he had one or two other errands to run.

First, he bought himself a travel-bag from Norwich market made out of dark blue nylon with lots of zips and pockets. Next, he went into the tiny travel agency in the prefabricated hut behind Castle Mound. He walked straight up to the bronzed and fragrant brunette with the scarf tied casually on the side of her neck and sat at the desk opposite her happy to spend the next half hour enjoying her radiant, if unconvincing, smile. But when he told her he was thinking of flying to South Africa on business she immediately handed him over to the short, fat manager whose shifty eyes did a quick appraisal of Colin's crumpled suit, his cheap travel-bag and his youth and decided he was wasting his time. To no-one's surprise Colin did not buy a first-class ticket to Johannesburg today, although he assured the manager that should he decide to do so at some stage in the future, his would be the establishment that would benefit from his patronage. The manager nodded indulgently and held open the door for Colin to leave, but not before giving him what he had really come for - the telephone number of the South African embassy in London. A few yards further up the street Colin went into a phone box and dialled the number.

He was disappointed to hear a very English-sounding voice on the other end of the line - he'd been hoping for something a little more exotic. The voice was friendly to the point of familiarity but grew cool when Colin said that all he wanted was the embassy's address. It was bad enough having to run the gauntlet each day of anti-apartheid protestors without having to be the one to furnish them with the location. But it relaxed again once Colin told the girl he was thinking of emigrating to the country and what he really wanted was the address of the visa department. This the girl was more than happy to give him, and having noted down the details, Colin replaced the receiver feeling pretty pleased with his own ingenuity. He had no intention of emigrating to South Africa or anywhere else. But later, when the balloon went up, the police would find all this information and waste time looking for him in foreign lands when all the time he would be in London with a new identity.

Back home now where Colin's mother was used to him being around the house at odd times of the day - he often did paper-work there or made use of the phone to make business calls. But Colin had never asked for letter-writing paper before. Muriel gave him a pad of her best pink Basildon Bond paper, but Colin said he didn't think that quite appropriate, so she gave him a pad of her second-best blue Basildon Bond paper.

Very little of the pad remained by the time Colin had composed his letter to his satisfaction. He sealed it in a blue Basildon Bond envelope and went out to post it to Embassy of the Republic of South Africa (Visa Applications), 8 Duncannon Street, London WC2.

While Colin was out this time he phoned Marcia at the office. He did it from the phone box opposite the entrance to the Lifeplan offices.

'Good morning, Lifeplan Assurance, how may I help you?'

'Marcia, it's me, Colin.'

There was a pause during which Colin thought he might have been cut off.

'Hello? Marcia? Are you still there?'

'Yes, I'm still here,' said Marcia, warily.

Colin's right knee began to bob nervously as he fumbled with the loose change in his pocket.

'Are you alone?' he attempted.

There was another pause.

'No. Kerney's in his office.'

'What about Slaker?' Yet another pause. 'Marcia?'

'Look, Colin. About last night –'

'Is he *there?*' he snapped.

'No,' said Marcia. 'He's out.'

'Good. I'll come up.'

'No, wait!'

Now Colin paused. If it were possible to hear another person's thought processes at that moment Colin would have heard Marcia's. He guessed what had happened: the events of the previous evening together with the alcohol had forged their conspiracy. But this morning, in the sober light of day with Colin just a disembodied voice at the end of a phone-line and Paul Kerney physically just a few feet away, Marcia had begun to have second thoughts. Colin had anticipated this might happen. If only he could get to her he was sure he would be able to persuade her to change her mind again.

Marcia had, in fact, been having those second thoughts - and third thoughts and fourth - from the moment the bus pulled away from the bus stop the previous evening. If truth were known, she persuaded herself, she hadn't *actually* promised him anything at all – had she? It was all talk wasn't it? Colin wasn't really going to try to steal names from the office files, was he? All morning she had been dreading Colin's phone call and had been rehearsing the excuse she was going to use when he did. Now that she was actually talking to him she was trying desperately to remember what it was she was going to say.

Putting on her most pathetic little-girl voice, she began again: 'Colin -'

But by now Colin was way ahead of her:

'Kerney must be going out sometime today,' he insisted, sternly.

'Well, there's nothing in his diary -'

'Marcia, Kerney *always* goes out for lunch.'

'As a matter of fact,' she said more confidently, 'he asked me to get him a sandwich. Honestly Colin, he did, on my mother's life.'

'Fine,' said Colin evenly. 'I'll wait downstairs in the car park and when you come down to get his sandwich you can hand over the list at the same time.'

'Oh,' said Marcia thinking quickly, 'I've already been out to get it. Ten minutes ago, in fact. You know that new baker's down the road? Sorry Pet.'

The lying bitch! Now he was getting quite angry. It was such a blatant lie that he was determined she was not going to get away with it. He took a deep breath to calm himself.

'That's all right,' he said angrily. 'I'll come back tomorrow. And if he doesn't go out tomorrow I'll come back the next day. In fact I'll keep coming back until you get me that list.'

'Colin, I never promised -'

'And you can explain to Kerney why it is I keep coming up to see you.'

Silence. As the seconds ticked by he could hear her breathing. At last she let out a long sigh.

'All right. Give me ten minutes and then come up. But *please*, Colin, don't let anyone see you.'

Fifteen minutes later he was back downstairs again clutching a thick manila envelope. He had gone up to the Lifeplan offices to find Marcia sitting at her desk. She'd put a cautionary finger to her lips and pointed to Kerney's open door. Then she had silently slid opened her desk drawer, pulled out the manila envelope and handed it to him, then just as silently shooed him out of the office. The whole operation had taken fifteen seconds.

Once outside again he walked quickly down to the park at the end of the street and sat on a bench holding the envelope in front of him. This was it. This was his Rubicon. Up till now it had all been planning and play-acting, but this was the first really tangible, the first *illegal* thing he had done. Once he opened this envelope there would be no turning back. Yet even now he could destroy the envelope, throw it in that litter bin over there and no-one would be any the wiser. But even as he had the thought he knew it was already too late. If he gave up now he would never know if he could have done it. He couldn't continue as he had been getting further and further into debt. No, the truth was he had no choice. He had to carry on. And the contents of this envelope really were his salvation - always assuming that Marcia had got him the right information, of course. Well, there was only one way to find out. With a resolute twist of the wrist he ripped open the envelope.

He gasped at what he found inside. Copies, not only of names and addresses of a dozen former Lifeplan clients, but of policies, letters and other documents that he hadn't even asked for, information that he could never have got by himself. It must have taken Marcia most of the morning to compile it – indeed, she must have had most of it already when he phoned, the crafty gorgeous little thing. On a small piece of paper clipped to the pile was a type-written message, unsigned:

Didn't know exactly what you wanted so I copied everything in each file. Twelve you said. I hope that's enough - it will have to be. <u>Don't</u> ask again!

Colin grinned to himself and kissed the note as if it were Marcia's own lips. He stood up unsteadily, walked to the edge of the road and was promptly sick in the gutter.

SEVEN

'*THRRROW* it!'

The command was insistent and George Smith, the Scotsman, now without his deerstalker or any item of clothing other than his singlet and a pair of baggy boxer shorts, was kneeling on a PT mat and trying with every ounce of strength he could muster to lob a child's plastic football across the three-foot gap that separated him from Mrs Dobrzynski, the physiotherapist. Not long after his wife died the previous Christmas George had had a stroke which took away most of the power in his right arm and leg. What strength had returned had come back fairly quickly and Mrs Dobrzynski was determined to bully every last ounce of it out of him. George sweated and grunted but judged the effort worthwhile since another couple of inches and he might just manage to hit Mrs Dobrzynski on her ugly Polish nose.

Sadie Collins' right arm was fine. It was her left shoulder she had broken when she'd fallen out of bed at her granddaughter's house. In her own bed in her own house Sadie always slept securely wedged between the wall on one side and her husband, Sid, on the other. But in her granddaughter's house the bedroom was the wrong way round, a fact she only remembered when it was too late. Sadie would be the first to admit, though, that the weights-and-pulleys machine she was presently harnessed to was helping her shoulder – even if it did take the rest of the week to get over one of Mrs Dobrzynski's sessions.

The door to the gymnasium swung briskly open and in strolled Brian, the group's regular ambulanceman and blessed angel of mercy. His appearance was the usual signal for everyone to stop the torture for the day. But Mrs Dobrzynski, in her starched white tunic and navy-blue slacks, was not going to be dictated to by a mere functionary of the Norfolk Ambulance Service. The session would end when she said it would, and not one moment before!

'Come *on*, George!' she barked as though he were three-years-old. 'Never mind Brian. We still have two minutes yet. Now, one last effort please. Pick up the ball and *thrrrrrow* it!'

Winifred didn't mind waiting a couple more minutes. She and Martha Hodge had completed their exercises a quarter of an hour since and were already dressed and ready to leave. Both were arthritic and both knew they had only one or two more sessions to go before Mrs Dobrzynski would pronounce them fit – or as fit as they were ever going to be – and ready to resume their lives as housebound invalids. In anticipation of this, Mrs Dobrzynski had already given each of them one of her special diet sheets that were supposed to get their weight down and so reduce the strain on their crumbling joints. This was a nonsense for both women. It was a nonsense for Martha Hodge because at just seven stone the loss of a single ounce would reduce her emaciated frame to that of a coat-hanger; and it was a nonsense for Winifred, too, because unlike Martha Hodge there was absolutely nothing wrong with her joints. That very morning she had been balancing on a chair cleaning the tops of her wall units when the ambulance arrived to take her to the hospital. Winifred was probably fitter than Mrs Dobrzynski and might even be capable of picking her up by her thick Polish legs and hurling her right over the top of the climbing frame. On days like today when the woman seemed to take a sadistic delight in bullying the likes of George Smith, she rather felt inclined to try.

At last all four cripples were dressed and heaving their creaking bones up the back steps of the ambulance with the help of the ever-attentive Brian.

'Ooh, thank God for the Norfolk Ambulance Service!' said Sadie Collins with feeling as Brian shoved her from behind. 'What *would* we do without them? What would we *do* without them?'

'They're good boys,' agreed Martha Hodge smiling across the aisle at George Smith.

'Dear-oh-dear,' chuckled George wearily.

'Yes indeed,' said Winifred adding her voice to the general chorus of approval.

'That's what we're here for,' said Brian who smiled and smiled, locked the back doors and gently drove out of the hospital grounds.

Winifred was always the first to be dropped off just as she was always the last to be picked up. She handed Brian the key with Albert's handkerchief attached as they laboriously approached the front door of number nine Ethel Smyth Close.

'Brian unlocked the door and pushed it open. 'Pooh! Bloody hell, Winnie, what a pong!'

'Winifred stopped and looked down at the fluffy white ball that was rubbing itself against her ankles and mewing seductively.

'Here's Tilley!' she cried. 'Tilley-Tilley-Tilley-Tilley!'

Had Brian not wrinkled his nose at that moment he might have wondered at the agility with which Winifred bobbed down and scooped up her familiar into her arms. But he had his eyes closed as the miracle was performed and he missed it.

'Don't I know it, Winnie. You ought to get that thing doctored. It can't be healthy being cooped up in a house on its own for hours on end.'

'Tilley's not a Tom!' snorted Winifred horsily. 'She's lovely, aren't you babe?'

Brian helped Winifred scale the inch high metal door-frame and into the hall of the bungalow. 'All the same,' he said guiding her into the kitchen. 'It really does smell bad in here.' Babe indeed!

'Well, I can't smell anything,' sulked Winifred, affronted. 'Tilley's a clean cat. You just don't like her.'

As if Brian could care. He had tried but probably wouldn't try again. If Winifred Jonah wanted to live in squalor that was her business. Antagonizing the patients wouldn't make his job any easier. In future he would hold his tongue - and his breath - and keep the peace. He helped her off with her coat and handed back her key.

'See you next week, Winnie,' he called as he closed the street door and walked back to the waiting ambulance.

From across the street Colin watched him go. It was a month since Marcia had handed him the list of twelve Lifeplan clients during which time he had visited each of them in turn - partly in order to put faces to the names but mostly to see if any presented any obvious problems. Three had:

The first was a widow who, after the briefest possible period of mourning following the death of her husband, suddenly appeared one day with a new hair colour, new bright outfit and new man - a neighbour who lived three doors away. A few days later the neighbour moved in and that was the last Colin saw of either of them. Good luck to her, thought Colin with a wry smile, and scratched her off his list.

The second was a very old and sick man who seemed to have an enormous family with many grandchildren. Since being widowed, he had been inundated with visitors who brought him flowers and gifts and took him out for frequent trips. If he lasted the month Colin would have been surprised.

The third was a frail little woman who survived her husband by a week at the end of which she herself died. Colin watched respectfully as the Cooperative Funeral Service went about their melancholic business.

Which left nine potential clients for Colin to choose from. Even so not all of them would be suitable. From Colin's point of view the perfect candidate for his attention would be an elderly widow/widower, recently bereaved, preferably frail and/or crippled, living alone in a quiet location, and - most important of all - visitor-free. The last thing Colin needed was a busy-body neighbour or relative turning up to interfere in the very private business he was intending to transact with them. Having assessed all the former Lifeplan clients a further four had to be removed for various reasons to do with location - busy streets, noisy neighbours, that sort of thing - and another who went to live with a daughter in Australia. Of the four remaining this one, Mrs Winifred Jonah, seemed his best shot.

The bungalow was at the end of a quiet cul-de-sac; a decent sum had been paid out by Lifeplan on the death of her husband and some of the money had clearly already been spent, as witness the new paintwork - a fact he could make use of later. Winifred Jonah was a frail and elderly and, judging by the way she hobbled onto and off the ambulance, wouldn't say boo to a goose. At first he hadn't been sure if the old woman he saw being helped from the ambulance was indeed Winifred Jonah. Her notes said she was only fifty-six and this woman looked a lot older than that, more like seventy-six. But he hadn't seen anyone else who fitted the description, and today he had heard the ambulance driver use her name. All the better for Colin if true. Only one relative, a nephew living in Norwich - far enough away not to bother too much about. There was some kind of home-help who came twice a week but stayed barely more than a quarter of an hour. No other visitors as far as Colin could see. She seemed ideal. There was just one problem: all the bungalows in Ethel Smyth Close were old people's bungalows with a warden living on site, and judging by the lights above the street doors there appeared to be an alarm system. This was potentially disastrous for if that alarm were triggered while Colin was in the middle of his delicate "negotiations" the entire project would be blown and Colin could even end up in jail. A pity because she really was the best candidate. But it simply wasn't worth the risk. Reluctantly, therefore, Colin had removed Winifred Jonah's name from the list, too.

But then two of his remaining three clients died in quick succession. The only one that remained was a Scotsman with the unlikely name of George Smith who had no family living south of the border but whose premiums were barely covered the cost of his wife's funeral.

Colin was appalled. There had to be someone he could use. He went back over his list again, but there really was only the Jonah woman. She was still his best bet - if it wasn't for that bloody warden. He decided he had to give her one last go to see if there was some way round the problem. His persistence paid off for after a couple of days sitting at the entrance to Ethel Smyth Close he realised that the warden had set times during the day when she wasn't around - usually coinciding with when the schools were going in or coming out. For half an hour in the morning and another half hour in the afternoon, therefore, Ethel Smyth Close was warden-free. All Colin had to do was make sure his visit coincided with the school bell and all would be well. He gave himself a pat on the back. Paul Kerney would have been proud.

As the ambulance glided slowly out of Ethel Smyth Close Colin leaned over his scooter pretending to fiddle with the brake. Then he sat up, removed his helmet and took another look at Winifred's details.

Interesting case, this one. The original application had been in response to a postal promotion that Lifeplan had run for a while last year. Another of Paul Kerney's brilliant ideas. The Jonahs had been one of the few to take up the offer and one of even fewer to have made a successful claim. The death certificate was unusual, too. Most of Lifeplan's clients died of age-related illnesses, but this one was different. There had been a coroner's inquest into the death of her husband, Albert. Colin didn't know much about coroners' courts but he had an idea they were only called in cases of unexpected or suspicious deaths. This one gave *Asphyxiation* as the cause of death and the report that accompanied it gave the circumstances as *Accidental*, although it didn't specify what kind of accident.

Accidental circumstances. To Colin's suspicious mind that was legal jargon for *suspicious* circumstances. He had a wicked thought: What if the old girl had bumped him off for the money? It happened – more often than is generally realised. Well, he chuckled, if Winifred really had done for Albert she hadn't got much out of it. How much did she get? A little over five thousand pounds. Five thousand pounds was nothing these days – although, he reminded himself bitterly, it was nearly double what he'd earned last year. And what had Winifred Jonah done to deserve this largesse? Nothing. She'd only been paying the premiums for three months - a total of £30. That was nearly seventeen *thousand* percent profit! Well, if Colin had any qualms about relieving the widow Jonah of a little of her windfall then that thought dispelled them once and for all. God, he'd done more himself for the money than she had! No, he had no uncertainties about taking a little of what, when you think about it, was really his due. With more than a little self-righteous indignation, he returned to the task in hand.

He'd more or less completed his study of the widow Jonah. The purpose of today's visit was to decide the right moment to make his move. Colin went over the plan again. Apart from the two hours this morning when she was at the hospital, Winifred Jonah had not left the bungalow all week. Each Thursday the ambulance picked her up at about ten-thirty in the morning and returned two hours later. Also on Tuesdays and Thursdays the home help came to the bungalow laden with shopping bags and left less than half an hour later. And that was it as far as visitors were concerned. The rest of the time there was no sign of life - no friends, no family. And a more secluded spot would be hard to find. Behind the bungalow were fields and all the neighbours on either side seemed to be elderly. The warden's bungalow was at the entrance to the close, eight doors away. He'd seen the warden. She was a harassed-looking woman in her late thirties. From all the toys on the front lawn she was evidently a mother with a young family which explained where she disappeared to twice a day.

So, when would be the best time to pay Mrs Jonah – the *wealthy* Mrs Jonah - a visit? Tuesdays and Thursdays were out. On the front of Winifred's file Colin confidently printed the word MONDAY in capital letters and underlined it. Right, he reckoned he was about ready to begin. If all went according to plan, by next weekend he should be in London, several thousand pounds richer and ready to begin a new life. As Colin zipped up his riding jacket and strapped his helmet under his chin he had one last look along the line of bungalows before turning round the semi-circle and riding slowly away.

He rode the twenty-one miles from Caisterbury to Norwich at break-neck speed to swamp his mind and stop himself from thinking, for now he had to face the most difficult part of his plan: having to tell his mother he was leaving on the following Friday to take up this fictitious job in South Africa. She would create a scene - Muriel always did when something nasty was about to happen that she could do nothing about. It was the same at the time of his parents' divorce. That had all been a huge embarrassment, although his sister, Helen, said it was just Muriel playing the abandoned wife. Even so, he was dreading having to confront her. But he could put it off no longer.

To his relief, Muriel only sobbed quietly while Colin packed his bag in his bedroom.

'Is that holdall going to be big enough?' she fussed. 'And these shirts look a bit worn at the collar.'

'I won't need to take much with me, Ma. Not at first. Different climate, see? I'll buy new clothes when I get to Jo'burg.'

Muriel screwed up her handkerchief into a ball in her hand. 'It's all so sudden. Couldn't they have given you more warning?'

'It's better this way. Honest Ma, it is. No need to draw out the agony.'

It was agony enough having to lie to her now. He returned to his packing unable to look his mother in the eye.

'You won't forget to ring me when you get there will you, darling? Let me know you've arrived safely.'

That was a point. Could he risk ringing her from London and pretending he was in South Africa?

'Reverse the charges, if you like. I won't mind. Your father will pay.'

No, he wouldn't be able to do that. 'I'm going to be up to my eyes for a while. You know how it is, a new job and all. And in a new country. I'll ring once I'm settled, okay? Look, don't worry. Nothing's going to happen to me.'

'But South Africa is so far away!' sobbed Muriel ready to break down completely.

Colin stopped what he was doing for a moment and put his arms round his mother. 'Ma, it'll only be for a while. I'll be back in no time, you'll see. I promise I'll be in touch just as soon as ever I can. But I am supposed to be working, remember?'

He surprised himself how fluently he was able to lie. If only it were all true and he really did have this fantastic new job in the sunshine. He had thought about the details for so long that they were almost real to him. He could almost believe it himself. And now he focussed his mind on the dream rather than the reality of what he was about to embark on and hoped his confidence showed in his eyes as his mother tearfully searched them for reassurance.

Muriel nodded bravely and wiped a tear from her eye. Colin pushed her gently away and told her to go downstairs and make some tea while he finished packing. He would be down in a minute.

Alone in his room, Colin took his passport from the drawer of his bedside cabinet and placed it on top of his shirts in the holdall. He'd only used it once in his life when he'd gone on a trip with his school to Luxembourg when he was sixteen. He hadn't needed it since. Not that he was going to need it now, either, but he could hardly leave it for Muriel to find when he was supposed to be 6,000 miles away. He would keep it in the holdall together with the majority of the cash he would be collecting over the next few days and tie it firmly on the back of his scooter. He intended to ditch the scooter first chance he got and buy that car he'd been promising himself for so long. He then planned to find a room – a bedsit or something for now – in an anonymous part of London and lie low for a while until he thought what to do next. That was as far as he had got with his planning so far. It seemed enough for the moment.

Somehow, though, in the back of his mind he knew, as he threw the blue nylon holdall onto the floor of his wardrobe and turned the key in the lock, that he would have to get in touch with Muriel sooner or later. By that time he would either be headline news or quietly living off his ill-gotten gains. He didn't really think anybody would come after him, especially if they believed he was 6,000 miles away. And he had chosen South Africa because he had an idea there was no extradition treaty there. He had taken Michael O'Donnelly's advice to heart about not being greedy. Who'd be interested in the little amount of money he was thinking of? If all went according to plan no-one would be bothering about such a little crime, least of all the police.

That evening Muriel made them both a nice fillet steak supper, Colin's favourite. This was going to be her farewell meal for him - even Muriel balked at the idea of seeing him off at London Airport, although she said she would look up at the sky to see if she could see his plane at the appointed hour. On Sunday evening she gave him steak again even though there were still five days to go before he left. Muriel couldn't eat her meal she was crying so much. In five days time her little boy will have gone to the other side of the world to brave to Great Unknown and make his fortune. What mother knowing that could have an appetite? What mother could eat not knowing when or even if she would ever see her only son ever again?

EIGHT

MONDAY 23rd June.

Zero hour. No more time for preparation now, no more excuses for putting off the deed. By this evening Colin would know if his plan was going to work, whether he was going to be among Life's winners or just another of its many losers.

The sun had been up since before five o'clock and Colin had watched it gathering its strength and with it the sapping of his own. Over and over he had rehearsed his lines until the words came back to him un-summoned as in a dream. But on this, the shortest night of the year, there was precious little time for dreams.

He went out before his mother rose at eight and rode his scooter at speed grateful for the mundane realities of a new working week. He ignored all speed restrictions, jumping lights and give-way signs. On any other day he would have been stopped half a dozen times by the police and almost wished he would today. But today he was invisible. Fate made him invincible.

Over the weekend Colin had finalized his plans. His first victim was to be the Scotsman with the quintessentially English name of George Smith. The first customer in any new sales pitch, as Colin knew only too well, is always the trickiest until he got his patter honed. Get this one right and the rest follow naturally. Colin had selected George as his first victim for several reasons: he lived alone in an isolated cottage in a quiet country lane well away from any neighbours so that should anything go wrong Colin would have a good chance to get away before the hue and cry could begin. He also lived alone with one son in Canada, while his nearest relative was an elderly sister who lived in Aberdeen. His name was so common it somehow stripped him of any personality. George Smith was just one member of a species - the *genus* Smith - and could thus be lost in a sea of other Smiths, like a vast shoal of identical fish, and so be wiped from Colin's consciousness as soon as the deed was done.

At eleven o'clock Colin parked his scooter among some trees a hundred yards or so from George's cottage and did a final reconnoitre of his target. The garden was still overgrown and as untended as it had been when he had first started watching the house nearly a month earlier. All to the good. That meant there had been no concerned neighbour lurking about, or worse, to arrive unexpectedly during the nest critical half-hour when Colin needed to be alone with his victim. Standing next to the house was the dark blue Ford Anglia that he had seen George polishing so lovingly on his first visit. The sight of it sent a new shaft of anger through Colin and sharpened his resolve. It was just the sort of car Colin might have bought for himself had things turned out differently. And it didn't look as if the car had been moved since he was last here. Doubtless it had been bought with some of the money George had received from his Lifeplan payout, money George had done nothing to earn, money that by rights should be Colin's. No, if Colin had any doubts about taking from George Smith he had only to remember the shiny blue car.

So, what was he waiting for?

Colin steeled himself for the coming confrontation. He knew once he started there was no going back. Had he forgotten anything? Just one final run-through before he went ahead:

On the death of his wife last December, George had received fourteen thousand eight hundred and eighty-nine pounds seventy-five pence as the beneficiary of a whole life policy in the name of his wife, Edith. Fourteen thousand eight hundred, thought Colin. Call it a round fifteen thousand. A nice tidy sum. Assuming he'd used, say, two thousand to buy the car, he had to have thirteen thousand left sitting in the bank. He could spare a little of it. It was only winnings, after all, just like any other form of gambling. And thirteen thousand - unlucky for some. Maybe George was superstitious and might even be grateful to have the sum halved. Because to be brutally frank, that was what life insurance really was - a gamble. Betting on somebody's life. In this case George had won. All right, it was tragic that George's wife had to die, but win he had nevertheless and had done no more for it than any punter on the Grand National. Colin was simply his book-maker in all but name. Without the likes of Colin to sell George the policy in the first instant he would never have received a penny of it. Colin knew only too well how much hard work it was getting them to invest in the first place. Looked at like that, all Colin was really doing was claiming his rightful commission.

But right or wrong Colin no longer had any choice. For over a month now he had done practically no work for Lifeplan. Even if Paul

Kerney didn't sack him for poor performance it would still take him months to catch up. His debts meanwhile were still mounting and he had paid none of them off. He had run out of options. He had to go ahead with his plan. George was the first. After this it would get easier he thought as he marched up the path to George Smith's cottage and knocked at the door.

Less than an hour later he was back on the Lambretta and racing out of Caisterbury along the Norwich road.

He had done it! It had been so easy, Colin couldn't believe how easy it had been! He had pushed, nudged, coaxed George Smith closer and closer to his goal, pressing him, wearing him down until his resistance was finally broken and he was like putty in Colin's hands. Paul Kerney went up in Colin's estimation for it was his techniques that had made it possible. What was it Kerney had said? "Only the best will succeed". Well, today Colin had proved he was one of the best. If only Paul Kerney could have seen his performance! He'd be so proud.

Colin had been charming at first, apologetic even. Such a tragedy coming on top of his wife's death like this, Colin was so very sorry. But it was all clearly stated on the policy. Had Mr Smith not read it? What a pity. It was always wise to read the document through thoroughly, including the small print at the bottom, before signing. But sign he did, and they were all bound by the legal requirements. Mr Smith must surely see that Colin's hands were tied. He had a responsibility to the other Lifeplan clients. Under the circumstances, all things considered, it was a terrible embarrassment but Colin had no choice in the matter but to ask Mr Smith to *give the money back.*

George sat down. At first he couldn't take in what Colin was saying. Give the money back? How could he give the money back? It was money due to him from his dead wife's life insurance policy. She'd paid in for years, regular as clockwork. Surely there had been some mistake.

No mistake. It was all in black and white on the policy. Did he not have his copy any more? What a pity for it was all there. The truth was he should never have received such a large sum. His wife's life had been grossly underinsured. A clerical error. Naturally Mr Smith was at liberty to challenge Lifeplan in the courts, but should he lose – and Lifeplan's solicitors were quite certain Mr Smith *would* lose – then he would have his own legal costs to find, plus Lifeplan's considerable costs and he would still have to pay back the original sum. The simplest thing would be for him to make a cheque out to Lifeplan Assurance (UK) Limited to the value of the benefit - (Here Colin made a show of looking up his notes) - fourteen thousand eight hundred and eighty-nine pounds and seventy-five pence. No cash please. As an agent of the company Colin was not allowed to accept cash. Colin would issue him a receipt for the amount and get on his way. Would Mr Smith care to use Colin's pen?

George went quiet as the enormity of what Colin was saying sank in. He sat dumbly holding the ball-point between the trembling fingers of his left hand staring blankly at the floor. He made no move to get his cheque book. He had no cheque book to get because he didn't have the money anymore. It was gone, all gone. He glanced out of the window at where the new Ford Anglia was glistening in the sunshine.

Colin looked at George's ashen face and felt suddenly desperate for the man. Say it was all right, Colin. Say it didn't matter, that it was just a mistake after all, a terrible mistake. Never mind, George, keep the money. Forget Colin had said anything or that he had even been there.

But then George mentioned the car. George didn't have all the money any more; he had spent some of it buying the new car. Like a trigger, it fired the next line in Colin's prepared script:

Oh dear, said Colin, seriously, that was a foolhardy thing to have done. George should have waited until the dust had settled before disposing of the money. He thought hard for a moment. Perhaps George could sell the car back to the dealer and recover the money that way -?

Here George guffawed in panic and contempt. *Sell* the car? Was he mad? And get what for it? Everybody knew that cars lost value as soon as they left the showroom. He'd never get anything like the four thousand he'd paid for it, he'd be lucky to get three. And besides, he admitted sheepishly, it wasn't just the car. George had bought other things. He'd been to Canada over the New Year to visit his grandchildren. There was no help for it. He simply didn't have fourteen thousand pounds or anything like. He sighed heavily and buried his head in his hands.

83

That was very rash, said Colin, his eyebrows knitting with concern, very rash indeed. It was difficult to see that anything could be done. An impossible situation, no way out at all that he could see. Lawyers would have to get involved - naturally. Unless...

George looked up, just as Colin knew he would. Unless...what?

Colin's tone instantly changed. He spoke rapidly, softly, like a priest giving absolution. He could see how desperate things were and he sympathized. Mr Smith wasn't the first client this sort of thing had happened to. There was just possibly a way out of the dilemma. It may be Mr Smith's only hope. So far only two people knew of the error: himself and the clerk who had drawn it to his attention. He used the word "error" advisedly because in effect the mistake was only on paper. Nothing yet had appeared in the accounts. The mistake had only just been discovered. Naturally, Colin was obliged to bring it to the attention of Lifeplan's auditors – it would be a dismissible offence not to. So, Mr Smith had to understand, what Colin was proposing was not without risk for himself.

By now Colin had George's attention. What was he saying? What was he proposing?

Colin took a deep breath and pursed his lips. He looked at George doubtfully. Finally he nodded. Very well. He could see George was a genuine case. Here's what he proposed: first, how much of the money did George actually have left? George shrugged. About nine thousand. In that case, it wouldn't be unreasonable for George to hand over half – four thousand five hundred - *in cash* and Colin would lose the paperwork.

For a moment George just stared at Colin in incredulous silence. Then the explosion came. He jumped to his feet. *Now* he could see what the game was. He didn't believe a word of what Colin had said. It was all lies! He should be ashamed of himself, trying to take advantage of a poor widower. There was no error in the paperwork. Colin had made it all up. He was a crook and he'd better get out of here now before George phoned for the police and had him arrested.

Colin was astonished. This wasn't in the script. By now George was supposed to be begging Colin to take the money and leave him in peace, not behaving like this red-faced fury flailing his good arm about and threatening retribution.

Colin had to think quickly. Yes, all right, he would leave if that was what George wanted. But he cautioned against getting the police involved. After all, what could he prove? It was George's word against Colin's. He'd deny everything. But if Colin did leave George had better be clear on one thing: there *had been* an error; George *did* owe the money to Lifeplan; and George had better rest assured that Colin *would* declare it the moment he got back to the office.

George snorted with contempt. He didn't believe a word of it. It was just more of his tricks.

Was it? Was George so sure? He'd already admitted he didn't have the policy any longer, so how could he check? It was quite a gamble he was taking. If what Colin was saying was true then he stood to lose everything – car, money, possibly his house and even his liberty. George was an old man. A case like this could go on for years. He might not live to see the end of it, maybe never see his grandchildren in Canada again. Was he willing to risk that?

On the other hand, what Colin was proposing was entirely without risk. He could keep the car and still have a few thousand pounds for his old age. It was up to George. The choice was stark: some of the money, or none of it. This was the only chance he was going to get. If Colin walked out of here today empty-handed George would have to face the consequences, whatever they were, alone. It was up to him.

In spite of his anger George hesitated, and at that moment Colin knew he had won. If only George had kept the policy he could check to see if what Colin was saying was true. His solicitor would know, but by the time he spoke to him it might be too late. Colin had made it clear that unless he left with the money today the deal was off. He still thought what Colin was saying was lies but it was just plausible to be true. What if he was right? George would lose everything. Was it worth allowing himself to be swindled in return for peace of mind?

It was while George was agonizing over this that Colin thought of his masterstroke. Like all flashes of genius it seemed to come from nowhere. If George was still unconvinced there was a simple way to settle the matter. George could discuss it with Colin's superiors and hear what they had to say about it. Without asking, Colin went over to the telephone on the sideboard and dialled his office number. After a minute he spoke to Marcia and asked her to put him through Paul Kerney. After another moment Colin held out the receiver for George to take.

George hesitated as the seconds ticked by. He looked at the receiver in Colin's hand and beads of sweat started to appear on his brow. It was enough. With an agonized shake of his head George collapsed into his trembling hands.

Colin replaced the receiver on its cradle. All the time he was holding the receiver out for George to take his hand had been covering the ear-piece so that George could not hear the voice of the speaking clock whose number Colin had dialled.

Colin followed on his scooter as George drove to his building society in Caisterbury High Street and waited outside while George went in and withdrew four thousand five hundred pounds in cash. Behind the Baptist Church Hall George handed over the money. He called Colin a few more choice names but Colin ignored that. He watched as Colin fired up the scooter and sped away.

NINE

IT annoyed Winifred, that comment Brian made about Tilley making the bungalow smell. She was sure it wasn't true. Cats are clean animals and very particular in their toilet habits. And Winifred always made a point of emptying Tilley's litter tray regularly. Perhaps it was something else that was making the bungalow smell – that's if there really was a smell and Brian wasn't making it up. It was times like this that Winifred missed Albert. The trouble was Winifred never did have a very good sense of smell, and very often things that other people found offensive she didn't mind at all. Cow muck, for example. Albert used to screw his nose up at it, but then he'd never lived on a farm. To Winifred the smell was as natural as fresh air and put her in mind of fields of abundant corn and aluminium churns of milk as fresh and white as alabaster. How could anyone possibly say cow muck was offensive?

All week since Brian made his comment Winifred had been going round the bungalow looking for signs of decay. She'd turned out cupboards, felt down the backs of chairs, poured bleach down the drains and opened windows. The trouble was, if she couldn't smell it when it was there, how was she to know when it had gone? Mrs Willet had never mentioned a bad smell, although she never stayed long enough to draw breath. Nor did Mrs Goffe, the home-help - but she wouldn't notice if a flock of bantams was nesting in the kitchen. She would have to ask Drew next time he came, except that Drew hadn't been over for a while. And that was another irritation. Not since she handed him the money for his van had she set eyes on him, in fact. Was he so ungrateful? No, he was probably too busy with his business and with the new baby to bother with his old auntie. She'd give him a ring next week if she hadn't heard from him by then to see how he was getting on.

That Winifred couldn't smell Tilley was no real surprise. She hadn't been able to smell much since the episode with the meat cleaver when she was a child. The cleaver had missed her uncle but he had struck back at Winifred sending her sprawling across the dairy and smashing her nose against the hearth stone. No doctor had been called. In fact, her uncle had refused even to allow Winifred out of the house until the bruising had gone down with the result that Winifred's nose mended awkwardly. Her sense of smell had never been the same since.

Winifred poured a little milk into a saucer and put the saucer on the kitchen floor. In a moment Tilley was there lapping it up. Well, at least the milk wasn't off or Tilley wouldn't touch it. Cats are very particular. There was nothing else for it, she supposed, and with a sigh of resignation Winifred tied her apron round her middle and set about cleaning the cooker.

The knock at the street door came while Winifred was on her hands and knees reaching into the furthest corners of the oven with a scourer. She almost didn't hear it. Who could it be? Just her luck to have visitors now. People with arthritic knees weren't supposed to be able to clean out ovens. Winifred switched off the radio and crept into the hallway. Through the frosted glass panel in the street door she saw the outline of a man holding what looked to be a briefcase by his side.

Winifred froze. Not the man from the council again! She thought she'd finished with all that. She glanced with agitation at her hands covered in grease and muck. He'd have her out of the bungalow in two shakes if he saw what she was doing. What a damned coincidence that he should arrive just that particular moment when she was up to her eyes. Or was it coincidence? Could it be that he could somehow see into the bungalow and had been spying on her waiting for just such a moment as this to pounce? No, she dismissed the idea. She was sure no-one could see in to the bungalow. She'd taken too much care to make sure they couldn't. But it was uncanny he should arrive today of all days. Maybe if she stood very still and ignored him he might just go away.

A second knock, more insistent than the first.

If it was the man from the council and she didn't answer the door to him, he could fetch the warden to open up with her spare key – Mrs Willet had no qualms about that. The least excuse and she'd be in. No, there was no help for it. Winifred would have to let him in. But she wouldn't offer him a cup of tea. Best to get rid of him as quickly as possible.

'Just a minute!' she yelled through the glass panel before quickly washing her hands and quietly shutting Tilley in the kitchen. Then she picked up her walking stick and hobbled to the street door.

Colin was sitting on one of Winifred's two new easy-chairs before she realised who he was.

'I thought you were from the council,' she guffawed, but just in case, she still wouldn't offer him tea.

Colin laughed, too. From the council, indeed! What a suggestion! Ha ha ha! He liked that. Ha ha! Very amusing.

Winifred didn't think it was that funny, but his good humour relaxed her a little. No-one bringing bad news could be so jolly. She sat facing him in the second easy-chair trying to conceal her greasy finger-nails, just in case.

Colin was courteous, if a little fidgety. He complimented her on the décor of the sitting-room, the patterned wallpaper and some of the trinkets she had on show.

'My goodness me, a shotgun,' he said, jumping up to examine the weapon hanging in the middle of the wall. 'Is it real?'

'It was my husband's,' said Winifred. 'It doesn't work.'

Colin seemed relieved. 'Ah yes, your husband,' he said sitting down again. 'It was partly him that I came about.'

'He's dead,' said Winifred levelly.

A nervous smile flickered across Colin's face to be replaced instantly with a concerned frown. 'Indeed. A great tragedy.'

They sat staring at each other in silence for a moment. Winifred had never been one for small talk. He seemed a funny little man in his crumpled suit, very young. Maybe that's why he was so nervous, the young are always lacking in confidence. They like to give the impression they know what they're doing, but they don't, not really. How could they? They'd not lived long enough to have had any experience of life. She remembered Drew had been like that before he was married. That soon made his grow up – and the children. That was probably it. This boy wasn't married. Winifred would be patient and let him do what he had come to do in his own time. Whatever that was.

Colin lifted his briefcase onto his lap, opened it, and took out some papers. 'The thing is, Mrs Jonah, there's been a bit of a problem.'

'Oh?

'Yes. I'm afraid there has.'

He was so very sorry. A clerical error. Albert's life underinsured. All clearly stated in the policy.

Gradually Winifred understood. The insurance policy had been a mistake. Drew always said the Lifeplan policy was too good to be true. Nothing new in that. Life was hard - if growing up on a farm taught you nothing else it taught you that. You don't get anything in this world for nothing. No free lunch. It was just like the man from the council all over again. And it was worse this time. The man from the council could only evict her from her home. This young man – this *boy* with the beautiful eyes - was threatening to destroy her life. Could he?

'Mrs Jonah?'

Winifred blinked back to the present. 'Yes?'

'You do understand what I'm telling you, don't you?'

Understand? Oh yes she understood. He was going to take her life away from her. Her new life that she had waited so many years to achieve. She was going to become a prisoner again. Winifred nodded slowly as Colin's voice grew fainter. She surveyed the room. It seemed to be decaying around her. The new wallpaper that Colin had so admired was turning back to nicotine brown before her eyes. The bright curtains hung limp and dank again. Even the furniture beneath her hands felt as though it was crumbling away to dust and decay as the young man spoke. And Drew's van too. Gone, all gone. Could this boy do all that? This handsome young man with his deep, seductive brown eyes that were so persuasive. Was this what it had all come too? All those years of terrible dreams. She thought she was forgiven. She was sure Albert had forgiven her. All for nothing. It had all been for nothing.

Colin was having difficulty getting through to Winifred. The old girl did seem to be a bit vague. Was she taking it all in? Was she even all there? She nodded but otherwise showed no sign of having understood a word he'd been saying. Did she appreciate the gravity of what he was saying? Maybe he should try another tack, shock her a little bit harder. He raised his voice just in case she was a bit deaf as well as daft.

'Didn't he?'

Winifred's eyes focussed back on Colin's as she realised he had asked her a question.

'I'm sorry?'

'Your husband, Mrs Jonah. Didn't he die under suspicious circumstances?'

Winifred caught her breath. He knew! Albert's death. The fire. He knew *everything!*

'Of course, there is a possible way out of this predicament.'

A way out. Could there be?

'I can see this is a genuine case. These furnishings. The new paintwork. You've clearly spent quite a bit of the benefit already so I doubt if you could pay it all back even if you wanted to. But there must be some of the money left. Am I right?'

Money. Yes, she must offer him money to go away. But what money? There was no money. Drew had had every last penny of it. No, she would get it back. Drew said it was just a loan. He would understand. He'd give it back to her. She would get it tomorrow.

Colin shook his head. 'Today, Mrs Jonah. I have to have the money today or I may be forced to go to my superiors and neither of us would want that, would we?'

Winifred gripped the arms of her chair. The little girl on the tricycle. The trees, the fields beyond. All dissolving before her eyes. She stared blankly at the young man seated in front of her. No, it's not fair. You can't do this to me. You haven't the right. This is my home. I must stop you. I *will* stop you.

'Milk?' Colin frowned, bemused by the suggestion. 'No thank you, I don't want any milk. But I wouldn't say no to a cup of tea.'

Colin darted up to hand Winifred her stick as she heaved herself laboriously out of her chair.

He was certain now that she would hand over the money just as George Smith had done earlier. He congratulated himself that he was getting better at persuasion. He knew it would be easier second time around. This time he hadn't even needed to use the fake call to the speaking clock. Mind you, he had begun to wonder there for a while whether he was wasting his time. Winifred was a bit simple. That's what comes of living among cattle and sheep. Makes you a bit woolly-headed. But she had seen sense in the end. In fact, she had been easier than George Smith. No histrionics or abuse this time. Winifred Jonah had put up very little fight at all. She'd been rather civilized about it all, even offering him a cup of tea.

Relaxing now that the difficult bit was over, Colin eyed Winifred's slow progression round the back of his chair and out into the kitchen. He heard the soft mew of a cat as she opened the kitchen door and took the opportunity to get out Winifred's file to go through it again.

Last February she had received five thousand pounds from Lifeplan, the smallest amount of compensation of the entire original twelve on Marcia's list. Hardly worth bothering with, really. He looked about the room again. Cheap wallpaper, tacky curtains and second-hand furniture. The whole lot couldn't have cost more than five hundred quid. So she must still have at least four thousand left. He could ask her for, say, two thousand. Less than that amount wouldn't be worth his while.

He congratulated himself as he snapped shut his briefcase. Who said crime didn't pay? By the end of the week he will have netted nearly ten thousand pounds - nearly four times what he'd earned in a whole year from Lifeplan. You have to admit, the thought was amusing.

It was the last thought he had before he simultaneously heard the thud and felt the searing pain in his neck.

More in surprise than pain, he stood up and reached a hand to his shoulder. A sheet of white light seemed to shoot across his line of sight and he blinked to clear it grimacing at the pain and flexing his shoulder against it. The second thud hit the exact same spot and this time he cried out and turned to see Winifred clutching what looked like a bottle of milk in her fist. The absurdity of the sight made him almost want to laugh. This crippled little old woman who a few moments ago was having difficulty hobbling out of the room with the aid of a stick was now standing four-square behind him and wielding a bottle of milk as a club. It really was very funny. He staggered out into the hallway with Winifred following close behind.

In the hallway he tried to get to the street door but his vision was blurring and he couldn't work out where the handle was. In front of him he saw a painting of a small boy with a tear in his eye and he lurched towards that instead. When the third thud struck home he no longer felt any pain but realised he was falling and reached out to stop himself. Had he fallen onto the painting he might have triggered the alarm button underneath. Not that it would have made any difference. At that moment the warden was half a mile away collecting her two sons from primary school. But in his confusion the painting became real and

Colin shifted his hand a fraction to avoid falling onto the little boy with the tear in his eye, and as the darkness finally engulfed him, he collapsed through the bathroom door.

PART TWO

TEN

HELEN sat imprisoned in her room. Although it was the last week of June she still felt cold huddled in her overcoat with no light, no heat, no way of making a cup of coffee, even. Angela had turned the electricity off before she left with Bryn that morning. That was reasonable, Helen supposed. It was the end of term and none of them was going to be back for three months. And someone had to wait in for the landlord to make his annual inspection of the flat. What was less reasonable was that Helen should be the one who had to do the waiting-in.

Strictly-speaking, Helen shouldn't be here at all. The flat was in Angela's sister, Deirdre's name and as far as the landlord was concerned Angela and Deirdre shared the flat together. But Deirdre had moved out six months earlier to live with her boyfriend, Steve. Angela and Bryn now occupied the main bedroom while another girl, Sue, had the second bedroom with her boyfriend, Ahmed. That left Helen with this box-room which was never meant to be a bedroom at all. Consequently, Helen had had to spend much of the morning stacking all her possessions into one corner in an attempt to disguise her bedroom as a store-room once more. When the landlord arrived she was to say she was just a friend who had been left the key in order to let him in.

Helen shivered wondering why she always let herself get into these predicaments. It had been the same when she and Angela had been undergraduates in Sheffield two years earlier.

Only that time Helen had been the one with the boyfriend.

Helen had done everything for Lionel. She'd cooked for him, washed his clothes, stayed in Hall in order to save her grant for him. Even when she was finally forced to admit that he'd been playing around with other women she still could not bring herself to leave him. She had been besotted with the man. And the worse he'd treated her, the more devoted she'd become. Her health had suffered; her degree had nearly suffered. Angela had warned her, shouted at her and finally moved her belongings out and into her own room. It had been the saving of her. And now it was happening all over again. Sharing this flat in Camberwell but travelling up to London on the tube every day, Angela had suddenly produced Bryn, a thirty-something divorced social worker and father of two. Helen had thought her friend had taken leave of her senses. Angela could have any man she wanted and yet here she was shacking up with some middle-aged hippy. It wasn't even as though Bryn were good-looking. God alone knew what she saw in him! But Helen knew. She recognized the signs: an infallible ability some women have to see only what they want to see. Helen had experienced it. Angela was experiencing it now. It was driving a wedge between her and her oldest friend but she had to see it through, to carry on living in this dreary, damp little room. For Angela's sake.

Still, there wasn't much to be done about it during the summer vac. Helen could hope that three months apart from Bryn might make Angela see sense – that's if they really were apart. Angela had said she was going up to Sheffield to see her parents, but she might not have done. She might have secretly gone off somewhere with Bryn. It was in the nature of the disease to lie, Helen remembered. Like anorexia. The symptoms were the same: Death by Denial.

The landlord arrived late and stayed too long. Helen wasn't a very good liar these days – out of practice. But gone he had and said nothing that betrayed any suspicion. Helen supposed she'd find out when the rent demand for next term came in. Too late now to worry. She had a last look around the flat, exorcised a ghost or two and heaved the heavy canvas bag - that held absolutely everything she could possibly want for the next twelve weeks - over her shoulder and left by the front door slamming it shut behind her.

It was raining. Helen quite liked the rain. It scattered less sturdy mortals and could clear a London street in seconds. Free now to advance in a straight line for a hundred yards, Helen decided to walk to the station. At Camberwell Green she stopped and looked at her reflection in a shop window. My God, what a sight! She was too tall, had always been too tall even when she was small. And ugly. My God, you're ugly, she told herself fiddling with a sodden brown curl that was plastered against her forehead. In her scuffed suede boots, her ankle-length overcoat and the canvas bag slung over her shoulder, she looked for all the world like one of the Yorkshire miners she used to see as an undergraduate at Sheffield. Only her ruddy complexion confirmed her as a country girl and even that seemed to be washing away with the London rain. She couldn't let her mother see her like this. Half way along Camberwell New Road she turned right into Wyndham Road and squelched into the *Cut Above* hair salon.

Half an hour later she emerged and the rain had stopped. A frizzled bunch of curls now sat on each ear and Helen wasn't at all sure they were an improvement, but the experience had had the required therapeutic effect. Pampering wasn't a familiar experience for her these days. She knew there was only so much that could be done with a face and figure like hers. Not that she was much bothered. Since Lionel, Helen had largely lost interest in that side of things preferring to devote her energies to more cerebral, and therefore sublimer, pursuits. At least, that was what she told herself. She had one more year to do at the LSE to get her Master's in Political Science and then she might think about boyfriends and babies and the next forty years. For the moment she had an excuse for putting all that out of her mind.

Before she noticed, she had walked right past the entrance to the Oval station and on round the curving brick wall of the cricket ground. The sun was beginning to shine between breaks in the cloud and Helen was experiencing that exquisite, light-headed feeling that comes at the end of one term with miles of time stretching ahead before the beginning of the next. And she was in no hurry to return to Norfolk. She shrugged her broad shoulders only to feel the weight of the canvas bag and with it a slight twinge as she remembered all the holiday work that it contained. This mildly unpleasant memory was compounded by the worse one that was waiting for her in Norwich.

Helen missed her father - she never pretended otherwise. *Before* – that is, before her father left - Helen had often thought there were two couples living in the Brearney household. No not *couples,* that was the wrong word; but two *pairs* of people, at any rate. Helen very definitely took after her father. They shared the same build, the same temperament, the same intellect. When her father had still been there Helen hadn't minded so much that Muriel doted on Colin. It had seemed fairer that way somehow, *symmetrical.* Helen was in no doubt which had been the stronger alliance. She and her father had complemented each other. Colin and Muriel were complementary, too, but they leaned rather than supported. It was a weakness.

But that was Before. Now, with her father gone, Helen was on her own and the symmetry broken, the household out of kilter. She felt peripheral to the bond between Muriel and Colin. The fact that they were both slim and good-looking and she wasn't just served to underscore the imbalance, and she'd noticed of late that she rather resented it.

Helen crossed the river at Vauxhall Bridge just so that she could walk past the Tate Gallery, and crossed back again over Westminster Bridge. On the South Bank promenade she looked down upon a filthy hag who quite obviously hadn't the first clue about how to actually play the squeeze-box she was thrusting aggressively under the noses of passers-by. Further along, an animated bassoon-player was embellishing a beautiful piece by somebody-or-other; Ravel, she thought, although she didn't know. She marvelled at the enormous pile of coins the hag had managed to amass and the pitiful few pennies at the bottom of the bassoon-player's box and wondered how all the Great Men with all their Great Theories would explain that little economic miracle.

Tired of walking now and having had a final cup of coffee in the Festival Hall cafeteria, Helen knew she couldn't put off the inevitable and longer. She walked across Hungerford Bridge, got the tube to Liverpool Street Station and from there caught the main-line train to Norwich. When she got off the train two hours later it was raining again.

'Helen, darling! What a lovely surprise! I wasn't expecting you until the weekend. Why didn't you phone from the station? I'd have come and collected you in the car, of course I would. Your hair's wet.'

Helen forced herself to smile at Muriel as she dropped her canvas bag on the hall floor and lightly kissed the proffered cheek.

'Hi Ma. Nice to be home.'

She dumped her overcoat unceremoniously on top of the canvas bag and went in to the sitting room leaving Muriel to gaze at the discarded pile as though she hoped it might spontaneously take itself upstairs.

In the sitting room Helen found two coffee cups, both still half-filled with coffee. She flopped down next to them and dipped a spoon through the milky film that had formed in one of the cups coating the back.

'I was just in the middle of clearing up,' said Muriel, slightly flustered. She gathered up the cups. 'Well, you must be hungry after your journey. Let me make you something. My, this *is* a lovely surprise.'

'It's all right, I had a sandwich on the train!' yelled Helen as her mother disappeared into the kitchen.

'You must want more than that,' called back Muriel. 'A big girl like you. How about some soup? I could make you some soup.' She returned a few minutes later carrying a tray of steaming mushroom soup, some liver pâté and half a baguette.

'What's this? Foreign food?' said Helen holding up the French stick. 'What's brought this on?'

Muriel sat down on the far end of the sofa 'Oh, I've been experimenting since you went back to college. All sorts of things. You'd be surprised.'

Helen ripped a lump out of the baguette and began to chew.

'Actually, the pâté was for Frank,' said Muriel smoothing her frock neatly.

Helen stopped chewing. 'Frank?'

Muriel laughed coquettishly. 'Oh darling, you remember Frank. He was here last Easter.'

'I wasn't.'

'No, that's right, you weren't,' frowned Muriel. Then, brightening, Muriel said, 'Oh, but you'll like Frank. He's a critic. A newspaper critic.'

Helen swallowed her bread and took another bite. 'What sort of critic?'

'Art critic of course. He has a weekly column in the *Norwich and Ipswich Times*. I met him at one of my events.'

Oh yes, Muriel's "events". Helen had forgotten about her mother's artistic side, which she only discovered after Helen's father left. Helen had long suspected there was more to them than just cultural improvement and now it seems she was right. Not that she could blame Muriel. It wasn't easy for any single woman, let alone one of Muriel's age, to get out and meet people – by which, of course, she meant *men* – or have any kind of social life, even in this day and age. Somehow she couldn't see Muriel, in her brightly coloured cardies and her patterned frocks, as a fully paid-up member of the swinging sixties. And musical soirées, she supposed, were preferable to bingo – or, God forbid, the WI! Besides, Muriel wasn't the sort to be comfortable in exclusively women's company.

'Frank's terribly sweet. A lot like your father in looks.'

'Looks can be deceptive,' said Helen scooping up a dollop of pâté.

'Oh, well I guessed you'd take that line,' sulked Muriel. 'But you needn't think I'm going to justify myself to you or anybody else. I don't see why I should. We share the same interests, Frank and I. And unlike some men I could mention Frank is a perfect gentleman. Goodness, darling, you haven't even met him and already you're criticizing him.'

'Don't have a go at me. I haven't said a word - yet.'

'You don't have to. I can tell just by the expression on your face what you're thinking. You're not your father's daughter for nothing. But there's absolutely nothing in it. Frank and I are just good friends.'

Oddly, the comparison with her father rather pleased Helen. 'Oh yes, Dad,' she nodded. 'What does he think of your fancy man?'

Muriel bridled. 'Frank is not my *fancy* man – I do wish you wouldn't bring your London vulgarities back with you. And I certainly haven't discussed him with your father. There's absolutely no need. The thought hadn't even crossed my mind. Besides, your father's not exactly been a monk, has he? And a woman has needs, too, you know.'

'Appetites,' said Helen scooping up more pâté.

'What?'

'Appetites,' repeated Helen licking the back of her knife. 'Not "needs".'

Muriel blushed again. 'I meant *companionship*. And besides, I'm a free agent, which was more than your father was when he took up with that woman.'

'Yvette,' said Helen throwing her head back against the sofa back in exasperation. 'Why won't you ever call her by her name?'

'Because it's a floozy's name.'

Helen guffawed.

'Yes, go on, laugh. In my day we had worse words than that for women who took men away from their wives and families. I was the one who was abandoned, remember, left alone to bring up two children.'

'Hardly children, Mother. Colin was fourteen and I was sixteen.'

'It's the principle that counts.'

'Anyway,' said Helen sitting back and crossing her legs. 'There was more to it than that.'

'Meaning?'

'Meaning it wasn't just sex.'

Muriel flinched at the word, much to Helen's satisfaction.

'Yvette gave him something he wasn't getting at home.'

'Well, I might have guessed you'd take his side,' said Muriel fishing inside the sleeve of her pink cardigan for a tiny embroidered handkerchief and dabbing bother eyes with it. 'I suppose he's told you all this, has he? Poisoning your mind against me. You're just like him, always twisting things round to suit yourself. I'm not surprised the pair of you discuss me behind my back. But then you always were Daddy's little pet!'

Too far. It always went too far. Wounds open so easily, blood congeals. Both women had been over it before and both knew there was little point in going over it all again. Like damp squibs they spluttered out. Even the regrets went unspoken.

Muriel stood up wearily and carried the plates in to the kitchen. After a minute Helen followed with her empty soup bowl. She looked at the back of her mother's head as she stood at the sink washing up and wondered if she had ever loved her.

'Where is my little brother, anyway? At work, I suppose, doing the deal of the century again.'

'Oh darling, you've missed him,' said Muriel sweetly. 'He's already gone.'

'Gone? Gone where?'

'To South Africa, of course.'

'South - ?'

Muriel turned to look at her daughter without stopping what she was doing. 'There's no use looking at me like that, I told you in my letter.'

Helen clenched her teeth. 'What letter? Told me what?'

'That he'd been offered this job in Johannesburg - or somewhere. Anyway, I did tell you. I must say, I was surprised that you didn't at least ring to wish him luck.'

'How could I when I didn't know?' Helen clenched her fists together and pursed her lips. 'How long has he gone for?'

'Oh, a year, I think.'

'A year!'

'Two, possibly. He left last Monday. And I did tell you, I remember distinctly. You find my last letter, you'll see.'

Helen stormed out of the room and came back with two sparingly-filled sheets of white Basildon Bond notepaper. Quickly skimming through them she held them out for Muriel to see.

'*This* is your last letter. Colin isn't even mentioned.'

Muriel squinted at the letter short-sightedly. 'Oh no, that isn't my last letter. I sent another after that. I don't use white anymore. You have a look. You'll see I'm right.'

Helen held her breath, stomped back in to the hall and up-ended her canvas bag. A blue envelope written in Muriel's tiny floral hand fell out unopened. Helen remembered it now arriving at the flat last weekend. With all the fuss about Angela and Bryn she had forgotten all about it. Slowly she turned the envelope over in her hands and still silently cursing, she ripped it open with her thumb.

ELEVEN

WINIFRED sat perfectly still in the kitchen, her arms stretched out on the table in front of her. She had been sitting like that for hours stock-still. The sun was slowly going down filling the room with a blaze of brilliant colours – yellows and purples and reds. But she hardly noticed it. Tilley was mewing for her supper and rubbing her head round Winifred's ankles, but she ignored her too. She was trying to think what to do.

Twice before she had been in this predicament, but on both those occasions matters had been taken out of her hands. Following the deaths of her aunt and uncle in the fire, it had been the police who had taken charge of the investigation, arresting those two boys. Not the least suspicion had fallen upon fourteen-year-old Winnie. Her lack of emotion had been put down to the shock of losing of her aunt and uncle in such a dreadful way. She'd lost her home as well as her only relatives. There being no Welfare State in those days, no foster homes, the church had helped and various charity organisations had all done their best to protect her from further emotional damage. Winifred having no other family, they'd found her a place in an orphanage and given her psychological as well as practical help. She'd not had to lift a finger.

With Albert things had been a little trickier. As well as the police there had been social workers, doctors, bereavement counsellors as well as representatives from the insurance company. Of these the police had been the most

111

tenacious, questioning her over and over until she was quite worn out. They had never come right out and accused her of anything but they remained unconvinced, she could tell. Everyone said that was just how the police were and she was not to bother, the prevailing opinion being that she had been through a terrible trauma and once again she had been regarded more as victim than perpetrator. Having got away with murder twice, she could be forgiven for thinking she was fire-proof – or at any rate, charmed.

This time, however, things would be very different. Try as she might, she could think of no convincing way of explaining away the body of a young man lying on the floor of her bathroom. At first she thought she should simply call the police and tell them everything: that Colin had tried to blackmail her and that she had feared for her life and had only hit out in self-defence. But that wouldn't explain how he came to end up in the bathroom or the blood on the hallway floor. In her initial panic she'd dragged Colin's body fully into the bathroom not daring to leave him where he had fallen in case anyone came. How could she explain how he got there? How was it possible a supposedly frail old woman was able to move a great big male body all on her own? And then there was the weapon, the bottle of milk she'd used to hit him with. Foolishly, she'd emptied the contents down the sink and washed it up cleaning off any evidence of blood and hair from the glass. Were these the actions of a victim? No, she could see this one was going to be far more problematic. If she was going to get through this she was going to have to find a more drastic solution.

Winifred dragged herself to her feet, went in to the sitting room and gathered up Colin's papers that had scattered over the floor, put them back into his briefcase and hid the briefcase down the side of the sideboard. It was growing dark now. She glanced out of the window. Nothing appeared untoward. Ethel Smyth Close was as quiet and empty of activity as it always was. She pulled the heavy curtains together. Then she took her sharpest carving knife from the kitchen drawer, pushed open the door of the bathroom and pulled on the light-cord flooding the room with light. Before her Colin's body lay propped up against the bath, his legs sprawled out on the white tiling floor. Winifred squatted down on her haunches and examined Colin's face. Two almond-shaped eyes seemed to be staring back at her. Such beautiful brown eyes, she thought. How could anybody with eyes like those be so evil? Then the beautiful eyes blinked.

'So. You're awake at last.'

Colin made no attempt to reply. In any case he couldn't. A thick piece of masking tape had been placed across his mouth. His hands were tied behind his back and his legs were bound together at the knees and at the ankles with strong rope. Winifred held the knife up so that he could see it clearly and let it glint in the light.

'If you cry out I'll use it. Don't think I won't.'

Colin nodded, so Winifred leaned forward, took hold of one corner of the masking tape and pulled it off.

Colin gasped and coughed. This was the first time he'd been able to breathe properly for hours. He was cold and stiff, the floor was hard and his head throbbed. Every time he tried to move another shaft of pain sliced through his neck sending a wave of nausea through him. He still couldn't fully comprehend what had happened to him. He recognised the woman was who was staring at him now in such a menacing manner: Winifred Jonah. But she looked quite different from the wizened little old woman he had seen hobbling onto the ambulance. The last thing he remembered was sitting in her front room waiting for her to do something – oh yes, she was going to make a cup of tea. And then, out of the blue, it was as if the roof had fallen on his head. The shock stunned him. The last thing he remembered before he finally blacked out was seeing her standing over him with something in her hand a bottle of milk.

He tried to push himself up against the side of the bath, but the pain was too severe.

'Water,' he croaked.

Winifred got up and went out returning a few seconds later with a glass of water and a flannel soaked in cold water. Awkwardly, she lifted him up by the shoulders and held him while he drank, then she laid his head back against the bath and applied the flannel to his neck.

'Thank you,' he whispered. His head was swimming. He closed his eyes but that seemed to make the nausea worse, so he opened them again. Winifred's face swam back into view and he tried to focus on it.

'Why are you doing this?'

'You know why.'

'Because of what I said?' He sighed heavily. 'Untie me.'

'No.'

'Untie me and I'll take it back. I'll go away and you won't see me again.'

'You say that now.'

'You think I'll go to police? Of course I won't, I'm not an idiot. I'm as much to blame as you are.'

'Yes you will. You'll tell and then they'll take my home away.'

He frowned trying to make sense of what she was saying. 'What are you talking about? No-one's going to take your home away. Why would they?'

'They will. You'll tell and then they'll make me leave.' She stood upright and started to leave.

This was insane. What had it to do with life insurance? His head was hammering again. He leaned back against the bath and closed his eyes.

'You can't keep me here. You'll have to let me go some time. My people will be looking for me.'

'Who's looking for you?'

'My office,' he went on. 'They know I'm here. They sent me.'

'To swindle defenceless old ladies?' She shook her head. 'I don't think so.'

'They may not know *why* I'm here, but they know I came. When I don't go in tomorrow they'll be looking for me. It won't take them long. Then they'll come. Maybe not tomorrow but the next day. Better to let me go before it's too late.'

'I can't.'

'Yes you can, of course you can. Look,' he said trying to sit up, 'I was wrong. Is that what you want me to say? I admit it. But so is this. You can go to prison for what you're doing. So far only you and I are the only ones who know about this. Untie me now and we'll forget all about it. You keep your money. I'll go away and we'll pretend none of this ever happened.'

'No you won't.'

'I will. I promise. You have my word.'

She gave a smirk of contempt and started to leave again.

'Wait!' His head throbbed and he had to wait till it settled a little. 'OK, you're right. No-one's coming. No-one knows I'm here. You're quite safe. And I won't say anything. Why? Because I'll go to prison too - for blackmail. Don't you see? So I won't tell will I? Just let me go.'

But Winifred was shaking her head again. 'I can't take the risk.'

'What risk?' he said exasperation, nausea and pain all rising together. 'I just said I won't fucking tell, didn't I?'

Winifred frowned and tutted. 'There's no need for bad language.'

He nearly laughed at that. What was wrong with the woman? Why won't she listen to him? He wouldn't say anything, truly he wouldn't. She was being totally unreasonable. Why? What was wrong with her? Then the penny dropped:

'My God, you did it didn't you? You killed him. Your husband - what was his name? You really did it.' He pulled back and started to whimper. 'Oh sweet Jesus.'

Winifred looked down. Tilley had come in and was rubbing the length of her body against Winifred's legs and still mewing for her supper.

'You see,' she said bobbing down and picking the cat up in one arm. 'I couldn't let you go now even if I wanted to.' And quietly closed the bathroom door after her.

In the kitchen Winifred opened a tin of cat food for Tilley, put it on the floor and then sat down at the table. By now the sun had gone completely and the room was in darkness, but she didn't want to switch on a light. She looked at the closed bathroom door. He was right. She couldn't leave him like that. But what was she going to do with him? If she released him he would go straight to the police, she had no doubt about that, in spite of his protests. Or he might return later and try blackmailing her again only worse next time. He already knew she was a phoney. No-one would believe she was frail and weak after this, so she was right when she said she would lose her home. But worse than that, he had found out the truth about Albert, and now she had practically admitted it. He could tell that to the police, too, and they would believe him because they already suspected as much. It would certainly overshadow anything he'd done to her. They might even commend him for it.

She slammed her hand down on the tabletop and glared at the bathroom door. Why did he have to come and spoil everything? She wished now she had killed him when she hit him over the head. A dead body was surely less trouble than a live one. Too late now. Besides, she wasn't a murderer, not really. What happened to Albert was his own doing. And it was the fire that killed her aunt and uncle, not anything she did. But to actually take a knife and put it to someone's neck... She shuddered. No, she couldn't do it. Not in cold blood. But she couldn't just leave him either. At the moment he was groggy but he wouldn't stay like that for long. Then he would get loose. Escape. Raise the alarm.

She would have to secure him better than that. And then there was the problem of where to keep him. On the farm she would have had no difficulty. Plenty of places on a farm - outbuildings, barns. But in the bungalow all she had was a small garden shed. That wouldn't do. He'd soon get out of that or attract attention. He would just have to stay inside the bungalow. But where? She looked about her. One bedroom. One sitting room. One kitchen. One bathroom. Hallway. Toilet. Not even a loft. She wasn't going to give up her bedroom. Besides, there was a great big picture window onto the street. Same with the sitting room. No, there was only one place: The bathroom where he was now. It was at the back of the bungalow and had a small frosted window. She would just have to make do without. That was no hardship. Bathrooms were luxuries. The farm never had a bathroom, or even a toilet for that matter. You washed at the kitchen sink or once a week in the tin bath in front of the fire. She could do that again. Fortunately in the bungalow the toilet was separate.

She was getting carried away with herself. Was she really going to incarcerate this young man? How long for? Tears of frustration welled up. Oh why did he have to come? And that wasn't the only problem. Tomorrow morning Mrs Goffe the home help was coming for the first of her twice-weekly visits. She couldn't put her off. On Thursday she'd be back again and later Brian would be coming to take her to the hospital. If she missed an appointment the warden would come fussing round wanting to know why. But she couldn't leave Colin here on his own. It was a nightmare.

First things first. He wasn't going to go along with her plans - far from it. He was going to do his best to stop them. So she had to think how she was going to control him. Wielding a knife over him was all very well while he was trussed up like a chicken. But he couldn't stay like that. She would have to untie him so he could move around at least enough so he could do his business. That was a point. She'd have to dig the old bucket out of the shed. What she needed was a way to control him but at the same time give him enough freedom to move around. It wasn't long before she thought of the gun. Albert's gun or rather, his father's. A side-by-side twelve-bore inscribed on a brass plate by the makers, W & C Scott of Birmingham and dated 1926. It had hung on the wall since they were married and Winifred had dusted it hundreds of times without paying it much heed. For all she knew 1926 might have been the last time it had been fired, although Albert had kept a box of cartridges somewhere.

She found them at the back of the drawer in the sideboard. She found Albert's tool-box, too.

Colin listened while Winifred screwed an old padlock harness on to the outside of the bathroom door, although he didn't know it was that. He listened, too, while she tested and re-tested the lock for strength and the key in the lock. He saw a spy-hole appear near the top of the door and heard the curtain rail go up over the door and the big heavy brown velour curtain that had hung as a draught-excluder in the flat in Caisterbury but had been too big for the picture windows of the bungalow. It had been too good to throw away. Winifred knew it would come in handy one day.

Then Winifred sat down again at the kitchen table and cleaned the gun the way she thought she remembered Albert cleaning it until it shone and the name-plate glowed yellow again. Opening the cartridge box, she took two of the little red cylinders, filled the barrels with them and snapped the gun shut. When she was ready, she pushed open the bathroom door.

For the past two hours Colin had been keeping up a continuous thumping against the hollow side of the bath.

'You can stop that now. No-one can hear you. This is the last bungalow in the street. There's only fields behind that wall. And next door is my neighbour, May Mitchell. She's eighty-four.'

She dumped the mattress on the floor and unrolled it.

'What's that?'

'Your bed.'

'I'm not sleeping on that!'

'Suit yourself.'

She put a bucket underneath the sink. Colin looked at it and wrinkled his nose. 'You must be joking.'

'I don't like this any more than you do. If you don't want to go in a bucket that's up to you. I'll empty it for you. Otherwise you can lie in your own stink for all I care.'

Colin said no more but watched in silence while she gathered up toothbrushes, toothpaste, creams - everything, in fact, from the bathroom cabinet and around the bath leaving only a bar of soap and a towel.

'And how exactly am I supposed to use them with my hands and feet tied?'

For answer, Winifred went out and came back with the gun which she cocked and lifted towards him. Colin's eyes widened at the threat.

'It works, so don't try anything stupid. I'm going to untie you now, but any nonsense and I'll tie you up again. Clear?'

Colin snorted, but he let Winifred cut the bindings – knees first, then feet, and finally his hands. As the cords snapped apart she stepped back smartly and levelled the gun at Colin's head. She needn't have worried. After six hours of lying on the floor with the blood-flow restricted to his limbs, he wasn't about to try anything heroic. He gently eased himself upright, flexed his knees and rubbed his painful wrists.

Satisfied, Winifred stayed no longer. She backed out of the bathroom keeping the gun trained on him all the while. Once in the hallway she slammed the door shut as quickly as she was able and snapped the padlock firmly into place. She pulled the brown velour curtain across the door, but then on second thoughts she drew it back again. It was heavy and thick and she wanted to be able to hear him should he try anything. Then she stood back against the opposite wall waiting to see what he would do next.

TWELVE

HELEN came down late for breakfast. Never an early-riser, it felt so good to be back in her own bed and in a decent-sized bedroom again that she luxuriated in both for even longer than usual.

After their row the previous evening, Helen and her mother had not spoken beyond the necessary civilities and they sat more or less in silence watching television until they went to bed. Neither woman was willing to back down but this morning Helen was feeling a little ashamed of herself. Quarrelling with her mother was no way to begin the summer vac, and it couldn't be allowed to continue for three months. It was because she worried about Muriel, innocent gadfly that she was, that she said what she did. She wanted to protect her mother from a harsh, changing world with which she was ill-equipped to cope. But as usual Helen went about it the wrong way blundering in with all guns blazing. What was needed where Muriel was concerned was tact and diplomacy - never Helen's strongest suit. She was better at straight-talking, which unfortunately came across as bullying. She knew it, but couldn't do much about it. It was one more trait she had inherited from her father.

If the truth were known, Helen actually agreed with a lot of what Muriel said. She was indeed a free agent having been divorced from Helen's father for nearly four years now. And Muriel was the injured party, technically-speaking, since her father was the one with the extra-marital affair. The problem for Helen was that being in the middle she could see both sides. If Muriel was naïve then her father had been dishonest – something unforgivable in Muriel's eyes. Honour, duty – these were important tenets to Muriel coming as she did from a world of family picnics and daddy-knows-best, cricket whites and Evensong. Helen's father had never fitted comfortably into the strait-jacket of convention that Muriel expected of him. He was an adventurer, and clumsy like Helen, not very good at hiding his tracks. The marriage was bound to end in failure. And when the end did come it was as dramatic as it was inevitable.

All the necessary formalities had been gone through: Yvette was named as her father's co-respondent; the requisite compromising evidence had been procured – and by that she meant staged photographs of the "adulterous" couple getting in and out of taxis together, not the more prurient type taken in hotel bedrooms - and a settlement agreed. But oh, what a pantomime it had been! England's divorce laws were positively medieval. To Helen's mind, if two people found they could no longer live together, the modern thing – the *civilized* thing - was to simply dissolve the marriage and part company without having to go through the farce of having to prove one or other was at fault. No-one was at fault. But if the relationship had been rocky before the divorce, what they'd had to go through in order to secure it had completely soured it. The whole business had been a trial for Muriel, in every sense of the word. She had been publicly humiliated and for that reason alone Helen felt she had to temper her criticism. After all, her father was the one who had escaped, and into the arms of the woman he loved and who truly loved him. Muriel, by contrast, had been left high and dry, too young to be put on the shelf and too old to start again. So who was Helen to cast brick-bats when her mother was at last showing an interest in another man, even one as disastrous-sounding as this - whatever his name was - *Frank*. She didn't like the sound of him. Art critic indeed! This needed nipping in the bud as soon as possible. What can Muriel be thinking of?

Helen plodded down the stairs, along the hallway and in to the kitchen. The hall clock said it was ten o'clock. She wondered where her mother was. She called but got no reply. Helen shrugged for no-one to see. It was a lovely summer's morning, the sun was streaming in through the kitchen window warming a little square of floor-tiling and Helen stood on this in her bare feet while she waited for the kettle to boil. Two women on the radio were discussing dietary tips. Helen switched them off and stuffed a huge doorstep of thickly buttered toast in her mouth. Then she carefully balanced her mug of tea and a plateful more of toast in two hands and turned to go in to the sitting room.

She nearly dropped the lot when she saw him. A great brute of a man filling the door-frame and barring her exit. If he hadn't been grinning she would have screamed – or she might have screamed had screaming been in her nature.

'You look as if you've got your hands full,' said the brute. 'Let me help you.'

'I'm quite all right, thank you,' mumbled Helen pushing her way between him and the door-frame.

'Sorry, I didn't quite catch that.'

She removed the toast from her mouth. 'I said, I can manage. Who are you? Oh, don't tell me: Frank.'

'And you must be Helen. I've heard so much about you.' He grinned again and held out his hand.

Helen didn't take it but stuffed another piece of toast in her mouth instead. She marched into the sitting room and planted her feet heavily on the coffee table between them and chewed aggressively. Initial impressions, in Helen's experience, are always the most reliable and her antennae were buzzing with danger signals. So, this man was supposed to be like her father, was he? He was nothing like her father, except in build maybe. For a start, he smiled too much. There's something very suspicious about a man who smiles too much. And then there was his age. One of Helen's objections to Bryn was that he was too old for Angela, and they were only seven years apart. There had to be closer to twenty years separating Frank and Muriel - the other way around this time. Muriel was old enough to be his mother. What on earth was the woman thinking of? And what was *he* thinking of? Helen glowered at him over the top of her mug.

Frank shifted awkwardly in the silence. 'Is there any more tea?'

'Help yourself. I'm sure you know where everything is.'

He disappeared to the kitchen returning a few minutes later with a steaming mug. 'Ah!' he grinned. 'The cup that cheers,' and sat down on the opposite chair.

'Mug,' said Helen with purposeful irony. 'Not cup.'

She studied him over the top of hers as she might a not very savoury-looking form of pond-life. She had to keep reminding herself not to be too critical of Muriel's friends. With that in mind she launched into what she thought was a perfectly reasonable opening gambit:

'Tell me, what exactly are your intentions towards my mother?'

Frank's eyebrows went up. 'I didn't think I had any.'

'I see. You're the sort of man who likes to flirt with older women, are you?'

'I wouldn't call Muriel old.'

'She's fifty. How old are you?'

'As old as my tongue and a little older than my teeth. How old are you?'

'You're thirty-five. Muriel told me.'

He shrugged. 'So?'

'Hardly compatible.'

At this Frank threw his head and laughed, crossed his legs. 'No, you've got it all wrong. Your mother and I are friends, nothing more.'

'Oh, I'm sure there's nothing more,' agreed Helen, unmoved. '*We* both know that. But does Muriel know it?'

'I'm not sure I follow.'

'Then I'll spell it out. I've heard about men like you, middle-aged, unmarried, the sort who only wants women as "friends".' She made it sound like child-molesting. She slurped her tea. 'Mind you, I don't blame you for trying. It can't be easy having to go to all those art exhibitions and ballets on your own. People snigger, tongues wag. It must be useful having a tame female on your arm. Anywhere near the mark yet, am I?'

By now Frank's grin had completely evaporated. He said, levelly, 'If you're suggesting what I think you're suggesting, then I'm afraid you're well off the mark. And impertinent.' He put down his mug and stood up. 'I seem to have offended you in some way. I'm sorry about that. You obviously don't like my company, so I won't impose it on you any longer. Would you tell Muriel I'll ring her this afternoon?'

'I might,' smirked Helen with satisfaction.

Just then Muriel came in through the French windows wearing sandals, voluminous shorts, a flowery blouse and a wide-brimmed straw hat. In one rubber-gloved hand she held a pair of secateurs and in the other a scrappy handful of French Marigolds, lobelias, white alyssum and a bit of fern.

'Ah! I see you two have met. Been having a nice chat, have you? What are you standing up for, Frank? There's no need to be formal. Sit down.' She picked a glass vase from a cabinet and headed for the kitchen. Frank sat down again frowning while Helen smiled at him smugly.

'Don't let us keep you if you've got something to do, Frank. Some garden fête to visit, perhaps?'

'Garden fête?' said Muriel coming back in and positioning the vase on the coffee table. 'I didn't know you were going to a garden fête today, Frankie.'

'Your daughter seems to think I spend my working day with fancy nonsense and then write about it for the benefit of the county's effete.'

'Do we have any in Norwich?' smiled Muriel removing a scallop shell ash-tray from the coffee table and pushed the vase into the middle. 'Move your feet please Helen, dear, you're not at college now. I'm afraid he's teasing you. Frank is a proper journalist. In fact, he was a war correspondent. In West Africa, wasn't it, Frank?'

'Ooh, a war in West Africa,' mocked Helen. 'First I've heard of it - Frankie.'

'Few people have,' said Frank. 'That's partly why I came back. To publicize it.'

'Bit of a come-down, though, isn't it? From international correspondent to art critic on a provincial newspaper.'

'Don't mock, darling,' said Muriel getting off her knees and sitting back on the sofa. 'Top jobs in journalism are not two-a-penny. It's only until something more suitable comes up. Isn't that right, Frank?'

'Come to think of it,' said Helen, still pursuing her own line of thought. 'I can't say I've ever come across you. What did you say your last name was again?'

'I didn't,' muttered Frank.

'Opie,' supplied Muriel. 'But he isn't using his own name. It's not that sort of a column. He writes under a pseudonym. Shanty...something or other.'

Helen's face suddenly lit up with glee. 'Not Chanticleer!' She screamed, threw herself back in the sofa and kicked her legs wildly in the air like she was peddling an upside-down bicycle.

'Ignore her, she's just showing off,' said Muriel spraying a fine mist onto her flower arrangement from a plastic bottle. 'Would you like some more tea, Frank?'

Helen was giggling uncontrollably. Chanticleer was the name of the *Norwich and Ipswich Times'* gossip column, a composite tagline for several different contributors, usually writing anonymously. Its stock-in-trade was any titillating bit of scandal about the famous - or would-be-famous - of East Anglia. Frank's job was even worse than she thought. He didn't write about the performances he went to see so much as the celebrities who went to see them. The stories were widely thought to be exaggerations if not outright invention. Not that anyone ever admitted to ever reading the column, although everyone seemed to know what was in it.

'Some famous names have written for Chanticleer,' said Frank, irritated despite himself. 'You'd be surprised.'

'I doubt it,' she giggled.

'Take no notice, Frankie dear,' said Muriel. 'She's like this with everybody until she gets to know them.'

Frank got to his feet again. 'Well, I'll have to get to know her some other time. I really do have to be going. I only popped in to say I managed to get two tickets for tomorrow night's performance. I'll pick you up at seven.'

Muriel let him kiss her on the cheek, then patted his arm.

'What are you going to see?' said Helen, irritated by this gesture of affection. When Muriel told her it was Noel Coward's *Private Lives,* she set Helen off giggling again.

'See you tomorrow night,' sighed Frank starting to leave. As a passing shot, he said to Helen, 'Your mother tells me you're going to be a politician. That wouldn't be the Diplomatic corps, would it?'

'Oh no,' said Muriel showing him out. 'Helen's following in Mrs Thatcher's footsteps. She's going to be Britain's second woman prime minister, aren't you darling?'

'Really, Helen,' Muriel said when Frank had gone. 'I don't know why you have to be so rude to my friends.'

'Oh Mother, he's just using you, can't you see that?' Helen was furiously shoving dirty linen into the top of the twin-tub.

'Yes, of course he is. And I'm using him. We're using each other. That's what relationships are all about as you'll find out for yourself one day when you've grown up enough to have an adult relationship.'

Helen pursed her lips. 'Do I have to remind you of Lionel?'

'No you don't, because you never let anybody forget. He's your excuse for everything. Well, not everybody is like Lionel. Certainly not Frank. You think you know but you don't.' Muriel felt flushed. She patted her hair nervously.

Helen was exasperated. 'It's precisely because of Lionel that I *do* know. Can't you see that?' she said fighting with a packet of washing powder trying to get the flap open.

'You just can't bare the idea that I found someone better than your father.'

'I don't think getting even with Dad for leaving you is a good enough basis for a relationship, that's all,' said Helen pushing her thumb through the corner of the packet and getting it stuck. 'How do you get into this bloody thing?'

'At least Frank doesn't cheat. He's kind and considerate.'

'Of course Frankie is until Frankie gets what he wants. All men are the same, devious and manipulative and -' Helen ripped the packet sending half its contents cascading over the kitchen floor. 'Damn!'

'Now look what you've done!' said Muriel bursting into tears. 'All over the floor. Oh, I can't take much more of this. First Colin, now you. I don't know what I've done to deserve such ungrateful children.'

Helen put her arms around her mother and held her tight. 'I'm sorry, Ma, I didn't mean to upset you. It's because I care about you. We both do, Colin and me. You do see that don't you?' But Muriel was blubbing and sniffling into her tiny screwed-up hanky.

Helen enveloped her mother with her big, strong arms. She was evidently feeling Colin's departure more than she was letting on. Helen knew how much she depended on Colin while she was away at college. It must have been quite a shock when he left, which doubtless Colin had done as insensitively and selfishly as he did everything else. And it was only yesterday, hardly enough time for Muriel to adjust. The last thing she needed was more emotional upset. Helen gritted her teeth and prayed to the heaven she knew wasn't there.

'I promise to be good and kind and understanding to my mother,' she mouthed silently. 'And to take care of my little brother, Colin, wherever he is at this moment in time.'

At that moment in time Colin was twenty-one miles away pacing the length of Winifred Jonah's bathroom. It didn't take him long. Three steps and he had it covered.

His terror of the previous evening had been replaced by self-disgust. For a few moments yesterday when Winifred had been leaning over him with the carving knife he had really believed she was going to kill him, and it is in moments like this that a man discovers things about himself. What Colin discovered he did not like, for he knew there was nothing he would not have done, no promise he would not have made to save himself. But then he told himself he had to humour her. She was clearly mad. Only a mad person could imagine they could keep someone locked up against their will in this day and age. But mad or not, she was right about one thing: no-one knew he was here. He'd been going over and over it in his mind but there was no-one, not a single solitary soul had the least clue where he was. Nor would anyone be looking for him. He'd gone to great lengths to make sure they wouldn't, even to the extent of laying false trails to throw them off the scent. If it wasn't so serious it would be a joke. No-one was going to help him. He could die here in this bathroom and no-one would know.

But it wouldn't come to that. There had to be a way to get out of here. If he kept a cool head he would soon be free. This was a modern brick bungalow not some medieval dungeon, it couldn't be that difficult to break out. All he needed was a plan of action. So let's see: the bathroom was about nine feet by five. The only door was the one into the hall. He had tried it last night but found it was locked on the outside. The Jonah witch had evidently been busy. He wouldn't be able to break it down without creating a commotion, and she still had that shotgun - assuming it worked, of course. He only had her word for that. Better assume it did for the moment.

By far his best bet was the little ventilation window. It was high up above the bath and barely a foot square. But it did open on to the back garden. He opened it now and looked out. Not much to see. A back fence and fields beyond tantalisingly just a few yards away. But the window was very small, far too small for anyone of his size to get through. Or was it? It was surprising how small a space you could get through if you needed to. He closed it again. For now he'd leave it. Best not to draw attention to it. The thing was, not to give anything away. Lure the witch into a false sense of security. Then when his chance did come he would be gone before she knew what had happened.

Earlier he thought he might do just that. Coming from the back garden, he heard a kind of clip-clip-clip. He jumped up onto the edge of the bath and opened the window. At first he saw nothing. Then he looked to his right and his heart skipped a beat. Over the side fence in the next garden he saw an old woman. She was standing with her back to him barely ten feet away hanging out washing and the clicking sound was clothes pegs being dropped into a wicker basket at her feet.

He started to giggle nervously. Then he heard himself call out, barely audibly at first but then louder, for help: Help! Please help me! I'm here, over here! Turn round! Next door, in the bathroom! Winifred Jonah's house! Please, help me, *please!*

The woman continued to hang out her washing. He tried again:

'I'm in the bathroom! Number nine! I'm locked in! Please help me, please -!'

He gasped. From the woman's left another figure slowly approached. It was the Jonah witch. Colin watched with mounting horror as she squinted in his direction, took something from her apron pocket and held it up for him to see. It was a brown paper bag which she blew into and held up behind the woman's head for a moment before bringing her hands together. Colin gasped as the bag burst with a loud bang. After a moment the old woman stooped again and picked up another tea-towel from the pile. Only when Winifred tapped her on the shoulder did the old woman turn round, startled to see Winifred standing there. She brought the damp tea-towel up to her heart and laughed her silent laugh. Colin watched in despair as Winifred mouthed the word "tea" into the woman's face to which she smiled and nodded with enthusiasm. She dropped her last peg into the basket and led the way back into her house with Winifred following.

A short while later she must have returned for he could smell food cooking - bacon. Few smells are more guaranteed to get the stomach juices churning than frying bacon. Truth was he hadn't given much thought to food but the aromas made him realise he hadn't eaten for nearly twenty-four hours. The smell was wonderful. The he saw the spy-hole darken and the sound of Winifred's voice:

'May Mitchel is deaf as a post, has been for years. And there's no-one the other side so you can forget about that.' She waited but Colin was determined not to respond. 'I've made you some breakfast. If you do as you're told you can have it. If you don't you won't eat. It's up to you.'

He almost told her to stick her food but stopped himself. He realised he needed food in order to keep himself alert and strong. Starving himself wouldn't do him any good. For now he would do what she wanted. Let her think he was being compliant and docile.

'All right,' he called back. 'What do you want?'

She told him to turn round and face the wall, then kneel down on the floor with his hands behind his back and his feet together. When he'd done that she unlocked the door and Colin allowed his hands and feet to be tied together with twine. Once he was secure she sat him down again against the bath, went back out to the kitchen and returned with a plate of hot food - bacon and egg.

He watched impassively as she dissected it into bite-sized portions and fed him like a child. The food tasted good but he wasn't about to tell her that. Compliance was one thing. Being sociable was quite another. When he had finished eating, she brought him a mug of tea.

'I've put two sugars in. I know you young people have a sweet tooth.'

She held the cup to his lips and he drank it silence. When he finished she stood up.

'There now, that wasn't too bad, was it?' When he still refused to reply she shrugged. 'Suit yourself.'

She went to examine the contents of his bucket. The smell didn't seem to bother her but Colin had to look away. She took it away without comment. He heard her empty it into the toilet next door and flush. When she returned she fixed the tape over his mouth. Then she pulled the mattress in close between him and the door and after a final look round, she closed and locked the door and drew the curtain across again.

Now, why had she done that? It was daytime, no-one would be coming. Or was there? Think Colin! Then he remembered: of course, it was Tuesday, one of the days the home-help came. He tried to remember what the woman was like. Not very old, mid-thirties at most. She certainly wouldn't be deaf like the old woman next door. If he made enough of a racket she was bound to hear him. Things were looking up. Maybe the nightmare will be over sooner than he had hoped.

Colin listened for the doorbell that would signal the arrival of the home-help. That was his first mistake, for this morning there was no bell. The first he knew that anyone was in the building was the sound of voices in the hallway. But before he had a chance to react he heard the kitchen door close and the radio being turned up to full volume. He thumped on the door – that was his second mistake. By carefully wedging the mattress up against it Winifred had muffled any noise. Frantically, he lay down on his back and with both feet he kicked at the door ten times, twenty. Still nothing. Panicking now, he tried again but then stopped. He could hear another noise start up: a vacuum cleaner. Colin thumped with all his might but whoever it was using the vacuum cleaner was singing – *singing*, for Chrissakes! At last the vacuum cleaner was switched off and Colin made one last desperate attempt to get the attention of the home-help. Then at last he heard the woman speak and Colin knew he was saved:

'What's that noise, Winnie? It sounds like it's coming from -'

But her words trailed off. The vacuum cleaner had started up again, drowning out the end of the sentence. Whimpering, Colin tried screaming through the tape but to no avail. He collapsed exhausted and in tears onto the mattress.

He heard nothing more until a few minutes later the bathroom door did open and Winifred stood in the doorway with the nozzle of the vacuum cleaner in her hand. Another moment and she put her toe on the button to switch the machine off.

'She's gone,' she said, and quietly closed the door again.

THIRTEEN

IT had been a close shave. As she packed away the vacuum-cleaner Winifred saw that her hands were shaking. The bungalow was small and although the bathroom was located at the back of the building Winifred was sure Mrs Goffe must be able to hear Colin's cries for help.

Winifred had been standing behind the street door since nine o'clock that morning watching through the glass panel ready to open the door before Mrs Goffe could use the bell. Mrs Goffe's official time was nine-thirty to ten, but Winifred wasn't taking any chances in case she arrived early for once. When Mrs Goffe finally turned up at nine-thirty-seven, Winifred had quickly and silently opened the door and beckoned her into the kitchen without a word. Mrs Goffe had been happy enough to be so shepherded, although she would have liked the chance to catch her breath and take her coat off first. But from the way Winnie put her finger to her lips Mrs Goffe was sure she was in for a treat.

Winifred Jonah had always been a bit of a disappointment to Mrs Goffe. Unlike most of the old folk she did for, she had never been particularly friendly or showed the least gratitude for Mrs Goffe's efforts on her behalf. She was even known to follow her round the bungalow on occasion while she was working, tutting at this bit of dusting or that bit of hovering. From the way she behaved you'd almost think she suspected Mrs Goffe of not doing her job properly. Well what did she expect on the wages Social Services paid? Like Mr Goffe said, if you pay peanuts, you expect monkeys, although she wasn't sure that was quite the right order of words. Today, however, Winnie seemed to want to be a mite friendlier than usual, even offering Mrs Goffe a cup of tea and a sit-down in the kitchen before she got started. Maybe Winifred Jonah was beginning to appreciate her at long last.

Confidentially, Mrs Goffe had always looked on her function as rather more than that of a mere char. More like a social worker herself, if truth were known, although she'd never get their wages – chance would be a fine thing! But a bit of appreciation now and again wouldn't have gone amiss. She regarded it as part of her duties to listen to their moans and groans. As she was fond of telling Mr Goffe, hers was often the only friendly face some of her old people saw from one week's end to the next. It was only natural they should want to unburden themselves to her - and you'd be amazed at the things some of her old folk told her. Get their life's stories, some of them. But not Winifred Jonah's, unfortunately. She had always been a bit aloof. Comes from growing up on a farm, Mrs Goffe suspected - farming folk were known to be a bit stand-offish. More used to animals than people, see? Winifred had never spoken much about herself, which was a shame because there were one or two areas that really sounded quite interesting. That business about her husband's death for instance sounded intriguing. Mrs Goffe would love to get to the bottom of that one. But Winifred had never been forthcoming no matter how often she dropped the hint.

Until today, that is. From the way she had been ushered in before she'd even had a chance to wipe her feet, Mrs Goffe was sure she was about to hear something sensational. But having been frog-marched into the kitchen, the door was slammed shut behind her and the radio turned up full blast. And *pop* music, for goodness sake! Who'd have thought Winnie Jonah would listen to that muck? And so *loud.* Couldn't hear yourself think. It was too much for Mrs Goffe. No juicy bit of gossip was worth the risk of one of her migraines. She didn't even finish her tea but made her excuses and got on with the vacuuming. Even so Winnie wouldn't turn the radio down. Kept it up full blast. She must be going deaf in her old age. And Radio One! Now, for herself, Mrs Goffe liked a nice romantic ballad sung by someone like Johnny Mathis. She knew all the words: *Look at me, I'm as helpless as a kitten up a -* . She rubbed the hoover nozzle furiously at a patch of carpet. Flipping cat hairs!

Tilley had darted out of the way of the thrusting vacuum-cleaner head and watched from the safety of the top of the glasses cabinet as Mrs Goffe quickly skated round the sitting room and into Winifred's bedroom where she switched off the machine in order to make Winifred's bed. It was during the resulting silence that she heard the thump and rustle in the bathroom. Winifred heard it, too, and watched with growing alarm as Mrs Goffe stopped what she was doing and stood upright to listen. Colin's muffled cry sounded faint and distant, but it was there. Mrs Goffe knitted her brow and cocked an ear, uncertainty clouding her voice:

'It sounds like it's coming from next door,' she was trying to say, but her words, along with the noises, were drowned out. As fast as she could but without hurrying, Winifred had grabbed the vacuum-cleaner and switched it on again. Mrs Goffe stood back in amazement as Winifred hobbled out into the hallway declaring that she would like to have a go at doing some of the cleaning. The bathroom – she thought she could manage the bathroom. Easy enough to clean even for her. Mrs Goffe needn't bother, she'd be quite all right. It did her arthritis good to have a bit of exercise. With a shrug of her shoulders, Mrs Goffe forgot the imagined noises, plumped up the pillows on Winifred's bed and, seeing from her watch that it was already five-to-ten, picked up her shopping bag and left just as Winifred's hand came to rest on the bathroom door handle.

'I'll bring your shopping on Thursday dear,' yelled Mrs Goffe as an afterthought through the letter-box, although she didn't think Winnie heard her above the noise of the radio and vacuum cleaner.

Yes, a close shave indeed. One false move while Mrs Goffe was in the building and the game would have been up well and truly. And it didn't end there. Winifred would have it all to do again on Thursday morning. And then later the same day Brian would be coming with his ambulance. At least with him it wasn't essential to come in, although he often did. Winifred would have to be ready and waiting on the doorstep. But how long was it going to be before one of them said something? She couldn't bar Mrs Goffe from the bathroom permanently. The woman had a nose like a ferret. She was bound to want to see why it was she was being kept out of there. And even Brian, normally so easy-going and disinterested, would start to wonder if Winifred was always waiting on the doorstep when he drove up. These little changes in routine never go unnoticed for long. Eventually someone would pass a comment and Winifred would have to explain herself, and the prospect terrified her.

God curse that boy! If he hadn't turned up she wouldn't be in this predicament. Things had been ticking along just nicely until he came with his evil designs. She hadn't asked for any of this, but as eggs was little eggs she was having to pay for it. Well, maybe she deserved it. Maybe it was just desserts for all the evil she had done in the past. Her aunt had had a phrase for that: it was God repaying debts without money. Maybe that was what Colin was, some kind of avenging angel – or avenging devil, more like.

Winifred threw back the velour curtain and with a resolute turn of her wrist, and unlocked the bathroom door. Colin was sitting on the mattress exactly where she had left him before Mrs Goffe's arrival – except he was looking a little more sullen than earlier. His normally perfect almond-shaped eyes had narrowed. What was that, resentment that he was losing the fight? No doubt he'd thought Mrs Goffe was going to be the one to set him free. Well, Winifred had shown him things weren't going to be that easy.

His hands and feet were still tied and he still had the sticking-tape across his mouth which Winifred now removed once again. She noticed him flinch when she did that and the skin around his mouth was looking sore from having the tape continually removed and re-applied. Too bad. Perhaps in future he'll think twice before picking on defenceless old ladies to bully.

'How long do you think you're going to be able to keep this up?' he asked spitting out the fluff. 'You won't be able to play that trick with the hoover twice.'

Winifred didn't reply but got on with cleaning the bath.

'I presume that was the home help - Mrs Goffe, is it? She very nearly heard me. Maybe next time she will. Let's see - Tuesday today. She'll be back again on Thursday, isn't it? Oh yes, and I'd almost forgotten: the ambulance comes on Thursday too. You going to use the hoover trick on him?'

Winifred stopped what she was doing and glared at him. How did he know about Brian? How come he knew so much about anything? He must have been watching her for weeks. The thought made her angry and fearful at the same time.

Colin saw the fear in her eyes and smiled at his little triumph. 'Didn't know I knew that, did you? I know all your little secrets. Lots of plates you got to keep spinning in the air. Sooner or later you'll drop one of them. Then I'll be out of here faster than shit out of a drain.'

'Don't worry,' she said breathless from her exertions. 'I thought of that. I thought of everything.'

'Really? Sure about that? What are you going to do when you need to go out? You won't be able to. You think I'm your prisoner, but really you're as much my prisoner as I am yours. You can't leave me here alone. In fact, you can't go anywhere or have anyone come here ever again.'

'Don't you fret about that,' she said vigorously polishing the mirror above the sink.

'I'm not the one who's fretting. I've got time on my side. You won with Mrs Goffe today. But what about next time? Or the time after that? I've only got to win once, remember, you've got to win every time. One day you'll make a mistake. Someone will ring the doorbell while you're on the loo then I'll kick up such a racket they'll think World War Three has started.'

She turned on him angrily. 'Then I'll just have to make sure you can't, won't I?' She snatched up the sticking plaster and made to put across his mouth.

He turned his head sharply away. 'No - please. Don't do that. Not yet.'

Winifred hesitated. He sounded so pathetic. 'Well you just watch your mouth then. I told you about talking filth.' She screwed the sticking plaster into a ball and threw it in the bucket.

Colin watched her for a few minutes swirling water around the bath.

'What's the ambulance for, anyway?'

'It's for my knees. My arthritis.'

Colin watched her leaning over the bath. 'Your knees!' he snorted. 'There's nothing wrong with your knees. Oh I get it. That's how you got this place. You're as much a con artist as I am. In fact, when you think about it, we're pretty much alike, you and I.'

Winifred rounded on him. 'What I got is mine by rights. I'm not like you. I'm not a thief.'

'No, that's right. You're a murderer.'

She very nearly swiped him across the face but managed to stop herself.

'You want to watch your mouth.'

She finished cleaning the bath and fished in her apron pocket for the padlock key.

He sat up swiftly. 'Hey, you're not leaving me like this, are you? Can't you untie me? You untied me last night. There's no-one else coming today.'

That was true. No-one coming to bungalow until tomorrow. She looked at his pleading eyes. He was still very young. Winifred went out and came back with the shotgun. She untied his feet and stepped away.

'What about my hands? Can't you untie them? I promise I won't try to escape.'

'No. I don't trust you.'

'But how am I supposed to -?' He nodded towards the bucket.

'You call me when you want to go.'

He snorted. 'What, and let you stick your hand down my pants? Are you mad?'

'I'll look away. Don't worry. No-one's interested in you.'

He frowned at her angrily. 'You are mad. You do realise that, don't you? I don't just mean a bit a bit dotty, I mean clinically bonkers.'

Winifred stood fiddling with the keys. 'I'm as sane as you.'

'I bet that's what's really wrong with you. Only a mad woman would do what you're doing. That's what the ambulance is for. It's the loony bus. It's not your bones that are cracked. It's your head. You're crazy. A crazy old mad woman.'

'You want to be careful what you say to me.'

He laughed. 'Careful? Of a crazy old witch?'

Furious, Winifred went out slamming the door shut and fixing the padlock. Behind the door she could hear him chorusing at the top of his voice,

'Cra-zy! Cra-zy! Crazy old witch!' he kept repeating over and over.

'Right, for that there'll be no dinner for you today!' she yelled back through the door. 'Nothing till you learn some respect!' With a furious sweep of her arm she threw the curtain across the door.

Winifred sat down in the kitchen before she fell down. Her hands were shaking and she clasped them together to steady them. She was suddenly very weary, weary of him, of the situation they were in, of the effort of having to think. She had hardly slept last night worrying about what to do next. She knew he was right. One day she would make a mistake, she might even have made one already with Mrs Goffe. And then what? Her life would be over. She lay her head on her arms and closed her eyes just for a moment and found her mind drifting back to a time long ago.

Every year when Winifred was a little girl a travelling circus set up on Town Green in Caisterbury and every year Winifred went. She loved to see the conjurers and the clowns. But what Winifred liked most were the acrobats, and one acrobat in particular: A young girl not much older than herself, a lone unicyclist, the darling of the show. Winifred thrilled to see her, so lithe and athletic, balancing her one-wheeled machine a hundred feet up on the high wire and longed to be like her. For her performance, no lights were permitted in the arena other than a single spot that picked her out against the dome of the big top, and from the ground it was impossible to see the safety-platform she was struggling to reach. But reach it she always did, and to triumphant applause from the audience far below. But then one day she fell. She missed her footing or something and the audience gasped as the figure fell like a stone. But all was well for there was a safety net. The girl bounced and recovered, did a somersault over the net and took a bow to the relief of the audience who exploded with applause.

To Winifred nearly half a century later, it seemed that that was how things were now. She knew she could not keep Colin locked up for ever, but for the moment she didn't know what else to do. Like the girl on the high wire, she was performing a dangerous balancing act with no clear sight of where she was heading. All she knew was that she had to keep going in order to stay upright, for if she stopped even for a moment she would certainly fall, and this time there was no safety net.

Winifred sat up again and ran her hands through her hair. She made some tea and drank it. Colin was quiet at last no doubt having worn himself out with his chanting. She had calmed down herself and thought she might relent and give him some food later. She went over to the curtained door and listened, but she could hear nothing. Maybe he was sulking. She carefully drew back the curtain and put her eye to the spy-hole but she could see nothing. That was odd. It was only early afternoon. She should be able to see daylight at least. Something seemed to be blocking the hole. She pushed her finger through' It felt sticky and she realised it was sticking plaster that was blocking it. As she did so she heard the sound of breaking glass.

Glass? What glass was there? She had removed everything in the bathroom that was made of glass. Then in a flash she knew. The window! He was trying to get through the window!

For a moment Winifred was too paralysed to know what to do. Surely he wasn't trying to escape through that tiny opening? Was it even possible? Desperate people are capable of feats that no normal person would even think to try to attempt, she of all people should have realised that. What a fool she had been! He must have been planning this all along. The curtain – she held its silky texture in her fist. That was what the name-calling had been about, to get her to draw the curtain across and muffle the sounds of him trying to escape. God, was she to have no rest! Angry with herself for her foolishness as much as with him for his perfidy, she fumbled with padlock taking longer in her haste than usual to release it. Somehow she managed to get it unfastened and she pushed against the door. It wouldn't budge.

Fool again! She had been so concerned about preventing him from getting out it had never occurred to her that he would want to stop her getting in. She had completely forgotten about the bolt on the inside of the door. And now she saw that he had pushed the mattress up against the door blocking it further. Frantically, she threw her weight against the door breaking the brass bolt and creating just enough of a gap for her to be able to squint into the room. She was right; he was trying to get out through the window. He was up on the side of the bath, one leg already through. But what she saw made her gasp. He had removed all his clothes and was completely naked but for his briefs, and his body was white, eerily white like a ghost. He had caked himself from head to toe with soap.

'Stop!' she ordered.

'Not a chance!' he called back.

Frantically, Winifred heaved against the door repeatedly until she had forced the gap wide enough to get the shotgun through.

'Stop! I mean it, or I'll shoot!' But he was already halfway out of the window.

Winfred pushed with all her strength, tears of frustration welling up into her eyes, blinding her. With one final Herculean heave she managed to get the arm that held the gun through into the room. She raised both barrels, aimed – and fired.

The deafening retort reverberated for several seconds in the hollow bathroom, then silence. Nothing moved. For a long moment Winifred could see nothing. Only as the smoke cleared at last could she see clearly into the room, and the first thing she saw was blood.

FOURTEEN

"THE Bourgeoisie Has Created More Massive And More Colossal Productive Forces Than Have All Preceding Generations Together." (Karl Marx).

Helen wrote the essay title at the top of the page, underlined it, and put down her pen. She hadn't intended starting her holiday assignment quite so early in the vac, but at least it got her out of the house. Muriel had spent most of the morning in the garden and had caught a chill. Helen was never very good with invalids, especially ones who played on their condition in order to get sympathy. That was what Muriel was doing – it was obvious. No doubt she was still angry with Helen for the way she had treated Frank and this was her way of punishing her for it. But Helen was only doing it for her own good. Muriel would eventually see she was right about him. But in the meantime she had Muriel's sulks to contend with.

It was one of the reasons her father had left, Helen remembered, these little emotional injuries of Muriel's. None of the usual reasons for divorce had applied to her parents' marriage, nothing as normal as wife-beating or abandonment, or even good old-fashioned adultery. Oh, Yvette had provided Muriel with the excuse she needed but the marriage had died long before Yvette came into the picture. Looking back, the signs had all been there: the absence of conversation, the cold politeness at mealtimes, the tacit acceptance of two people living in the same house but leading separate lives. What Helen had been too young to realise at the time, and what Colin had never fully appreciated either, was that it wasn't their parents' fights that was the danger signal but their silences, for aggression means passion and there can only be passion when two people care about each other. Not that there hadn't been plenty of rows at the beginning, quite violent ones, when Muriel first realised where her father had really been spending those weekends when he was supposed to be away on business. But once the rowing stopped, that was a clear sign that the end was near, and sure enough, it was shortly after that the solicitors' letters started arriving. Colin had simply assumed that because they were being civil to each other all was well. So it came as even more of a shock to him when the split came. Poor Colin. He never did understand subtlety.

Even so, Muriel had contrived to make it look as though she had thrown their father out. Pride made her do that. While her husband's assignations had been discrete Muriel hadn't bothered about them. It was only when the affair became public that she'd had her attack of righteous indignation, ordering him from the house at the point of a gun, no less. And what a farce that had been! Helen had seen it and almost laughed, Muriel waving the enormous weapon about in her tiny feminine hands. It was her father's service revolver which had long rusted as he must have known, yet he had allowed himself to be ejected from his own house with nothing but two suit-cases and what remained of his self-esteem all piled up on the pavement outside.

Muriel had kept the rest – the house, the furniture, and of course the children. Her father had only his freedom and his Yvette. Helen thought he had the better deal.

Helen could disengage herself too, she supposed, but she only walked the mile-and-a-quarter to the County Library for a couple of hours of peace. With three full months of Muriel's company – exclusive company, it seemed, now that Colin was gone, too – no doubt she would be doing it again. Her essay could be written at leisure and she'd only have to see Muriel at mealtimes. For now, at least, the library would be her sanctuary.

She scratched her way crab-like along the single row of economic books finding little of any use: Adam Smith's *The Wealth of Nations* and one or two treatises by John Maynard Keynes. Most of the rest were pocket theories on how to get rich quick without really trying. That was easy, Helen thought: just write a book about it. Tucked at the end of the shelf was a dog-eared copy of the *Communist Manifesto.* Helen brandished it ostentatiously back to her desk hoping to unnerve the little old ladies who were exchanging their *Mills and Boon* romances. None noticed.

Back at her desk, Helen laid the little yellow paperback to one side while she rummaged in her canvas bag among the dozen tomes she had filched from her college library. She didn't notice the shadow fall across her desk. It was Frank's shadow.

'Aren't you hot in that lot?' he said to the upturned mountain of overcoat, university scarf and suede boots.

'What?' She was struggling to dislodge a volume of encyclopaedic dimensions from her bag. 'Oh, it's you,' she said, and pushed a lock of wayward brown curls from her eyes.

'Need any help?'

She dumped the book on the desk-top and pushed her glasses up onto the bridge of her nose. 'Do I look like a weak and pathetic girly to you?'

'On the contrary.'

'Then why do you feel you keep having to offer me help? I'm quite capable of unpacking my own bag, thank you very much.' She pushed the encyclopaedic volume away from her knocking the little Communist Manifesto on to the floor. Frank bent down to pick it up. But before he handed it back, he read the title.

'And?' she inquired holding out her hand.

'Nothing. It's obviously just meant to make an impression. I'm not impressed.'

She snatched it from his grasp. 'What are you doing here, Frank? Shouldn't you be out haranguing some miserable second-rate actor for that cheap rag of yours?'

'You mean Norfolk's finest? No, not today. There's a limit to the amount of culture anyone can take in a week.' He rotated his head trying to read the title of her essay.

Helen covered it with her hand. 'Then what is it you want? As you can see, *I'm* trying to work,'

'Your mother asked me to come. She said I'd find you here. She was concerned that we started out on the wrong foot yesterday and asked me to try to make amends. I told her it would be a waste of time.'

'Frankie dear, it's not that I don't like you - which I don't, by the way. It's just that you're a user.'

'I don't know how you can say that when you know nothing about me.'

'I know enough. Muriel is easily impressed. She can't see beyond the fact that she has the attention of an attractive younger man. She's flattered, that's all. I, on the other hand, can see right through you.'

'Muriel would be deeply offended if she heard you speak about her like that.'

Helen removed her glasses and smiled her sweetest smile. 'Look Frank, why don't you give it up? You're not really interested in Muriel - at least, not the way she thinks you are. To you she's just a…' she searched for the word. '…an accessory. Like a handbag. And about as much use. Don't get me wrong, I'm not blaming you. People in your position don't have any choice but to resort to subterfuge. I understand that. But Muriel doesn't. She thinks you really like her – as a woman, I mean. But we both know that's not possible, don't we? All I'm asking is that you be honest enough to tell her, that's all. I'm sure she'll still want to be your friend – as will I. But it has to be a friendship based on honesty.'

Frank glanced about him. People sitting nearby were ostentatiously not meeting his gaze. One sniggered.

'I do wish you'd drop this nonsense,' he muttered under his breath - a request Helen was pleased to ignore. Indeed, she raised her voice even louder.

'I don't know why you're being so defensive. I'm on your side, truly I am. I think it's awful the way people like you are treated in this country. What chaps get up to with other chaps in the privacy their own bedrooms as far as I'm concerned is no-one's business but their own. Live and let live, I say.'

Frank's face was by now as red as Helen's smile was bright. 'You can be real cow, can't you?' he muttered through gritted teeth.

Helen noticed, because he made sure she couldn't help but notice, the bearded librarian who had been glaring at them for some minutes from behind the counter and was now making his way over to them. In whispered tones of barely suppressed annoyance, he suggested that if they wanted to continue their discussion would they kindly do so outside.

'Why?' said Helen putting her glasses on and glaring back at him.

'Because this is a public library,' said the man.

'A temple of learning and scholarship,' agreed Helen, 'where, one would hope, all knowledge is sacred.'

'Yes,' agreed the man with infinite forbearance. 'But there are rules.' He left the sentence hanging unable to bring himself to name the subject he was referring to. Helen had no such scruples.

'Oh, can't we discuss queers and poofs in these hallowed halls?' she said loudly.

'If you wouldn't mind,' insisted the man holding out his hand for Helen to leave.

Helen glanced round at the sea of faces now turned towards her. 'We wouldn't wish to offend delicate sensitivities,' she said gathering her books together. 'Come, Francis. Let's go and frighten some horses somewhere.'

Out in the street, the morning was sunny and warm as they trudged down Rampant Horse Street, a name Helen thought singularly apposite under the circumstances.

'Since you've managed to get me thrown out of the library,' said Helen to the despondent Frank, 'you can buy me a coffee.'

'Got *you* thrown out? I'll never be able to show my face in there again.'

'Don't be such a wimp! You don't care what that little bearded bigot thinks, surely? Oh, come on,' she said stomping up the steps of Jarrold's department store.

'I don't know why I'm doing this,' said Frank putting his wallet back in his pocket and sitting at the window table of Jarrold's café that Helen had chosen. 'I must be a masochist.'

Helen shoved the debris of the previous occupant of the table to one side and bit deep into her doughnut squeezing out a great eruption of raspberry jam. 'Think of it as an investment. I may yet be nice to you. Come on, fight back if you think I've misjudged you. Convince me you're worthy of my mother.'

'I don't see why I should. What do you want to know?'

'You were in Africa, you said. Start with that. Where was it?'

'Where is Nigeria? I would have thought with your university education you'd know.'

'That is the sort of thing people who haven't been to university always say,' said Helen licking jam from her thumb. 'For your information, university students are not taught every single piece of knowledge known to man. If they were they'd be studying for thirty years not three, and even then they wouldn't know a hundredth of what there is to know. Which makes that comment of yours a really, really, *really* stupid thing to say. I meant, what were you doing in Nigeria?'

He gave up. 'I was a freelance journalist.'

'Covering some fictitious war.'

'Covering a real, bloody, nasty war, yes. But that was only for a few months. Before that I was in Kenya.'

'Covering a different war, no doubt.'

'No, as a matter of fact I was burying my wife.'

Helen stopped shovelling sugar into her cup. She didn't know whether or not to laugh or frown. Would anyone lie about a thing like that?

'I'm sorry,' he said. 'I shouldn't have blurted that out.'

'No, that's okay. Erm, how…?'

'In childbirth. Not something that's supposed to happen in this day and age, is it?'

'No it isn't. I'm sorry, truly I am. What happened?'

'He lived. He's nearly two now. Charles - or that was the name we wanted to give him. I suppose he might be called anything by now.'

She frowned and shook her head. 'I don't follow.'

'It's complicated.' He stirred his coffee slowly then put his teaspoon down in the saucer. 'Actually, that's not quite true what I said just now. I mean about being married.'

'I see.'

'No, I don't think you do. My wife was Kenyan. We were married, but according to tribal custom. Most Kenyans these days are Christians, you see?'

Helen didn't see, but she nodded anyway. 'What about your son? Where is he now?'

'Still in Kenya, living with his grandmother – along with a few dozen aunts, uncles, cousins. You know what these big rural families are like. I expect it's the same in Norfolk.' He laughed at his little joke, but Helen could see he didn't really think it funny any more than she did.

She sipped her coffee thoughtfully. 'Tell me to mind my own business, but if your son is in Kenya, what are you doing over here?'

'Getting enough money together to go back.'

Helen pulled a face.

He nodded. 'I was writing a series of articles for one of the Sunday supplements. One of them was about big game hunting - which, by the way, was how I met Delia. She was part of a conservation group. I was warned how politically sensitive the ivory trade was, and how much money was involved, but I went ahead and wrote the article anyway.'

'Delia was your wife's name?'

He smiled indulgently. 'They don't all live in mud huts and pick maize for a living. I didn't think the piece I wrote was particularly contentious. Unfortunately, the Kenyan government didn't agree. I had to leave Kenya pretty smartly, which is how I ended up in Lagos.'

'And then you managed to get thrown out of there, too.'

He looked up. 'How did you know that?'

'Just a wild stab.'

He sat back. 'Well, that's about it, really. I returned to the U.K., needed a job and decided to come back to Norfolk – my family are from a village just outside Yarmouth. The *Norwich and Ipswich* offered me this one. It was the first paper I worked on when I first started out. It's not ideal, but beggars can't be choosers.'

'Meanwhile, you've still got to get your son back from Kenya, or have you given up on that idea?'

'I think about little else. But it's easier said than done.'

'That's terrible,' said Helen genuinely outraged. 'Can't the Foreign Office or someone help? That's their job, isn't it?'

He laughed. 'The last thing the British government wants – especially this one - is anything that smacks of the old colonial power still trying to run things in one of Her Majesty's former colonies. I'm afraid my problems are way down on the priority list.'

Helen stirred her coffee thoughtfully. 'How much of this does Muriel know?'

'Not much. I haven't told her anything about Delia - or Charles.'

'Don't you think you should?'

He shook his head. 'You're quite wrong about me and Muriel, you know. She's a good friend who came along just when I was at a particularly low point. I don't intend working for *Chanticleer* for ever. I'll go back to Kenya once the political situation settles down. It's only a matter of time.'

Could he be that naïve? About some things Muriel was very old fashioned. It was quite likely she saw these social outings with Frank as some sort of elaborate courting ritual. In her eyes, that was how a gentleman was supposed to behave. Nor would she regard the fifteen year age difference between them as particularly onerous. After all, Helen's father was at least that much older than Yvette. What was good for the old goose is good for the old gander. Helen wondered if she ought to tell Frank of her fears. The trouble was she had made such a hash of things so far might well think her intervention was just one more ruse to separate them. Much as it went against the grain, Helen had to admit that she just might, possibly, have been wrong about him.

They finished their coffee. Helen stood up and heaved the canvas bag over her shoulder.

'I do wish you'd allow me to carry that for you. People are giving me funny looks.'

'You know what, Frank? You're a dinosaur.'

'For wanting to help a lady?'

'For thinking this lady wants your help.'

She followed him down the escalator again and out of the building. They walked along in silence each lost in thought. Helen had no idea where they were going. She simply followed his lead. If he crossed a road, she crossed it. If he turned a corner, she did too. They seemed to be walking for miles and were now in a part of the city she didn't know very well. Eventually they entered a modern glass office block which she decided must be the offices of the *Norwich and Ipswich Times*. Inside the marbled entrance hall people were milling around singly and in groups, descending stairs, entering lifts. They walked up to a set of high-speed lifts and stood facing each other either side of the doors and Frank pushed the call button. This, Helen decided, would have to be the parting of the ways. She couldn't follow him up to his office, nor did she want to. When the lift arrived they would say goodbye and she would walk back to the bus station. She wondered vaguely, while they waited for the lift to descend, which floor his office on.

The lift arrived and the doors opened. People got out.

'Well, I'll see you this evening, no doubt,' said Helen, holding out her hand.

'Oh yes, *Private Lives*,' said Frank, taking it.

The lift doors closed again.

'Aren't you getting in?' said Helen.

'*Me?* I was following *you*.'

Helen fumbled in her pocket for her glasses, put them on and scrutinized the company name-plate next to the lift door.

'Idiot!' she growled.

She heaved her canvas bag back onto her shoulder before turning on her heel and stomping out of the building. 'Colman's Mustard, indeed!' she muttered nearly tripping down the steps in her haste.

FIFTEEN

COLIN was pacing the bathroom again, this time hearing his bear feet slapping against the cold floor tiles. He was angry and he was in pain: angry with himself because he had come so close to escaping only for his nerve to fail him at the last moment. Another few seconds and he would have succeeded in squeezing his torn and bruised body through the tiny fanlight and out into the cool evening air. And what a sight he would have made running through the streets of Caisterbury in just his briefs covered head to toe in a thick film of lather which had lubricated his exit. But he wouldn't have cared about that for he would have been free! Now the bloody stuff was drying on his body and flaking off him like a second skin.

It was the blast from the shotgun that had stopped him, the paralysing shock of the explosion which the hollow space of the bathroom had amplified tenfold. Up to that moment he had never believed the gun actually worked, but now he knew it definitely did. It had been a sobering experience. And simultaneous with the bang he'd felt a sharp pain in his right ear. Most of the shot had missed him and embedded itself in the plaster above his head, but a few pellets had nicked his earlobe causing it to pour with blood making the wound appear far worse than it was. The resulting confusion of pain, noise, blood and dust had stunned him just long enough for the witch to get the door open and the gun inside. By the time Colin recovered his wits she was already aiming again, and this time he had no doubt she would have hit her target squarely. There was nothing left to do but give up and clamber back inside.

He stopped pacing to stand in front of the mirror and gingerly remove the blood-encrusted piece of toilet tissue that he had been holding against his ear. Half his earlobe was missing but it looked worse than it was. But what angered him the most was the realisation that he had blown his best chance of escape, for within minutes of forcing him back into the room and locking the door the witch was out in the garden nailing strips of timber over the outside of the fanlight. With each hammer-blow receded the last chance of escape through that route.

God, she must be feeling pretty smug with herself. He wouldn't put it past her to have set the whole thing up, deliberately leaving that window unlocked just to tempt him. She knew it was there. Just hours earlier she'd seen him trying to attract the attention of the old woman next door through it. She must have realised he'd try to use it. She was playing him like a fish, feeding out the line, and then just when he'd run about as far as he could, reeling him back in again. She was trying to wear him down mentally. Well, he'd show her he was stronger than that. If she wanted psychological warfare, she'd get it. Three times now she'd managed to frustrate his efforts at escape. She was probably expecting him to be demoralized and bitter by now. Well, he'd be the opposite. He'd be nice to her, flatter her, make her *like* him, and that way get her to drop her guard. Then when she was least expecting it he'd pounce.

What other choice did he have? He knew now for certain that no-one was looking for him. If asked, his mother would say he was in South Africa. It would be weeks before she started to wonder why she hadn't heard from him and longer before she tried to locate him. He didn't have weeks. If he wasn't out of here within days he would go mad – that's if the Witch hadn't killed him already. In any case, who would Muriel ask? Lifeplan? What would they tell her? That Colin had left the company. She already knew that. They wouldn't tell her he'd left without giving notice because companies don't reveal that sort of information, not even to mothers of former employees.

Who else could she ask? Marcia? She wouldn't say anything. She didn't *know* anything, not really. He hadn't told her what he intended doing with the list of names he'd wheedled out of her. Even if she guessed the reason she would be too frightened of losing her own job to say anything. No, he had to face it, there was no-one. No cavalry, no knight in shining armour was coming to his rescue. He was entirely on his own.

Anyway, one thing he could not afford to do was simply sit around waiting for something to turn up. The only way he was going to get out of here was by using his own guile. And that wasn't the great advantage he first thought it would be. If today had taught him anything it was not to underestimate Winifred Jonah. That had been a mistake that had put him right back to square one. She might be mad but it was the madness of cunning. And psychologically he was back at the beginning, too. He was going to have to begin the whole process of building up a rapport with her again. Only this time he was going to have to be more subtle about it. He was going to have to smile at her, charm her, flatter her and convince her that he meant it, God help him. And all the while he was being nice he would be hating her, the witch, the ugly, foul, evil old *witch*.

Winifred couldn't stop shaking. No longer merely trembling hands, her whole body shivered uncontrollably as she thought about what had just nearly happened. How could she have been so stupid? She thought she had been so careful. She thought she had covered every eventuality. But then, who would have dreamt that anyone would try to climb through such a tiny opening? And he had very nearly succeeded. Another minute and he would have been out through that window and off, and her life would have been over. God, he was wily and clever that one. He'd lulled her into a false sense of security pretending to be a poor vulnerable puppy when all the time he was a cunning little fox. She could almost admire him for it.

In horror she threw the shotgun away from her across the kitchen, but almost immediately she snatched it up again. She fumbled to remove the spent cartridge which she buried in the bottom of her waste bin. Then she scrubbed her hands in carbolic to rid them of the smell of sulphur. Could anyone smell it in the air? She couldn't, but that didn't mean anything given her lack of smell. She opened a window and the back door to get a draught through.

Her next thought, once she had regained the ability to think again, had been to board up that ventilation window. For once not caring who might see her, she rummaged in the shed until she found some old planks and nailed them over the outside of the window. It was only when she got back indoors again that another and far more worrying thought occurred to her: Someone must have heard the shot. How could they not? She still had ringing in her own ears though it was several minutes after the blast. Surely any moment now the warden - or the police - would be hammering on her door. And he would hammer too, and shout and kick and do everything he did this morning only this time they would hear him and again all would be lost. Winifred brought her two trembling hands up to her face.

She listened for the tell-tale noises, but she heard – nothing. Not a sound came from the bathroom, either. What was he doing in there? What new treachery was he constructing even as she waited that she hadn't thought of? Fearful of what she might find, she returned again and again to the spy-hole to check, but saw only his ghostly white figure pacing up and down, up and down, up and down.

As the minutes ticked by and no-one appeared, her heart began to beat less violently and at last her breathing returned to normal. Maybe that old myth about gunshots being mistaken for cars back-firing would account for it. But cars didn't back-fire anymore - at least, not modern ones. She peeped nervously out of the sitting room window. All appeared normal in the Close. Maybe the police were hiding round the corner waiting to pounce. At last she garnered enough courage to unlock the street door and pull it towards her. It didn't, as she half-expected, fall in under the weight of a dozen policemen. All was quiet and normal outside. There was even birdsong which there wouldn't be if anyone was about. She crept down the garden path to the edge of the road and looked up and down it into the gathering gloom. The Close was empty. Completely empty of people. And it was then that she realized why no-one had heard the gunshot, or if they had would not have paid it much attention: it was because of the time of day. Half an hour earlier and the kids would still have been coming home from school. Half an hour later and they'd be out in the street again playing in the long summer twilight. But just at that moment, the exact moment when Winifred had pulled the trigger, fathers were still at work, mothers were preparing the tea and their children were sitting in front of television sets.

Heady with relief, Winifred closed the street door as silently as she could. Once again she had survived - but only just. Whichever gods were watching over her they had not yet slept. It is said that those who the gods wish to destroy they first make mad. Given what her tortured mind had been through in recent days and months, it was a wonder she retained any sanity at all. Now fully recovered and in command once more, she had to deal with him again. She found the shotgun again and with a steadier hand this time she broke it open and filled the empty breach with a fresh cartridge before snapping it shut again. She knew, as she turned wearily towards the bathroom once more, how it would be. He would be sullen and abusive again as he had been when he first realised he was her prisoner. But that was all right for it would mean he knew that he had lost, and that was all that mattered.

When she got the door open she saw he was sitting on the edge of the bath. She entered, gun-barrel first. The sight of him shocked her. As much of him as she had seen through the spy-hole had not prepared her for this. He looked awful, an alien thing, almost unrecognisable naked in his new white skin that was flaking off in patches leaving pinkish areas underneath. More like an insect than a human being. A piece of blood-soaked toilet paper was stuck to his right ear, and on the wall above his head was an area of shattered plaster the size of a dinner-plate. Otherwise all seemed as it was before. There were no more holes that she could see, nowhere he could wriggle through.

He did not speak when she entered. That was all right. It was what she had expected. Besides, Winifred was not in a mood for discussion. She had decided what she was going to say to him, and having said it she would leave him alone to mull it over.

'I warned you what would happen. So, no dinner for you tonight.' That was it. That was all. She started to back out again.

To her bewilderment, his face broadened into a brilliant smile. 'Fine,' he grinned putting up a salutary hand.

She stopped and looked at him.

'Well, it's fair enough. Like you say, I knew the rules. I broke them. Fine. Truth to tell, I'm not all that hungry.'

Winifred didn't know how to respond. 'So long as you know.'

He nodded. Without taking her eyes off him and keeping the gun held level, she stooped to grab a corner of the mattress with her free hand. She'd already decided she was going to remove it in case he tried to use it to block the door again.

'Take it,' he told her cheerfully. 'No honestly, I don't blame you one inch. Take it, I don't need it.'

What new game was this? He was being friendly and compliant when he should be morose and difficult. It was making her nervous.

'Don't you think you can sweet-talk me out of it 'cos you can't. I'm taking it and that's all there is to it.' Winifred set her jaw and started again to back out.

'Absolutely,' grinned Colin. 'Take it. I couldn't agree with you more. Er, there is one thing, though. Do you think I could have a bath? And maybe a change of clothes. I know it's a bit of a cheek, but my suit – well, I'm sure you can smell it.' He pointed to the crumpled pile on the floor that he had thrown down in his haste to escape.

No, she couldn't smell it any more than she could smell the gunpowder or the sluice bucket. But others might – Mrs Goffe, for one – and that wouldn't do at all.

'There's no hot water. Not till tomorrow.'

'Never mind. Cold baths are good for you - character-forming.' He grinned again. 'And it would be a shame to waste all this soap, don't you think?' He pulled his fingernails across his chest leaving five pink tramlines in their wake.

'I'll fetch a towel.'

Once the door was closed she padlocked it again - just in case.

What was he up to, acting like nothing had happened? Did he still think she was a fool? Did he expect her to behave as though nothing had happened? Asking for a bath! If he thought he was going to get round her with jokes and silly smiles he was mistaken. Oh yes, she knew what he was up to; he was just trying to confuse her. But that was all right. Let him think he was getting the better of her with his posh words. Meanwhile she would be getting her way. He could have his bath, it was no skin off her nose - although it might off his, she chuckled. See, Mr Clever-pants, I can make jokes, too, Mr *Smelly*-pants! And he could have a change of clothes, too, so Mrs Goffe couldn't smell him. He'd have done better to stink the place out, he had no sense. That was another point to her. If it's a battle of wits he wanted she could oblige. They'd soon see who was the smarter out of the two of them.

Christ what a bitch! No food, and now no bed either. She's really going to make him pay for trying to escape. What did she think he was going to do, sit around and do nothing? This punishment for bad behaviour, she was just being vindictive. But he was determined not to let her see it bothered him. That way she will think she's won and if she did that he might as well give up. It was psychological warfare and he had the better brain.

He was sure now that his strategy of placating her was the right one. Subtlety unnerved her, he could see that, she didn't know how to handle it. He was smarter than she was and that was what was going to get him out of here. Make light of everything. Let her think he was treating it all as one big joke. It will take time but it will work. Already it was paying dividends: she was going to let him have a bath. A point to him. Just a little point, but next time it will be something more, and a bit more and bit by bit he will have calmed her again. Then just when she thought all was well he'd strike again. And next time there would be no mistakes.

Winifred took him some of Albert's old clothes. She didn't know if they'd fit him and she didn't much care. Probably they wouldn't: he was taller and broader than Albert. He looked to be back to normal after his bath although he was still naked with only the towel wrapped round his middle. Keeping the shotgun steadied on his face, she held something out for him to take: it was a hank of cotton wool soaked in TCP.

'Antiseptic,' she explained.
'I know what it is.'
'For your ear.'

He thought she was being kind but really she wasn't. She didn't want the wound getting infected on top of everything else. The toilet paper dressing had come off in the bath and she could see that quite a chunk of the lobe was missing.

He accepted the wad reluctantly. 'Didn't trust me with the bottle, eh?'

'You don't need more than a drop.'

Good, he thought, that was very good. Keep her guessing. The more uncertain she was the more likely to make mistakes. He held the pungent-smelling wad against his ear and grimaced at the pain. 'Christ!'

'It'll sting for a bit,' said Winifred. 'But then it'll do it good.'

'Too bloody right it stings!' He nodded to the clothes folded neatly over Winifred's free arm. 'Those for me?'

'My husband, Albert's. He only wore it once. It's clean.'

'It stinks of mothballs.'

Did it? Winifred didn't know. 'I'll wash your one.' She bent down to exchange the neat fresh clothes for the jumble of stale ones.

'I must say the room service in this hotel is simply tops. I shall be recommending it to all my friends.'

Winifred pursed her lips together tightly. 'Still making jokes?'

He shrugged. 'What else is there to do?'

Winifred threw his suit into a corner of the bedroom. Despite her determination not to let him get the better of her here she was all wound up again. She must try to keep control. He wanted her to lose her patience with him, that was his plan, she could see that now. But as long as she kept her cool he wasn't going to win because ultimately she held all the cards. He could make his jokes and give his clever replies but in the end he would do what she wanted. He would see that cooperation was in his best interests. Because the more he did as he was told the better life would be for him.

She picked the jacket up from the floor and as she did so something fell out of a pocket. It was an envelope bulging with bank notes. Winifred had never seen so many together all at once. She counted them and whistled. There was over four thousand pounds mostly in fifty pound notes. Winifred had never seen a fifty pound note before let alone held one in her hand. She wasn't even sure it was real. She counted the notes again: four thousand five hundred pounds. That was almost as much as she had received from the insurance people when Albert died. But then she realised what it meant, where the money must have come from, and then awe turned to anger.

It was stolen money. That was the only explanation. She wasn't the only Lifeplan client Colin had been swindling. It had never occurred to her before but now it made sense. Of course there would have been others before her. How many others? And her money would have added to it - her *Albert's* money. He was an even bigger crook than she realised. A regular Ronnie Biggs.

In her anger and frustration, Winifred stood outside the bathroom door. Inside she could hear him whistling as he tried on Albert's clothes, *whistling!* So, he thought he thought he could fool her, did he? Well, he wasn't free yet. He was still her prisoner. And if she had anything to do with it, that was how he would remain. She listened for a few moments, her fists clenching and unclenching spasmodically. Then with an anguished, almost feral cry she raised both fists high above her head and brought them down with all her might upon the door. Behind it, the whistling stopped.

SIXTEEN

'I'VE been thinking,' said Muriel. 'Isn't it time we heard from Colin?'

'Hm?' Helen was lying on her back on the sofa frowning over her *Guardian* crossword and trying to think of an anagram for *rhubarb*.

'After all, it has been nearly three weeks. You'd think he would have written by now just to say he'd arrived safely. What do you think? It's a puzzle.'

'It certainly is,' muttered Helen.

Muriel came in to the sitting room and stood squarely in front of her daughter. 'Well?'

Helen dropped the newspaper on to her chest and looked up. She could see her mother was in earnest. 'When did he leave?'

'Two weeks ago last Monday. Eighteen days.'

Helen hadn't the faintest idea how long it took for a letter to arrive from South Africa. It was not a part of the world she cared to think about very much. Eighteen days didn't sound very long to traverse six thousand miles.

'Any day now, I should think.' She went back to her crossword. 'You worry too much, Mother dear. Give the boy a chance to get settled in. He's probably got more important things on his mind than writing home to mummy.'

'More important than putting his poor mother's mind at rest?'

Muriel's cold, so pitifully noticeable all week, had temporarily dried up. In her concern about Colin she had forgotten about it. She couldn't concentrate on two things at once.

'I would have thought that if a letter could get here in five days he could have sent one to me in eighteen,' she said distantly.

'Hm,' agreed Helen.

Muriel picked up the glass vase from the coffee table with a yellow-gloved hand and inspected the dried skeletons of flowers. Only the bit of fern had any life left in it. The odour of decomposition offended Muriel's nostrils and she held the vase at arms-length until she could get it to the kitchen sink.

'What letter?' Helen had followed her mother into the kitchen.

'The letter that came for Colin. Didn't I mention it? Oh well, I put it in the bureau. It arrived the day before yesterday. I can't think why they sent it to him here when he's already over there.'

Helen fought back her exasperation. 'If it arrived two days ago, Ma, why didn't you open it? It might be something important.'

'That's precisely why I didn't open it. You can't go around opening other people's letters, especially official-looking ones. It's all right,' she continued flushing with irritation. 'I was going to send it on to him - just as soon as he gives me his new address.'

Helen mentally counted to ten. It was a familiar story. As far back as Helen could remember Muriel had never dealt with official documents leaving all such matters to her husband. Even now rate demands, electricity bills, telephone bills – anything in a brown envelope or with one of those little cellophane windows - were forwarded on to him at his new address, unopened. He had to pay them, so there was no point in distressing herself unnecessarily. Muriel would only open letters she had been expecting or ones whose handwriting on the envelope she recognised. It was a line of reasoning completely alien to Helen. Having spent most of her adulthood in one educational institution or another, communal life was second nature to her. In the flat in Camberwell bills were shared, problems halved. Everything was discussed from overdrafts to boyfriends – which amounted to much the same thing. The word "personal" was not in her vocabulary.

'I will be patient with my mother,' Helen muttered to herself. 'It's not her fault.'

She found the letter, a long white one, in the bureau and turned it over in her hands. She could see why it had arrived in only five days. In the top left corner of the envelope was the coat of arms of the Republic of South Africa – a lion and a springbok - but the stamp was British, not South African. The postmark said it had been posted on the second of July at five-fifteen p.m. and it had originated from somewhere in WC2 – a London code. Without further hesitation, Helen ripped open the envelope with her thumb.

It was a very brief letter, only one short paragraph long, and signed by someone in the visa department of the South African Embassy. The contents made no sense to Helen at all.

'This letter makes no sense to me at all,' she said slowly returning to the kitchen.

'I warned you not to open it. And just look at the state of the envelope! Honestly, Helen, you have no respect for other people's property. I'll never be able to stick it back together again.'

Helen read the letter again. 'Where would Colin get five thousand pounds from? That's more than he earns in a year.'

'I don't think so,' said Muriel reaching for a tea-towel. 'He gets a good salary from Lifeplan. And in this new position he'll be earning even more.'

'Don't be silly, Ma, Colin never has any money. He owes me a tenner, and I know for a fact he's borrowed money off Dad.'

Muriel went quiet. The thought of Colin borrowing money off his father rather than her was a great disappointment. She wiped her gloved hands on the tea-towel and took the letter from Helen. A moment later, she handed it back.

'I expect it's some kind of advance. This new job is supposed to be a promotion.'

'What exactly is his new job?'

'I'm not sure. The same as his old one, I expect. Only better. Oh, I don't know, you'll have to ask him yourself.'

Helen was thoughtful. 'It says here that he can apply for work in South Africa on condition he has a valid return ticket to the UK and sufficient capital to support himself in the meantime. What do you make of that?'

The words meant nothing to Muriel. She imagined it was some kind of insurance jargon. Helen understood the words but not their meaning – at least, not in this context. In fact, the whole tone of the letter was odd. It wasn't the sort of letter sent to someone who already had a job but rather someone who was thinking of visiting the country in order to look for a job. But Colin was already fixed up by the time the letter was sent, wasn't he? She looked at the postmark on the envelope again and compared it with the date at the top of the letter. Both dates agreed, Friday the second of July: eleven days *after* Colin had supposedly left the country.

'Mother, are you sure Colin's gone to South Africa?'

Muriel didn't even bother to turn round to reply. 'What a silly question, darling. Of course I'm sure. I helped him to pack.'

In the library Helen found it difficult to concentrate on her essay. She had a dozen huge volumes open on the desk in front of her but she wasn't looking at any of them.

She didn't know why the letter should bother her so much. It wouldn't at all surprise her to discover that everything Colin had told Muriel turned out to be fantasy and that there never was any high-powered job waiting for him in South Africa. The story hadn't rung true when Muriel first told it to her. It would be entirely within character for her younger brother to have made the whole thing up just to impress Muriel who was gullible enough to believe it. She remembered all the nonsense when he first joined Lifeplan about how he was going to earn a fortune in his first year only to end up getting less than a shop assistant. Muriel, of course, had accepted every word he said without question.

But then, Colin had always been able to pull the wool over her eyes. Muriel's brilliant son.

To everyone other than Muriel Colin had always been a disappointment particularly to his father who'd had ambitions for both his children. Not that Colin wasn't bright, but his abilities had never been tested having left school as soon as he turned fifteen just weeks before sitting his 'O'-levels and got a job. The normal rules of life didn't apply to Colin and formal education especially he regarded as a mug's game. Like Helen, he had the chance and the ability to go to university if he wanted to, but he spurned it. He knew best. In his philosophy you got on in life through your wits and not because of what was written on a piece of paper.

Now all this rubbish about a promotion to the Johannesburg office of Lifeplan Assurance. Would someone with Colin's qualifications – or rather, *lack* of qualifications - be offered such a post? Would a tuppeny-ha'penny outfit like Lifeplan even have an office in Johannesburg - or anywhere else outside Norfolk, for that matter? Helen doubted it. More likely it was another empty promise made by that wise-guy boss of his, Paul Kerney, to keep Colin in his present underpaid position as a junior sales rep. Some yarn about future prospects if he worked hard and did well - that sounded more like it. Colin hero-worshipped Paul Kerney but he always sounded like a slippery character to Helen. She was convinced nothing would come of this new job and in time the whole matter would be quietly forgotten and never mentioned again.

But if that was the case, what was this letter from the South African Embassy about? It certainly looked genuine enough. Was Colin seriously thinking of going to South Africa to work, albeit not in Lifeplan's Johannesburg office? And whatever made them think Colin had five thousand pounds? Colin didn't have five thousand pence! He would find the South African government harder to hoodwink that Muriel. So if he wasn't in South Africa, where the hell was he? Eighteen days since he left, Muriel said. He must have gone somewhere. Helen suspected some scheming was going on but she couldn't work it out, the twists and turns of her little brother's devious mind had always defeated her. Well, there wasn't much she could do about it. She opened the library copy of John Stuart Mill's *Principles of Political Economy* and started to read.

A figure skulking behind the newspaper boards caught her eye. She got up and went over to him.

'Frank, what are you doing here?' she said in a loud whisper.

'Do I need your permission? It is a *public* library,' he replied in a softer one.

'Muriel put you up to this, didn't she?'

'She doesn't know I'm here – this time.'

'If you don't go away I'll tell the librarian you're annoying me and get you thrown out. Remember what happened last time.' She looked over at the front desk. Today it was occupied by a fat woman in a cardigan.

Frank smiled. 'I told her I'm here to do research. I think she likes me.'

'Look Frank, what do I have to do to get it through to you that you are not welcome? I ignore you and you fail to notice. I insult you and you come back for more. Is one Brearney female not enough for you? Do you want to bed us both?'

She had meant to embarrass him. She embarrassed herself more. It wasn't at all what she had intended to say but it was too late now to retract.

That evening the three of them ate dinner in silence. Muriel's cold had returned with a vengeance and she wasn't feeling up to refereeing another battle royal between Helen and Frank. She tried to engage them both in conversation but ended up having separate conversations with each. At last her exasperation got the better of her.

'Are you two still at loggerheads with each other? For Goodness sake! Call yourselves adults?' She slammed the serving spoon down on its plate.

Muriel sniffed her way through the egg mayonnaise and coughed over the chicken supreme. The sherry trifle she didn't think she could face at all and more than she could three hours of Rossini later. Frank had gone to a lot of trouble to get the tickets; it would be a crime to waste them. In any event, *The Barber of Seville* was not really her cup of tea, so perhaps Helen would be a dear and go in Muriel's place, 'If you think you could bear each other's company, that is.'

Helen went with Frank to the theatre. During the second act when Figaro and the count have to break into Dr Bartolo's house in order to

185

rescue Rosina, the balcony window got stuck. It wasn't in the script and for that reason Helen laughed. As she turned to Frank with childish delight she saw that he had been looking at her.

*

Colin was winning - slowly, but winning nevertheless, of that he was certain. He'd been here for three weeks now and look at the concessions he had wrung out of Winnie-the-witch: first the clothes, then the mattress came back; not forgetting hot water for baths. Even the food had improved, and as long as he did as she asked, she no longer withheld his food. That was important, because he needed food to build up his strength for the final showdown. And that was coming any day now, he could feel it in his bones. Just one chance, that was all he needed, just one.

Of course, he'd had to prove he could be trusted. It was no good just telling her, he had to *show* her. That was important. After that business with the fanlight she was hardly likely to take his word for it, and he couldn't blame her for that. (He saw now that he would never have been able to get through that window, it was a ridiculous idea. He told her that, too.) He had to prove he was worthy of her trust. And he had done. Several times.

The first time was when that char-woman came again. The witch had done the same as she did on previous occasions – starved him the night before, tied and gagged him and she locked the door. This time, though, he told her she needn't have bothered, and he promised to be on his best behaviour and not even try to attract her attention. 'Scouts honour!' he'd joked and put three fingers up to his temple. Naturally the witch was sceptical, but Colin had been as good as his word. It was important to be truthful some of the time, that way when the moment came for a real lie she would believe him. When Mrs Goffe arrived he had sat quietly on his bed, not making a sound. He heard Winifred speaking to her, telling her what jobs to do and which rooms needed cleaning and which didn't – not the bathroom, of course. He smiled at that – of course not the bathroom. And then he heard the hoover starting up, just like always. When Mrs Goffe switched it off and she came near the bathroom door Colin held his breath – silent running, he told the Witch with a wink of his eye - until he heard her go away again. It seemed to have worked. Mrs Goffe didn't bother trying to get into the bathroom this time. When she had gone the witch came in to free him. Colin looked pleased with himself.

'See?' he'd said to her. 'I told you I'd be good. You needn't have worried.'

His performance must have impressed her because he got an extra rasher of bacon that morning. And it was the same when the ambulance came. The doorbell went on the dot of ten-thirty – they're so punctual those people. Colin listened carefully. He heard the witch open the door and greet the ambulance man – Brian, he heard her call him. She put a saucer of milk down for the cat, the street door closed and the bungalow was silent for two hours. And even though the Witch wasn't there to see, he had remained absolutely still the whole time, hadn't so much as breathed. He told her so when the ambulance brought her back. She said she believed him. That was important the fact that he had earned her trust. And to prove it she put extra custard on his jelly at lunch.

She was warming to him, he was certain. Not long now. He'd have her eating out of the palm of his hand, the witch, the ugly, foul, flea-ridden, filthy old *WITCH!*

No-one's arrived. If they know he's here they aren't coming to rescue him. Either they don't care or she's wrong about where that money came from she found in his pocket. But she was sure she wasn't wrong. Four thousand five hundred pounds was an awful lot to be carrying about. Whoever it belonged to they didn't seem to be in too much of a hurry to get it back. She'd seen nothing on the local television news or in the Free Press. Well, Winifred had a good use for some of it at least. There were two mouths to feed, now, and she had been wondering where to get the money to pay for the extra food. No need to worry about that anymore.

At some stage she must get out to a shop, even if it was just the corner shop at the end of Lady Astor Crescent although she disliked going in there. For one thing they kept such ridiculous hours, opening from nine till five and closing for lunch. Who closes for lunch in this day and age? Then there was the fresh produce that was anything but fresh. And the prices! No wonder supermarkets were taking all their trade away from them. Besides, Winifred much preferred to go direct to the farmer. She was, after all, once a farmer herself.

With the possibility receding of someone coming to look for Colin, Winifred had grown a little reckless of late. Just a few risks, nothing too serious, to see what would happen. He seemed much more compliant of late. The other day she went into the bathroom with the shotgun slung over one arm just to see what he'd do. It wasn't loaded, and she had her knife at the ready in her other pocket in case. As she expected, he didn't do anything. She knew what he was up to. He thought he could get her to drop her guard and then suddenly make a dash for it if he thought he could get away. But she was onto him. She was playing him along. Let him think he was hoodwinking her. Lately she'd even taken to leaving the gun in the kitchen. The first time she did that was by accident, she had simply forgotten about it. From then on she often left it behind in the kitchen, and each time she felt a little stronger, a little more confident. She was testing him, and each test that he passed she rewarded him for his good behaviour: gooseberry crumble for his tea one day, Albert's small radio to listen to the next. He seemed willing to please – eager, in fact. It was almost as if these little rewards were the purpose of his good behaviour. She knew the real purpose was for him to escape. He talked about escape quite openly now but as if it were some distant goal to aim for, nothing real. It was almost a game, like he never really meant to do it. He'd start sentences with things like, 'When I get out of here.' Another time it was, 'You see, I *am* trustworthy.' Just like Drew was as child. She could almost hear her five-year-old nephew: 'You see, Auntie Winnie, I *am* a good boy really, you see?'

All right. Let's see who's fooling who. On Wednesday evening Mrs Goffe's youngest pushed a note from his mother through the door saying she wasn't feeling too well and wouldn't be in the next morning - not for the first time. Winifred didn't tell Colin that. She acted as if Mrs Goffe was coming the next day as usual. She went through the usual routine the day before Mrs Goffe's visits: She didn't feed him Wednesday night and bound and gagged him as usual on Thursday morning. At nine-thirty she acted as if Mrs Goffe were there, pretending to talk to her, telling her what wanted cleaning that day, and then Winifred got the hoover out and did the work herself. When she switched the machine off again she had crept over to the bathroom door and listened. Not a peep out of him. She looked through the spy-hole but he was just sitting on his mattress looking like he was holding his breath. Seems he was as good as his word.

An hour later she did it all to do again for the ambulance. She told Colin he was trusted to be on his best behaviour since Winifred would be going out and he would be left entirely on his own for a whole hour. If when she came back he had been good, she would give him a nice treat for his supper. Of course she didn't go to the hospital. She'd gone out to the ambulance as it drew up and told Brian she wasn't feeling up to Mrs Dobrzynski's ministrations today. Brian had been all understanding and said he hoped she felt better next week and driven off without further ado - one less job for him today. On the way back into the bungalow Winifred had pushed the doorbell to see if it prompted any reaction, but he'd been quiet as a lamb. She was impressed. Maybe he was being a good boy after all. Later, she made him a jelly trifle as a reward for being on his best behaviour.

SEVENTEEN

'WHAT'S this?'

'What does it look like. It's a wheelchair.'

'I can see it's a wheelchair. What's it for?'

'You sit in it – strapped in, of course. I'll let you into the rest of the house like I promised.'

Colin wasn't sure.

'It's perfectly safe,' Winifred went on, hastily. 'It was Albert's.'

Colin pushed the wheelchair backwards and forwards. It wasn't exactly what he'd had in mind when he'd got her to agree to let him have a bit more freedom as his reward for the weeks of obedience. He had expected to be allowed to wander around unfettered. That was his plan. This wasn't the same thing at all.

'How am I supposed to make it move if I'm strapped in?'

'I've thought of that,' Winifred explained enthusiastically and she sat in the chair to demonstrate. 'I've taken the foot-rests off. You can drag yourself along using your feet, like this see? I've tried it so I know it works.'

'Albert's, you say?'

Winifred nodded.

Colin wheeled it backwards and forwards again.

Winifred pursed her lips. 'Of course, if you don't want it – ' She made to wheel it away.

'No, wait,' he said putting out his hand. 'I'll try it,' and hopped onto the seat.

Winifred produced a piece of rope from her pocket. He barred his teeth, but she lifted the shotgun. Colin shrugged and put his right arm on the wheelchair arm for her to tie together. Then she produced a longer piece of rope and tied it round his middle. She let him keep his left arm free.

'Now I think we're ready,' she said rising to her feet again.

'For what?'

'Dinner, of course. Something special today. A special treat.'

Colin sat on one side of the kitchen table while Winifred prepared the meal. It was to be lamb chops. She'd been saving them for just this occasion knowing it was inevitable to come sooner or later. Anyway, it had to be lamb chops. There wasn't anything else in the larder.

Colin was idly manoeuvring the wheelchair with his free hand on one wheel. He managed to do a complete circle. 'They're quite nice these bungalows, aren't they? Quite spacious.'

'They're all right,' agreed Winifred. She was peeling potatoes at the sink keeping the gun propped up against the sink close at hand, just in case.

He laughed. 'You know, I've been in this bungalow for a month now and this is the first time I've been in the kitchen. First time other than the sitting room I've been anywhere.'

'You could have come sooner - if you'd kept your promise.'

'What promise was that?'

'Your promise not to try to escape.'

He put his head back. 'W-e-l-l, you didn't really expect me to, did you?'

'No, not really,' she agreed, and dropped a peeled potato into a saucepan of salted water.

'You know, we get on quite well, don't you think? I mean, who would think looking at us now that I was your prisoner?'

Winifred didn't reply.

'I mean, look at us. We make quite a good team. I reckon when you finally let me go we'll stay good friends. I'll probably come round and visit. Would you like that? Me coming to visit?'

'That would be nice,' agreed Winifred.

'So you agree, then? That you will let me go one day?'

'We'll see.'

Colin sighed heavily. 'Is there anything I can do to help? I'm quite good in the kitchen. I always used to help my mother peel potatoes.'

'What would your mother say if she knew that you were a blackmailer?'

'Ah, but what would your mother say if she knew you were a kidnapper?'

'I never had a mother.'

'Don't be silly. Everybody has a mother.'

Winifred threw the second potato into the pot. 'You don't want to be talking about things you don't know nothing about.'

He raised his free hand in a placatory gesture. 'All right, I'm sorry. You never had a mother. If that's what you want.'

'It's the truth.'

'Well, if it's any consolation, I never knew my father all that well. They're divorced, my parents.'

'That's a shame,' said Winifred with genuine feeling.

Colin beamed at her. 'Do you really think so? You know, you're not a bad old girl really, are you?'

Winifred got the chops out of the meat safe and chopped an onion.

'What about me? You quite like me really, don't you? Go on admit it. I know you do.'

Winifred did not look up. 'You came here to steal from me, that's all I know.'

'Oh, you're not still going on about that, are you?'

'It's why you're here.'

'I know, but to be honest, I doubt whether I would have taken your money, you know? I mean, how much was it you got? Five thou? Hardly worth my while.'

Winifred kept her own council. She was thinking of the four thousand she found in his wallet.

The chops crackled and spat in the frying pan and the potatoes steamed up the kitchen window. Eventually it was ready to serve and Winifred put his plate down on the table in front of him first.

'There's tinned pineapple and cream for afterwards.'

'Yum-yum!' said Colin.

Because he had only his left hand free, she cut his meat up for him into bite-sized pieces and put a fork near his left hand. As she bent forward to put his plate down he did something that neither of them had anticipated: he kissed her on her cheek. Winifred blushed but said nothing, and neither did he. It was difficult to know who was the most surprised. Colin put a piece of the meat into his mouth and started to chew. It was while Winifred had turned away to put a final spoonful of peas on her own plate that the moment Colin had been waiting for patiently for so long finally arrived. There was a quick movement outside and the back door suddenly opened inwards.

'Oh, sorry, I didn't see you.'

A young, flaxen-haired girl stood in the doorway. She was a pretty girl, about sixteen or seventeen years old, with her hair in plaits and wearing a man's shirt. On her lower half she wore Wellington boots and grey corduroys. The sleeves of the shirt were rolled up to the elbows. One hand she kept on the handle of the open door while in the other she clutched a basket. To Colin she looked wonderful, so full of life, bright and rosily healthy with an outdoor complexion and her sparkling green eyes were wide with surprise and curiosity.

Colin stared at her in amazement. His mouth dropped open revealing a half-chewed piece of lamb.

She gave him a friendly, inviting smile. 'I thought Winnie was here. Is she about?' She looked searchingly behind him as though she expected Winifred to pop out of a cupboard above his head. When Colin still didn't reply she took a step forward and put the basket down on the kitchen table. Then her eyes took in the wheelchair, the food cut-up on his plate, the saliva that was beginning to dribble out of his open mouth, and she decided something.

'I'll just leave the eggs and milk here then, shall I? Tell Winnie, Lindsay brought it. Can you do that? Lindsay from the farm? I expect she'll know when she sees it.'

A sort of strangulated gargle came from Colin's mouth. He tried to speak but couldn't get it out. The words seemed to stick somehow in his throat. Lindsay waited, but still nothing came. So she shrugged, gave Colin her sunny smile again, and bounced out closing the door after her.

From behind the door Winifred emerged as white as a sheet. She was still holding her half-filled plate in her hands with a lamb chop, boiled potatoes and frozen peas on it. Colin started to tremble. His body seemed to go into spasm. The wheelchair rocked backwards and forwards. Winifred put down the plate and went to him putting her arms round his shoulders. He was going blue in the face.

'It's shock,' she said. 'Try to breathe slowly, don't force it.'

For a minute she just held him while he wept quietly, tears rolling down his face, his whole body shuddering in her arms. 'I was so close, Winnie,' he whispered. 'I could have made it. One word, that was all I needed, just one word and I'd have been free.' He was sobbing pitiably, terrible wails of tears.

'Ssh,' said Winifred. 'I know, I know.' She stroked his hair and put her cheek on his forehead, rocking him like a baby.

'I couldn't do it. I c-couldn't d-do it!'

'I know, hush now.'

'Please, Winnie. Please let me go. I promise I won't tell. I won't say a word. You can trust me. You know you can trust me now. I've proved it. I've been a good boy. Haven't I?'

'Oh, how I wish I could,' she said with all sincerity. 'But I can't let you go, you know I can't. If I did I'd lose everything.'

'But you wouldn't,' he sobbed. 'I promise you wouldn't, I promise. Please, I can't stand it any longer. Please let me go. *Please!*'

Winifred continued to rock him in her arms like a baby. Then he started to spasm again, a hand going out to the table in front of him. And before Winifred knew what he was about he had found the fork. With a terrible cry of despair he slashed at her.

She staggered away from him but not before he'd caught her on her left arm. The fork stuck in so deep that she had difficulty in pulling it out. When she did blood flowed from the tabmarks in tiny red rivulets.

'Oh!' she cried. 'Now you show your true self. I knew it! Lies, tricks, you haven't changed! Let you go? *Let you go?* When this is the thanks I get? Ill never let you go. You'll stay here till you die, you hear me? *TILL YOU DIE!* '

Colin barred his teeth like a madman, tears and spittle spilling out of him, his eyes wild with anger and despair. He roared at her:

'I'll kill you if you don't let me go! I'll kill you, you witch! Do you hear? I'll *kill* you!' He flayed about indiscriminately upturning the plate of food off the table, spinning the wheelchair, slicing the air with his fork.

Winifred stared at him in horror. He looked ugly, inhuman, his face red to explode and saliva frothing at the mouth. Angry and in pain from her wound, she grabbed the hand that held the fork and twisted it off him. Then she spun the wheelchair knocking the table out of the way and propelled him towards the bathroom while he flailed his free hand behind him trying to grab and bite her. It was Albert all over again.

'You're not fit to be with people,' she barked. 'You're an animal. You belong in a cage, and that's where you're going! And you'll never come out again!'

'No!' he screamed. 'NOOOO!!' his feet frantically dragging along beneath the wheelchair as Winifred shoved him back into the bathroom, slamming and locking the door and throwing the curtain across. She dropped to the floor and put her hands over her ears yelling herself to drown out his terrible howls of despair.

EIGHTEEN

TUESDAY 15th July.

The Feast of St Swithin. The legend that the weather on St Swithin's Day governs that for the next forty days held good for forty hours only. Torrential rain, that started late on Wednesday night turning roads into rivers and rivers into lakes, stopped abruptly at 2 p.m. on Friday afternoon. By Saturday the skies had cleared to leave a still, misty haze across the meadows and wheat fields of south Norfolk.

Winifred had not been out of the bungalow since the day Colin attacked her, nor had he been out of the bathroom – or his box, as Winifred increasingly came to think of it. Fortunately, Mrs Goffe had not turned up on Tuesday of the following week or on the Thursday. There had been no further note of explanation so Winifred had no idea of the reason. Had anyone asked, Mrs Goffe would have blamed the floods. It might even have been a reasonable excuse. It didn't occur to Winifred to ask for excuses. She was just thankful that she had been spared the need to think up another reason why Mrs Goffe could not go into the bathroom.

But Mrs Goffe's absence had brought to a head Winifred's one problem that had been increasingly concerning her and which now could be ignored no longer: the desperate food situation. The cupboard was bare. Not that it had mattered much in recent days: as punishment for Colin's vicious attack on her Winifred had refused to feed him. Too bad. She had warned him. He knew what the consequences would be if he disobeyed her again. He had to learn that such behaviour would not be tolerated. The carrot had not worked, now it was time for the stick.

Even so, she knew she would have to feed him again eventually and for that she needed provisions. The groceries Mrs Goffe brought, when she did deign to come back to work, was only ever enough for Winifred's needs. Ordering more would simply arouse Mrs Goffe's already sharp curiosity. And Winifred could hardly be seen to be lugging heavy shopping bags from the town week after week, not if she was supposed to be a cripple. The only other avenue open to her she herself had already blocked. In her panic over what Lindsay might have seen – or worse, what she might report to others - Winifred had told the girl that the young man in the wheelchair was Albert's invalid nephew who had been staying with her for the weekend but had now gone back to the home where he usually lived. Lindsay accepted the explanation without question, but it also meant that Winifred was stuck with her regular weekly order from the farm of half a dozen eggs, four pints of milk and seven rashers of bacon – once again only enough for one.

The solution came to Winifred, quite literally, from out of the blue. It was a beautiful summer's day, not a cloud in the sky. Hadn't she told Drew that she would come and visit him and Susan and the children as soon as the weather improved? For some reason Drew had missed this month's visit to Caisterbury. With all that had gone on that had been no bad thing. Fending off Mrs Goffe and Brian had been difficult enough, she would never have been able to fool Drew. She guessed the reason he hadn't been was probably to do with the new van he was going to buy with the money from Lifeplan; money, she need hardly remind herself, that that creature had tried to steal from her. But Drew could have phoned to let her know how he was getting on. It was, after all, her money. It was so unlike him to be ungrateful. Never mind, she would pay him a surprise visit in Norwich and set things right. This way she would kill two birds with one stone since she could see the new baby and do a really big shop away from prying eyes at the same time. Yes, a trip to Norwich was just the ticket.

She went into the bathroom to tell Colin what she had decided to do. He didn't seem much interested. Since the attack he hadn't seemed much interested in anything. In fact, he hadn't spoken a word since that day, just sat in his wheelchair, now more or less permanently bound to it, and glared at her. Sulking like a big baby. Well, that was too bad, too. He only had himself to blame. He didn't ask how her arm was, she noticed. Painful, would have been her answer if he had. She still had it wrapped in a bandage. It would serve him right if she waited until it was properly mended before she even attempted carrying heavy bags of shopping. She wouldn't, of course. Unlike him she kept her word. She said she'd feed him and she will. She told him what she was doing then gagged him and locked him in his box. She'd only be gone a few hours. He'd be all right until she returned - too bad if he wasn't. Then she telephoned *Nitenday* cabs. The taxi took her to the bus stop outside Barclay's Bank in

Caisterbury town centre, and by half-past one she was in her seat and on her way to Norwich.

'Aunt Win. What a surprise.'

Pleasant surprise would have been more welcoming. Winifred beamed at her nephew. Susan looked a bit distraught when she opened the door just now. No doubt she was feeling the strain of coping with a new baby.

'I haven't come at a bad time, have I?'

'No. No, of course not. It's nice to see you.' Susan attempted a smile. She was holding the new baby in her arms and he grizzled sleepily with his head buried in his mother's arm. Winifred poked a finger into his sleepy face, but he just grizzled again and turned away.

'Drew's out the back working on his van,' said Susan wearily. 'Do you want to go through?' She closed the street door after Winifred and then disappeared into the kitchen.

Huh, Winifred thought, and walked through the house and out the back door into garden. She had a mild presentiment that all was not well but couldn't put her finger on what was wrong. She certainly hadn't received her usual friendly welcome. No doubt Drew would tell her if something was wrong.

Drew's greeting was, if anything, even cooler than Susan's had been. He was in a boiler suit, covered in grease, and lying on his back underneath his van which was up on bricks. He didn't immediately stop working when Winifred appeared although she was sure he had seen her.

'Well, this is a fine way to greet your old aunt. Aren't you pleased to see me?'

Drew got up from under the van, wiping his hands on an oily rag. 'Sorry, Aunt Win. Yes, of course I'm pleased to see you.' He kissed her lightly on her cheek. 'How are you?'

'Better for that. I thought since you hadn't been this month I'd pay you a visit instead.' She paused for the mild admonition to sink in. 'I said I would, when the weather improved. Do you remember?'

Drew nodded. 'I remember.'

Winifred looked at him with concern. She repeated what she said to Susan. 'Have I come at a bad time? I thought Susan seemed a little tired. Has the baby been keeping you up?'

'No, the baby's fine.'

'Well then, what is it? Something's wrong, I can tell.'

'Nothing's wrong,' he said impatiently.

Winifred knew when he was lying. Something was worrying him, but if he wouldn't tell her then there wasn't much she could do about it. She tried one last tack. 'Everything's all right between you and Susan, isn't it?'

'For God's sake, Aunt Win. Everything's fine. Honestly. Stop going on.'

She drew herself up. 'Is this the new van?'

For a moment Drew didn't answer. Then he burst out laughing.

Winifred was starting to get cross. 'Now what have I said?'

'Is this the new van? Does it look like a new van?' said Drew finally unable to restrain himself. 'Do you think I'd have spent all of today and most of last night working on it if it was new?' He threw the oily rag at the open bonnet. 'This is my old van, and it's knackered.'

Winifred shook her head uncomprehendingly. 'But I thought you were going to buy a new one. That was what the money was for. The money I lent you. What have you done with it?'

He just stared at her. 'Don't you know? No, you don't, do you? I can see you don't. Oh, I'm sorry, Aunt Win. Really, I am so sorry.'

'Know *what*? Sorry for *what*? ' Her eyes were filling with tears of frustration.

She was trembling. He'd forgotten she was an old lady and with all his own concerns he had also forgotten his manners, too. He took her inside, and while Susan made them all a cup of tea, Drew gently explained:

'There was no money, Aunt Win. The cheque you gave me bounced.'

'Bounced?' The familiar yet alien word floated towards her from out of a grey mist.

'The bank returned it. I thought you knew. Surely, you knew? The same thing must have happened to you with the cheque you got from the insurance company.'

He went on muttering about the cheque, but Winifred wasn't really listening. She was trying to understand. It was true that the cheque from Lifeplan had come from her bank along with an accompanying letter. She remembered now, and other letters that came later, all in red ink. But never having had a bank account before she had not understood them. She'd intended asking Drew about them the next time he came to visit. But he never came, so she never had a chance. And what with all the business with Colin – .

'It's *his* fault,' she said suddenly. 'I knew it! I knew he was a lying, thieving creature.'

Drew looked quizzical. 'Who, Aunt Win? Who are you talking about?'

'Never mind.' She fumbled in her bag for the money from Colin's jacket. She had intended spending some of it on provisions. She thrust the envelope into Drew's hand. 'This is for you. Take it. Buy that new van.'

Drew glanced at the contents of the envelope and was dumbfounded at what he saw. He could see that it was considerably more than the two thousand she had originally given him.

'I don't understand. Where did this come from?'

'It's Lifeplan money. Take it.'

Drew quickly thumbed through it and whistled. 'There must be over four thousand pounds here. Aunt Win, I can't take all this.' He held it out for her to take back.

But she recoiled from it as if it were a poisoned chalice. 'Yes you can. I don't want it. None of it.' She staggered to her feet.

Drew looked helplessly at Susan.

'I'm going now,' said Winifred hobbling towards the door.

'But you only just arrived,' protested Drew, standing also.

'Doesn't matter. I have to go. I have things to do. Important things.'

Drew followed Winifred to the front door still protesting, but she was already half way down the street and deaf to his calls.

Winifred lumbered down the road unaware of where she was going or what she was doing. Images came together and separated again like the coloured crystals in a kaleidoscope. Nothing seemed to hold its form for more than a few seconds before the whole was agitated again and another jumble appeared. But the same words kept playing over and over in her mind: *He* did it. It was *his* fault. He had ruined her life and now he was trying to ruin Drew's. In her mind's eye she saw Colin seated on his wheelchair, his eyes fixed and his fingers extending outwards like the tendrils of an evil creature poisoning everything they touched.

She tapped her stick along the pavement like a blind person. She had to do something, she was sure, something important, but what was it? Food - that was it. Yes. It seemed almost an irrelevance now but she was sure she needed to buy food. She crossed over the road and walked into a supermarket.

The bright lights, warm atmosphere and soft music of the supermarket calmed her a little like a warm bath. There were other customers milling about but she didn't see them as she roved mechanically down one aisle and up the next. Familiar items swam before her and swam away again. She stopped at a display that seemed particularly beckoning. Brown eyes beseeched her; gentle eyes implored her. Of course, that was why she had come. Smiling at the cute faces on the tins, she reached out and dropped the items into her shopping bag.

She didn't notice the man in the dark suit following her. He had seen her come in to the supermarket and fail to pick up a wire basket and then watched from behind an aisle as she took items off the shelves and put them into her own shopping bag. When Winifred joined the checkout queue he signalled discreetly to the girl on the till and went himself round to the far side of the checkout by the door ready to pounce when Winifred tried to leave the store. But when it came to her turn, Winifred paused for a moment in front of the checkout girl and then, smiling still, she emptied her shopping bag onto the conveyor belt.

'Is that everything?' asked the girl peering over the cash desk.

'Yes, thank you,' said Winifred, and held open her bag to show it was empty.

As Winifred fished in her purse for the money, the checkout girl raised her eyebrows at the man in the suit who shrugged and walked away.

Back at the bungalow, Winifred propped her walking stick against the street door and took off her coat before going into the kitchen to unpack her bag and pile her purchases on the table. She had bought nothing but cat food, tins of the stuff. Tilley was rubbing her body against Winifred's legs and mewing with anticipation. Winifred opened a tin of one of her favourite recipes, scooped out half the contents into her bowl and put the bowl on the floor. Tilley was there in a moment relishing the treat. Then Winifred got a second bowl down and emptied the rest of the tin into that. Then she picked up the shotgun and went in to the bathroom.

Colin was still sitting in the wheelchair exactly where Winifred had left him three hours earlier. His arms and legs were bound and a wide piece of masking tape obliterated his mouth. Only his eyes were capable of expression and they narrowed and fixed on her as she came towards him. Winifred drank in his expression with satisfaction.

'Look what I've brought,' she said holding the bowl out for him to see. 'Dinner.'

PART THREE

NINETEEN

HELEN would never have believed it of herself. After all that she had said about and to Angela and Muriel, to have committed the same crime herself that she had so earnestly warned them against. And worse, to have done it in such a cowardly, underhand way.

Muriel would have to be told. Helen would never be able to live with herself if she were to continue deceiving her mother. And when she did tell her, Muriel will remember Helen's attempts to separate her from Frank and assume they had been part of her plan to get him for herself. *And she'd be right.*

If she were honest she would have to admit that she had been attracted to Frank from the moment she first set eyes on him. Why else would she have treated him so badly? Frank knew. He as good as said so on the drive home from the opera. Not for one minute had he believed her little acts of aggression towards him. What amazed Helen was that he felt the same way about her. Plain, short-sighted Helen. Helen the academic. Helen the man-eater.

One thing was for certain, however: she couldn't continue living under Muriel's roof. It would be insult on top of injury. If nothing else she wouldn't be able to bear her drifting around the house snivelling into her tiny hankies and playing the wounded lover day after day. Frank said Helen was over-reacting once again; that Muriel never saw him in those terms – the poor, innocent, naïve fool. But what did he know? He was a man. Helen knew different. She knew Muriel would play the victim and what was more, wallow in the role. She remembered the way her mother had been at the time of her divorce. It ha been a performance worthy of one of the soaps she was so fond of watching on the box.

Helen turned on her side to look at him and saw that his eyes were already open. His bare arm lay outside the sheet and it came up to caress her cheek and brush away a stray curl from her forehead. He blew lightly on her face making her blink.

'You do a lot of that,' she said.
'What?'
'Watching.'
'It's my job to watch people.'
'Is that how you knew? I mean, that we would - '

He placed a finger against her lips as if speaking the words would break the spell.

They were in his flat. The room was hot and sticky with the unrelenting humidity of a July afternoon. Lying so close together, she could smell him: his eyes, she thought, or just him. It made her tingle with pleasure and she inhaled his man-scent deeply, her shoulders quivering in the moist atmosphere.

'You're shivering,' he said, pulling up the bedclothes.
'No, it's not that.'
'What then?'
'I don't know what to.'

He turned on his back and looked up at the ceiling. 'I thought we'd settled it. You come here to live with me.'

'What, in this poky little room?' she laughed. 'How long would we last before we were at each other's throats? I know what living in a confined space can do to you. It drives you insane eventually. You should see my room in Camberwell.'

'Then go back to Muriel.'

'You know I can't do that. Besides, I have to be back at college in a few weeks. There's no simple answer.'

He sighed heavily and put an arm over his eyes. 'Then I'll come to London with you.'

'And do what?'

'I don't know. Get a job on a London newspaper, sweep streets - I don't care. I just want to be with you.'

'With just our love to keep us warm?' She laughed. 'We'd end up hating each other. Besides, I told you, I live in a box. We'd go insane within weeks.'

'Be adventurous for once in your life. Sometimes I wish you were more like your mother.'

'I thought it was *not* being like my mother that you liked about me.'

'It *is*. I *do*. Now you're twisting everything I say again – as usual.'

'As usual,' she nodded closing her lips tight.

He was such a little boy, his pride so easily hurt. Of course she wanted to live with him, go to London, get a place together. But she had planned something similar once before with someone else who, in the heat of a summer's brief affair, had promised her everything and in the end given her nothing. It was a mistake she had no intention of repeating. And then there was his son in Kenya. He hadn't even mentioned him yet. What if Frank suddenly had to leave England and go to him? Or worse, have the child come over here? No, it was all too impractical. It was too – *adventurous*. Helen wanted to say all this to Frank. She wanted him to understand. In time, maybe he would understand. But for the moment she found frustration where there should have been trust and she threw off the bedclothes and got up.

'There's a simple solution to all of this,' she said aggressively putting on her jeans. 'I'll go back to London today - now.'

He sat up watching he struggle into her boots. 'Are you serious?'

'It's the obvious answer. It will solve all our problems – yours, mine and Muriel's. Forget me Frank. Go back to your son in Kenya.'

'Now you're being ridiculous.'

'Am I? We'll see.'

'Helen come back! Helen? Helen!' He pulled the sheet up over his head as if that could drown out the thud of the street door being slammed after her.

Muriel was standing in front of the wardrobe mirror in her bedroom where she had come to change her blouse. It was too hot to wear the same one all day and she took the opportunity, now only in her bras and skirt, to appraise herself.

She was fifty. Not a bad figure for a woman of her age. She put that down to her even temperament, a determination not to let the problems of the world bother her more than they had to. Yes, she had kept her looks, of that she was confident; keeping her men was proving more of an effort. She hadn't seen Frank now for three weeks. He had rung once to cancel an engagement they had planned for a performance of *Waiting for Godot* at the Maddermarket theatre. That had been no great loss. If truth be told, she'd much rather be sitting at home with her feet up on the couch and a box of Cadbury's Milk Tray open watching *Coronation Street* on the television. It had to be more satisfying than listening to a couple of old tramps jabbering about nothing for two hours.

When she joined the Norwich Arts Appreciation Group back in November, she hadn't intended remaining a member for ever; just long enough to make a new circle of friends with whom she could have coffee mornings and the occasional artistic *soirée*. But then Frank had come along and more or less took over her life. She'd been flattered by his attentions, of course she was, what woman of her years wouldn't be by a man fifteen years her junior? Not that he knew it was fifteen; she'd told him ten, and that was bad enough. She may be a bit inexperienced where men were concerned – her husband had been her first, her *only* boyfriend - but she knew enough to realise it was important to at least *feign* an interest in what pleased him. That had been her mistake with Helen's father. As a husband, Henry Brearney had always been her intellectual superior. But Muriel was from a generation that had been brought up to believe the role of a wife was to support her husband; to be a decorative *accoutrement* to his brilliance, not to compete with him. This new equality between the sexes she frankly found exhausting. And all these interminable trips to theatres and art galleries wore her out, physically as well as mentally. A woman of *her* age, she started to think, then crowded the thought out of her mind. A woman of her *age* wouldn't have breasts like these. That was what men really wanted. She cupped her breasts in her hands and pushed out her chest. Yes, not a bad figure, considering. Not that Frank had had them, of course. Not yet. He wasn't the sort to take advantage. Nor, incidentally, was he the sort of man Helen tried to make out - she'd never believed that for a moment. A woman has instincts about these things, and Frank she knew was a *real* man; a *gentle*man. But even the promise of future endearments seemed to be not enough these days. She hadn't heard from Frank since that phone call. It was humiliating. Helen would say *I told you so* in that insufferable way she had of always being right, telling her he wasn't worth bothering about. But Frank *was* worth bothering about. He was all she had to bother about.

Downstairs the street door slammed and she heard Helen thumping up the stairs. Muriel quickly finished dressing.

'Ma, are you there?'

'In here, darling!' Muriel yelled through the bedroom door.

Helen softly opened the door to what was once her parents' room but was now just Muriel's. She looked at the slight, feminine figure adjusting the top button of her pink blouse and thought how delicate and fragile she was as if the draught created merely by opening the bedroom door would blow her away.

Helen took a deep breath. 'Ma, I'm leaving.'

'Are you, darling?' Muriel was picking lint from her navy-blue skirt with forefinger and thumb. 'Where are you going?'

'I'm going back to London.'

Muriel looked up. 'But why? I thought the new term didn't start for weeks yet.'

'I-I can't concentrate here. Too many distractions. I'll be able to work better at the flat.'

'In that tiny boxroom?'

'Angela's away, I can use her room. Anyway, I've decided. I'm going.'

'Well, if you think it's for the best, darling.'

'It is.'

Helen turned to leave the room but stopped on the threshold with her hand on the door-knob. She couldn't leave it there. She had to face up to her responsibilities however unpalatable they were. Helen may be a lot of things, but she was no coward. Gritting her teeth and shutting her eyes, she spoke the words she knew would destroy the butterfly behind her:

'I've been seeing Frank, Ma. That's why I'm going.'

'Seeing him? Whatever do you mean?'

'We're lovers. Frank and I are lovers.'

Behind her, Helen heard the gasp as Muriel collapsed on to the bed.

*

'It's only me, dear!'

Mrs Goffe knocked at Winifred's street door a third time and then tried the handle. It opened. That was most unlike Winifred to leave the door unlocked. Maybe something was wrong. With a *frisson* of anticipation, Mrs Goffe inched her way into the bungalow calling out Winifred's name all the while. She found her sitting at the kitchen table gazing into space.

'There you are!' said Mrs Goffe with a mixture of relief and disappointment. 'Didn't you hear me knocking?' Mrs Goffe came nearer. 'Are you all right, dear?'

'I'm fine,' said Winifred without shifting her gaze.

Mrs Goffe put her hand on top of Winifred's. 'Gosh, you're cold. You look as if you've been sitting here all night. I'll make you a nice cup of tea. That'll warm you up.' She filled the kettle at the sink and put it on the gas.

Winifred barely noticed. She had indeed been sitting there all night. All weekend, in fact, since she came back from Norwich. After she gave the animal, the *creature*, his food she came in here and sat down. She hadn't even taken her coat off. And here she had remained staring into space.

Mrs Goffe put two bags of shopping down on the table. 'I know it's only Monday, Winnie, but I thought I'd better pop these round since I didn't manage to get here last week. Shall I put them away for you?' Without waiting for a reply she started opening cupboards.

'Goodness me! Well, Tilley won't be going hungry this winter, will she?'

For the first time Winifred stirred. A grin slowly spread across her face. 'They're not for Tilley. I've got another pet now.'

Mrs Goffe faced her, arms akimbo. 'Is that so? Well, I'm sorry Winnie, but don't expect me to fetch and carry for another mog. Mr Goffe says I'm here for my old people, not for their menageries. My back is quite bad enough, thank you very much, not unless Social Services made it worth my while, which they won't. What's its name? I only hope it's a bit cleaner than Tilley. You know, Winnie, I've been meaning to say but that Tilley does make the place smell. Are you sure it's not a tom? If so you ought to get him done – you know, *thingy'd*. Two cats will make this place smell like a zoo. If Social Services come round they'll think I'm not doing my job properly.'

'He's not a cat.'

'Oh, a *dog*. Well, that's not so bad. At least a dog can do his business in the garden. Where is he now? In the garden?'

Winifred grinned. 'He's in his box.'

'*Kennel* Winnie, please,' said Mrs Goffe measuring out three heaped spoonfuls of tea. '*Box* sounds like a cage. I do so hate to see animals caged up, don't you? That's why you should let Tilley out now and again. What did you say his name was?'

Winifred frowned.

Mrs Goffe looked at Winifred and tutted. 'Our last dog was called Holly. Well bitch, I suppose I should say. Poor old thing was fourteen when she died – that's ninety-eight of our years. Not a bad innings. Mind you, I'd never have another. The *mess!*' She thought for a moment. 'Tell you what, I've got her old lead at home somewhere. Shall I bring it next time I come? Shall I? Would you like that? I don't want any money for it. Oh dear. Have you done something to your arm?'

Winifred looked at the wound Colin had made with the fork.

'That looks nasty. Goodness, are they teeth marks?'

'No!' frowned Winifred pulling away.

'They look like teeth marks to me. I should get a tetanus jab if I was you. You can't be too careful these days. Where did you say you got this dog from?'

'I didn't.'

'And that bandage needs changing. Is that blood?' Mrs Goffe tutted. 'You know, you really should take better care of yourself, Winnie.'

Mrs Goffe went out into the hallway.

These old folk. They live alone, don't take proper care of themselves. In the end their minds start to go. Mrs Goffe saw it all the time. Winnie Jonah had gone downhill rapidly since her husband died. Tragic really, because Mrs Goffe never really believed Winifred was as bad as she made out. But it's not just the body. It's the mind, too. One minute they're as sane as you or I, and then the next -. You can never tell. Now, let's see: where would Winnie keep her crêpe bandage?

She went over to the bathroom.

Ah, now here was a prime example of what she was talking about. Winnie had suddenly got it into her head not to let her clean in there. Not that Mrs Goffe was overly bothered about that, these old girls can have some very unpleasant personal habits, *very* unpleasant. And here was that great ugly curtain still drawn across the door. Whatever did Winnie want that for? What's she hiding in there?

Mrs Goffe slid the curtain away from the bathroom door:

What's this? A padlock? Well I never! What on earth can that be for? And a hole! Mrs Goffe never heard of such a thing! A hole drilled right through the bathroom door! The *bathroom* door! Wait till she told Mr Goffe about that! She went up onto tip-toe to peer through the tiny squint.

'What are you doing?'

Mrs Goffe spun round to find Winifred standing just behind her with her fists tightly clenched.

'Oh nothing, dear. I was looking for a bandage for your arm, that's all.'

'I haven't got any. And I told you. My arm's fine.'

'Please yourself, I'm sure,' said Mrs Goffe, blushing pink. 'I was only thinking of you.' She nodded at the bathroom. 'You still don't want me to clean in there, I see. Well, whatever it is you're hiding in there, better not let the warden see. I won't say a word of course, that goes without saying, none of my business. Some kind of hooch is it?'

Outside there came three blasts of a car horn.

'That'll be Mr Goffe come to pick me up,' said Mrs Goffe bustling gratefully towards the street door. 'The tea's made, you only have to pour. I'll see you on Thursday then, shall I? I'll bring some crêpe bandage next time I come. And I'll bring that dog-lead too. I won't forget.'

And then she was gone out the street door.

*

Helen was in her room packing, and crying as she packed. Helen didn't cry. It wasn't in her nature. But the emotions of the past weeks had caught up with her at last and she couldn't see very well though the mist that veiled her eyes. She threw all her books into her canvas bag and made a mess of it. Then she tried to pack her other things and made a mess of that, too. The trouble was she'd taken out too many books from the library and now didn't have room in her bag. Maybe Colin had a spare one she could borrow.

She went into her brother's room realising by its unfamiliarity that she hadn't been in there for years. The thought reminded her that he, at least, had got out. Whether he was in Johannesburg or wherever, he was well out of it. She wept at not having seen her little brother on this trip and now she didn't know when she might see him again. She made a promise to herself that as soon as she had sorted things out she would get in contact with him. Someone had to make the effort. It was clear he never would. She found Colin's table tennis trophy that he'd won as a teenager and she held it to her breast. He wouldn't miss it. She could always return it if he asked for it. She'd take it with her to London as a keepsake. She ran her hand along the old school photograph still on the wall and fund Colin's eleven-year-old image and her thirteen-year-old one. You couldn't mistake Colin. Even in this black-and-white picture his eyes burned out at you. She let her fingers linger there for a full minute remembering the day. Then, with a resolute twist of her wrist, she unlocked the wardrobe door.

On the floor of the wardrobe was a blue nylon holdall. It didn't look empty but there was no other suitable bag for her to take. She lugged it out and plumped it down on the bed pulling the zip fastener across in one tug.

Helen flew past Muriel's room, down the stairs and out into the street, her mind wild with unspoken imaginings. She didn't know where she was going but her feet carried her along a familiar route. In ten minutes, breathless from running, she burst into the building, her eyes frantically searching the cloistered rows.

He was there.

Frank's expression was a mixture of simpering pleasure and relief as Helen advanced towards him. 'Helen. I knew you'd come back.'

'Oh shut up, Frank!' Helen felt every eye in the place on her and she backed away from the bearded librarian who was leering menacingly in her direction.

'Come on!' She grabbed Frank's arm. 'I need a drink.'

In the pub Helen gulped down her half-pint of lager and shook her head vigorously.

'Never mind about Muriel, this is more important. Look!' She threw something down on the table and stared hard at Frank.

He picked it up. 'What is it?'

'What does it look like? It's a passport. *Colin's* passport. I found it lying on top of some clothes in a holdall in the bottom of his wardrobe.' She looked at him expectantly.

Frank examined the document. It was current. A regular UK passport. The photograph was of a fair-haired young man staring out at him. The rest of the passport was blank except for a small rectangular stamp on page six for BELGIE-I 1971. He handed it back to Helen.

'So?'

She snatched it from him. 'What do you mean "so"? Are you thick or something? It's Colin's passport. He's supposed to be in South Africa. He can't be if his passport's here, can he?'

Frank sighed. 'Well obviously he didn't go.'

'Oh brilliant. I can see you're wasted on the arts desk. The question is *why* didn't he go? And more importantly, *where* is he now?'

'Minding his own business, I should imagine,' said Frank growing irritated by her insults. 'Which is probably what you should be doing.'

'It is my business. Colin's my baby brother.'

He picked up the passport and flapped it at her. 'Hardly a baby.'

She waved a dismissive hand. 'You know what I mean. I feel responsible. God knows someone has to.'

'Maybe he changed his mind about going. Or he got a better job offer.'

She snorted. 'What job offer? There never was a job offer. All that rubbish about a promotion. I knew it was too good to be true.'

'Well there must be some truth in it or why else would he contact the South African embassy? Remember the letter? And why pack his passport if he wasn't going to use it?'

'Yes, I was wondering that. I know - it's because Muriel helped him pack. He did it to convince her.'

'Seems a little extravagant even for Colin,' said Frank reaching for his beer.

She scowled at him. 'How would you know? You've never even met him.'

'Only from what you've told me about him. A bit of a fantasist you said.'

'Exactly. Which is why I'm suspicious. He's up to something, take it from me.' She stood up.

'Now where are you going?' asked Frank with trepidation.

'Back to the house. Coming?'

He demurred. 'I...can't. I am supposed to be working.'

Helen smirked. 'Don't want to face Muriel, you mean. Fine, I'll go on my own.' She started to leave.

'What are you going to tell her?'

'Muriel? Nothing. I'm going to do what I should have done weeks ago. I'm going ring Colin's office and find out what's going on.'

TWENTY

THE police found Colin's scooter two streets from where he had parked it. Someone had removed the crash helmet weeks before by cutting through the chin-strap that had secured it to the underside of the seat. The helmet now lay discarded and useless at the back of a garden shed on the other side of Caisterbury, the child's box-cart for which it had been stolen lying on top of it with a broken back axle.

Mrs Campbell at number eighteen Emmeline Pankhurst Close had alerted the police to the scooter. For the past week since the schools broke up for the summer holidays, some of the older boys had been wheeling it up and down the Close despite its flat tyres and bent handle-bar. The smaller boys, including her nine-year-old Michael, had tried to copy the older ones, only the scooter was too heavy and one of them was going to have a nasty accident pretty soon. She told the shirt-sleeved constable that she thought the scooter belonged to someone in the next street.

The constable took down the details of the make and licence number and started to knock on the doors of Catherine Parr Close. Then he moved on to Edith Sitwell Close. By the time he got to Ethel Smyth Close he was hot and had had enough. With all the residents in Ethel Smyth Close being pensioners or invalids he didn't think it likely the scooter belonged to anyone there. He phoned through the details to his station who ran a vehicle check. When he phoned in again an hour later they told him the scooter was registered to someone living in Norwich and arranged for a local garage to pick it up.

*

All the way back to the house Helen had been steeling herself for the inevitable confrontation with Muriel. When she got there the house was empty. She knew where she'd gone – to her sister's in St Alban's just as she had done when she first discovered her husband's infidelities. She was conforming to her previous pattern of behaviour. Just to confirm it, Helen phoned her aunt. Yes, Muriel was there.

All well and good. The last thing Helen wanted right now was having to fight Muriel on two fronts - over Frank and over Colin. Helen put the phone down and breathed a sigh of relief. She then found the number of Lifeplan Assurance (UK) Ltd in the telephone directory and dialled it. At first she got the engaged signal, but when she redialled she heard the high-pitched tone that usually means the number is unobtainable. The third time she tried she got the unobtainable signal again, so she rang the operator who told her the number was unobtainable.

'I realise that,' said Helen mustering all the patience at her command. 'That's why I've rung you. Can you try it again for me, please?'

The operator tried again but came back a minute later to say the number was still unobtainable.

'What exactly does that mean, "unobtainable"? Is the phone out of order, heaven forfend?'

'All I can tell you,' said the operator, 'Is that the number is unobtainable. Sorry.' The line went dead.

Helen snatched at the phone book and read the address of the Lifeplan offices. It wasn't far. She could walk.

Lifeplan's door was locked when she got there. Helen looked at her watch. Half past two. Perhaps they were all still at lunch. She looked through the letter-box. On the floor the other side of the door was an enormous pile of mail that Helen thought looked far too big to have been from a single delivery. She went next door to the shoe shop.

The owner of the shoe shop greeted Helen's enquiry with a sick laugh. He, too, would like to know what was going on. He owned the premises and had been sub-letting the upstairs rooms to Lifeplan for the past three years. They owed him six weeks back rent not including the four since they did a bunk.

'When was the last time you saw any of them?' asked Helen, her heart thumping now with apprehension.

'The last week in June,' said the shop owner. 'They were here on the Friday and gone by the Monday and I haven't sent hem since.' He pulled out a well-thumbed copy of the *Norwich and Ipswich Times* dated Wednesday 7th July. 'Here, read for yourself,' and he went off to serve a customer.

The article was on page two under the headline, NORWICH INSURANCE SWINDLE. Helen read the three columns rapidly.

'They owe millions,' said the shop owner coming back. 'Seems they've had been in trouble for some time, couldn't pay the claims.' He shook his head. 'I'm only the landlord. I'm the last to know.'

'What about the agents?' asked Helen.

'They've been done, too, poor sods. No money for wages, see? I thought you were another one.'

'Another one?'

'A rep. They've been turning up all week. I've been thinking of putting a notice up.' The man scratched his neck thoughtfully.

'Was Colin Brearney one of them by any chance?' asked Helen.

The man shook his head. 'Didn't give any names.'

'Fair hair, brown eyes, early twenties?' Helen persisted.

'Sorry love.' He went off to serve a customer.

Helen folded the newspaper and walked out the shop. She found a phone box and dialled the number of the *Norwich and Ipswich Times*.

'Frank Opie, please.'

She waited while the switchboard operator put her through

'Frank? Don't you read your own bloody newspaper?'

'What are you talking about?'

Helen read the article out to him over the phone.

'Well yes, now you come to mention it, I did know about it.'

'*Now I come to mention it?* What the hell do you think we've been talking about all morning? Some journalist you turned out to be!'

'Hang on a minute,' Frank protested. 'I only knew Colin worked for an insurance company. I didn't know it was Lifeplan. That's a major story. If he's mixed up in that -'

'Not *if*, Frank. Not any longer. He's in this up to his neck.'

'What are you gong to do?' he asked dreading the reply.

'I'm going to the police.'

'No – Helen – wait! You could be doing more harm than good. Let's just make sure of our facts before we get the police involved.'

'You and your bloody facts,' said Helen dismissively. 'By the time we get the facts anything could have happened.'

'Well, just don't mention Lifeplan to the police. Not yet.'

'Oh, don't worry,' snorted Helen. 'That's not what I'll be seeing them about.'

At the police station the desk sergeant was very polite, very charming. Helen had to wait while he took down the particulars from an irate businessman who was reporting the theft of hubcaps in broad daylight while he was having his lunch in the park. The desk sergeant pointed out, very politely, that if the theft happened in the park then it was really the Parks Police he should be talking to. But he took a note of the details in any case. When the businessman had left, the sergeant folded over the top sheet of his note-pad and smiled, pen poised, ready for his next customer.

'I want to report a missing person.'

'Name?'

'Helen Brearney. It's my brother, Colin who's missing.'

The sergeant wrote the name at the top of his pad.

'And how old is the little chap?'

'Twenty-one.'

The sergeant put his pen down.

'What makes you think he's missing?' he asked very politely.

'Because he hasn't been home for four weeks and we don't know where he is.'

'Have you tried any of his friends? Girlfriend perhaps? Or a relative?'

'Yes yes, we've done all that,' lied Helen. 'And as far as I know he doesn't have a girlfriend.'

'Had a family row, did he? Went off in a huff?'

'No no, nothing like that. He's just left. Gone. Vanished. Without trace. *Compris?*'

'Well I'm sorry, miss, but if he's over twenty-one he can do as he pleases, he doesn't need permission. Not even his sister's. It's a free country.'

That was debatable as far as Helen was concerned. 'What if he's had an accident?'

'Have you tried ringing the hospitals?'

'I can't ring round every hospital in the country, can I? Good God!'

The sergeant's smile, always on the point of fading, now dissolved completely. He leaned across the desk and lowered his voice.

'Look miss, have you any idea how many thousands of people go missing every year in this country? For all sorts of reasons. Most turn up sooner or later. If your brother's been gone for only four weeks then the chances are he'll come back of his own accord just as if nothing has happened. Unless, that is, you know of a particular reason why he shouldn't?'

Helen opened her mouth to tell him about Lifeplan, but remembered what Frank said and closed it again.

'Then take it from me, this time next week he'll be back wondering what all the fuss was about.'

'And if he doesn't turn up next week? Or next month? Or next year?'

'Then come back and we'll talk again.'

'Fine. And in the meantime he might have been smashed over the head by someone with a brick and his body dumped on a bit of waste ground.'

'Look,' said the sergeant, 'if you're really that concerned then why not try the Salvation Army? No, I'm not joking. They're very good at tracing lost relatives. I can give you their address if you want it. But if you want my advice, go home and wait by the telephone. He'll get in contact when he's ready. Mark my word.' He winked and smiled and turned his attention to a young mother and three screaming children who had just barged in through the door.

'Useless bunch of – !'

'I did warn you,' said Frank lying lengthwise on the Brearney sofa.

'You told me not to mention Lifeplan,' said Helen throwing the copy of the newspaper with the article in it at his head. 'Perhaps I should have done, he might have taken a bit more interest.'

'Or his colleagues might be round here now turning the place over. Muriel would really love that.'

'You're not in Kenya now, Frank.'

'And you think that sort of thing doesn't happen here?'

'All I know,' said Helen trying to concentrate on tangibles, 'is that at the same time that two managers of Lifeplan vanish with the company's assets my brother, who happens to work for them, also disappears. In addition, he packs a bag full of clothes lying on the top of which is his passport. He's also been corresponding with the visa section of the South African Embassy which, as we all know, is a favourite destination of criminals since there's no extradition treaty between them and us. Now, call me paranoid but that all seems to add up to something.'

'Well, I admit it does *sound* strange, but do you really think your brother could be mixed up in a major insurance fraud? I mean, *Colin?*'

'That's the second time you've mentioned his name something like that,' said Helen suspiciously. 'Do you know more than you're letting on?'

Frank had been studying the newspaper article again. 'You say Colin hasn't been seen since June the twenty-first. It says here that Kerney and Slaker went missing on the second of July. That's nearly two weeks later.'

'So?' said Helen impatiently.

'So why didn't they all go at the same time? Assuming they were involved in the same thing.'

'Covering their tracks?'

Frank shook his head. 'No, I don't think so. Those other two were Lifeplan's most senior managers. Colin was a junior sales rep. What could he possibly know that could be of use to them?'

'Maybe he found out something and they kidnapped him.'

'Now you're being ridiculous.'

'The fact remains that Colin has gone,' Helen said, patiently. 'And there aren't any Lifeplan offices in South Africa, I've checked.'

'Do you want to know what I think?' said Frank seriously. 'I think Colin's disappearance has nothing to do with Slaker and Kerney. I think it's something else entirely. It was a pure coincidence that those two managers happened to do a bunk round about the time that Colin did his disappearing act - note I said *about* the same time. I also don't believe Colin had any intention of going to South Africa. He just wanted everybody to think he was. That letter from the embassy was just a smoke-screen.'

'And what reason would that be, genius?' asked Helen, exasperated.

'If we knew the answer to that we'd know everything. The important thing is his passport is here. So he must still be in the country. Start from there.'

'Well, that's something I suppose. This morning you were all for forgetting the whole thing.'

'I still think there's probably a perfectly innocent explanation. be a perfectly innocent explanation for all of this. One thing is for certain: if he really was involved with this insurance business you wouldn't need to go to the police. By now they'd be knocking on your door wanting to talk to you.'

The words were barely out of his mouth when the doorbell rang. Helen went to the window to see who it was.

'Frank, it's a policeman.'

'Do you want me to go?'

'No. I'll answer it.'

Frank could hear voices in the hall but not what they were saying. Helen was only gone a few minutes but the waiting was intolerable. When she came back she was as white as a sheet.

'They've found Colin's scooter. And I've just found this on the hall table.'

She held out a letter addressed to Colin. It was from his bank manager reminding him of the loan he had taken out and asking why the repayments had not been kept up since March.

'He's been planning this for months.' Helen looked at him shakily. 'Frank, I'm scared.'

'Calm down,' he said. 'It may be a blessing in disguise. If his bike is in Norwich then the chances are he is, too.'

235

'We've got to find him, Frank. Wherever he is. I've got to know if he's all right.'

'Salvation Army?'

Helen just glared at him. 'We'll put an advertisement in the newspaper – your newspaper, the *Norwich and Ipswich Times*. It's worth a try. You write it. Tell him to contact me, Helen, at this number. That's all. Don't give any reasons. And for goodness sake, don't breathe a word of any of this to Muriel.'

'Don't worry,' said Frank sincerely. 'I shan't be saying anything to your mother.'

Helen put her arms round Frank and pulled him close to her. 'Oh Frank. I've got this awful feeling, I can't describe it. I think something terrible's happened to Colin.'

TWENTY-ONE

DREW didn't contact Winifred immediately he heard about the Lifeplan swindle. He'd been too preoccupied with putting his life back together again. Being a plumber by trade he'd long harboured the dream of going into business by himself and becoming his own boss but never really had the capital to do it. Frankly he'd always been nervous of the idea and the fact that he didn't have a decent set of wheels was the excuse he needed to do nothing. Winifred's offer of a loan had been the spur he needed to take the plunge. Urged on by his wife, Drew had quit his job, bought a whole load of new tools and put a down-payment on a new van.

Only, between resigning and buying the van Winifred's cheque had bounced leaving him with no van, no job and no customers. He did try to get his old job back but by then it was too late - his boss had already hired a replacement. In desperation, Susan had urged him to contact Winifred again but this he had been reluctant to do. He hadn't been too keen to accept her money in the first place; going back to her a second time smacked to him of begging. He promised Susan he would contact Winifred soon, but he never did preferring instead to soldier on with the few tools he did have and his clapped-out A40 van until it finally gave up the ghost. When Winifred turned up in the summer it was like a miracle. And this time it wasn't a cheque she brought but cash, and more than enough for the new van and new tools.

In the days following Winifred's visit he'd had to rush round organising things. The tools he had bought new, the van very nearly new. Only when all that was settled and Drew had time to think about other things had he made the connection between the Lifeplan swindle and the bounced cheque and realised Winifred had been just another victim of those two Lifeplan managers. It was then he had his attack of remorse over what he had privately thought about his aunt – and the names Susan had not so privately called her. Once again his aunt had come up trumps. And there he had been punishing her by not paying his usual monthly visit to Caisterbury. It shamed him to think how selfish he had been and how hurt she must be by his behaviour.

Well, it was time he put matters to rights. It was Thursday. He could afford to take one day off and spend it with his aunt. Whether he could afford it or not, he was going to. Kissing his son and his wife for the first time in weeks, he bought the biggest, most luxurious box of chocolates he could find and set off in the new van for Caisterbury.

The ambulance drew up outside number seven Ethel Smyth Close at 12.26 p.m. Brian wasn't able to stop directly in front of Winifred's bungalow because someone had parked a grey Bedford van, nearly as big as the ambulance, half on and half off the pavement, but he got as close as he could. Not bothering to switch off the engine, Brian opened the back doors and let down the step.

On board were three of Brian's regulars: Martha Hodge, Sadie Collins, and Winifred. For some reason George Smith had not been keeping his appointments in recent weeks. But that was often the case, in Brian's experience. Old folk are always falling ill over something. Brian wouldn't be surprised if he never saw George again. He was unlikely to see Winifred again after today, either, as it was her last day at the hospital her course of treatment having come to an end. In her hand she held three scruffy carnations and a card – the gift of Martha Hodge. Brian waited patiently while Martha clutched Winifred's plump hand in both her spindly ones and made her promise faithfully not to forget her.

'You will come to the Halloween party, won't you Winnie? Sadie and I are coming as witches, aren't we, dear?'

'Ooh!' screamed Sadie, rocking about in her seat. 'Can you imagine? Me in a pointed 'at!'

'*Do* say you'll come,' urged Martha earnestly into Winifred's face. 'Sunday the thirty-first of October at the Mission Hall in Well Street - you know it? Brian's kindly volunteered to pick us up and bring us home again, haven't you, dear?'

Brian smiled. For once he didn't mind the extra duty. Double time for four hours' work most of which he would spend propping up the bar at the back of the hall. A doddle. No alcohol of course, Well Street being a Methodist Mission, but he wouldn't have been able to drink anyway as he was driving.

'I expect I shall,' said Winifred. ''Though I don't know what I shall wear. Well, goodbye all.'

Winifred allowed Brian to take her arm for the last time and she leaned heavily towards him as she slowly made her way round the side of the ambulance.

'Wo-there, Winnie! A little more water with it next time!'

Winifred didn't rejoin the jest. She was swaying unsteadily and peering intently towards her front door. Drew was seated on the doorstep. When he saw Winifred he stood up and started up the path towards her.

'Looks like you've got a visitor,' said Brian.

'Yes,' said Winifred unsteadily.

'How long have you been waiting?' Winifred asked him once they were inside the hall and the door closed.

'About ten minutes. I couldn't remember what time your session ended.'

'Well, you can't be expected to remember everything.'

'I'm sorry I haven't been for a while. What with work and the new baby and one thing and another.'

'Oh well, you're here now.' Winifred smiled. They went into the kitchen.

'You sit down, Aunt Win. I'll make us a nice cup of tea, shall I?' He handed her the box of chocolates he'd bought on his way over. 'Soft centres. Your favourites.'

'Very nice,' said Winifred.

Drew went to fill the kettle the sink. 'Are you having problems with your drains, Aunt Win? There's a funny smell in here.'

'I can't smell anything.'

'No, I was forgetting. You don't have a sense of smell do you?' He lit the gas under the kettle. 'Would you like me to have a look while I'm here?'

'No. It'll be all right.'

Drew sat down, opened the chocolates and held the box for Winifred to choose. 'Quite like old times, isn't it?'

'Yes,' smiled Winifred and popped an orange cream into her mouth.

Suddenly Drew put up a finger. 'Listen to that.'

Winifred stopped chewing. 'Listen to what?'

Drew cocked his ear. 'Silence. I'd forgotten how quiet it is here. After all the traffic noise in Norwich. You know you're very lucky living where you do.'

'Yes,' agreed Winifred. 'I suppose I am.'

Drew put out his hand to hers and spoke earnestly. 'Look, Aunt Win, I know what you've been going through these past few weeks.'

'Do you?'

'Yes, I do. And I want you to know I'm sorry – well, for the way I've behaved. I've been very selfish. But I didn't understand, you see? About the money, I mean. It must have been awful for you, too thinking you had it one minute and the next, gone. I'm amazed you managed to get any of it back. According to the newspaper those two crook managers disappeared with the lot.'

Winifred gazed blankly at him. 'Yes.'

'One of the lucky ones I suppose.'

'I suppose so.'

The kettle started whistling and Drew got up to turn the gas off. He made the tea, found the sugar in the cupboard, got the milk from the fridge, sat down again.

'You know, that really is a terrible smell. Are you sure you don't want me to check round for you?'

'Quite sure thank you.'

Drew looked over his shoulder and for the first time noticed the brown velour curtain pulled across the bathroom door.

'I expect it's a dead rat,' said Winifred.

Drew nodded. 'Could be.'

He turned back in his seat, smiled, drank his tea and offered his aunt another choice of the chocolates.

TWENTY-TWO

THE advertisement went into the Friday edition of the *Norwich and Ipswich Times* and also the *Eastern Daily Press* just to make sure the whole of the eastern counties were covered. It was the same wording every week, just two lines: COLIN - RING HELEN - URGENT followed by Muriel's telephone number. Nothing else. Helen had deliberately omitted using the Brearney name. If by some stroke of luck Colin did happen to read it he'd recognize the telephone number and know who it was from. It was a long-shot but she didn't know what else to do. Doing something, no matter how trivial, made her feel better.

By the end of the third week Helen was beginning to lose her enthusiasm for the idea. It seemed just putting a woman's name and telephone number together in the small ads of a newspaper brought out every weirdo from under whatever bit mucky rockery his sick imagination inhabited. One particularly persistent and inventive caller finally had to be told to go boil his head and he got quite abusive when she did so. Frank thought this all highly amusing. But it wasn't the smutty phone calls that bothered Helen so much. If the ad attracted that kind of caller then perhaps the police were taking an interest, too. Even if they were, Frank didn't think they would connect the ad with the Lifeplan fraud. But the longer it went on the more nervous Helen was becoming.

Muriel had returned from her sister's and that was another problem. Frank refused to come to the house while Muriel was there, and Helen was equally reluctant to stray too far from the phone just in case Colin did ring – or worse, if Muriel should answer an obscene phone call. So they were having to consult each other by telephone themselves. Life in the espionage world was becoming very complicated.

At least Muriel hadn't thrown Helen out of the house as she had expected. In fact, Muriel hardly said a word since her return confining herself mostly to her room. The only time Muriel had spoken was to ask for Frank's address - it seemed he had never given it to her, much to his relief, and he absolutely forbade Helen to divulge it.

'The last thing I need at the moment is your mother turning up on my doorstep,' said Frank when she told him.

'You haven't got a doorstep. Just keep looking over your shoulder and if you see a short, middle-aged woman following you with a Tommy-gun - *run!*'

Helen would dearly like to talk to her mother, to get it all out in the open and not bottle up resentment. These long, meaningful silences were just an irritation - something else she shared with her father. Normally she might have forced the issue, gone in to Muriel's room and had a stand-up row, if that's what it took to clear the air. But she had enough on her hands sorting out Colin. Muriel and her hurt pride would have to wait. Not that much was getting sorted out. The weeks were drifting by and nothing seemed to be happening. The only phone call other than obscene ones had been from Angela who had rung to say that she had married Bryn during the vac and to find out when Helen was coming back to the flat. Helen had been evasive. This was one subject she couldn't discuss even with her oldest friend.

Then one afternoon during the last week of September the telephone rang. Helen was in the kitchen trying once again to grapple with her holiday assignment. As she entered the hall she caught sight of Muriel coming out of her room at the top of the stairs only to disappear again as Helen picked up the phone. At first Helen thought it was going to be another heavy breather when she could hear nothing at the other end of the line and was about to whistle very loud and very close to the mouthpiece when she stopped. A voice on the other end had spoken her name. A female voice:

'I'm Marcia. Marcia Pike. I used to work with Colin.'

Helen held her breath.

'Hello? Is anybody there? This is still Colin's number, isn't it? Colin Brearney?'

'Yes,' Helen managed to breathe. 'Yes, it is. I'm Helen Brearney, Colin's sister. Colin Brearney is my brother.' She silently bit her lip at her stupidity.

'Only, I looked it up in the phone book,' continued Marcia, oblivious. 'And it doesn't say *Colin* Brearney, only *Henry* Brearney, so I wasn't sure if I had the right number.'

'Henry Brearney is our father,' said Helen. 'Do you know where he is? Colin, I mean.' She looked up the stairs and cupped her hand over the mouthpiece so Muriel couldn't hear.

'I'm sorry, what did you say? I'm afraid this is a terrible line.'

'Look,' said Helen turning her back on the stairwell, 'it's a bit difficult to talk at the moment. Do you think we could meet somewhere?'

'I'm not sure.'

'Please. It's very important that I speak to you. You do you know what's been going on don't you?'

Helen could tell by the pause that she did. 'I can't really leave the house, though. My mum'll be back at five and I ought to be here.'

'That's all right. I can come to you.'

'I don't know.'

'Half an hour. That's all I ask. Then I'll be gone. Please. I'm very worried about my brother.'

Seconds ticked by while Marcia thought about it. 'Long as you're gone by five.'

'I will. Hang on while I get a pen.'

Helen ran back in to the kitchen to grab her pad and wrote down the address Marcia dictated.

'I know where that is. I'll be there in fifteen minutes.'

No sooner had she put the phone down than she picked it up again and rang the number of Frank's office.

'Frank? Drop whatever you're doing and meet me at the end of the street in ten minutes. There's been a reply to the ad. What? Of course it's important; I wouldn't be asking if it wasn't. It's someone who used to work with Colin. I think she may know something. What? I can't speak up. Muriel's upstairs. Look, I'll explain when I see you. Just get over here as quickly as you can.'

She put the phone down and ran out of the house. Then she ran back in, grabbed her notepad and pencil with Marcia's address on it and ran out again.

The first mists of autumn were shrouding the trees lining the street where Marcia lived with her parents as Frank and Helen drove up and parked outside. It was a prosperous middle-class suburb of Norwich. All the houses in the avenue were identical 1930's semis with stuccoed brick walls, Dutch gable ends and arched vestibules open to the elements.

The door to Marcia's house was opened by a shapely, slim young woman in a yellow tracksuit with red tightly-curled hair, red nails and red lips. She looked like a banana that had been dipped in rosehip syrup.

Marcia took a step backwards when she saw that there were two people standing on the step.

'Oh. I was only expecting one.'

'This is Frank,' said Helen introducing him. 'He's just a friend. You can ignore him.'

'Well, I suppose you'd better come in.'

Flustered, Marcia offered her two guests a cigarette from an onyx cigarette-box in the sitting room. When Helen declined for both of them, Marcia took one herself and lit it from an onyx lighter.

'Sorry, do you mind?' She held up the white stick.

'No, you carry on,' smiled Helen.

Marcia began by confessing her utter bewilderment over what had happened. Lifeplan was such a nice company, the people so friendly. As she told the police when they interviewed her, she'd had absolutely no idea what was going on there. You could have knocked her over with a feather. Helen had no difficulty in believing her. After two minutes of interview she didn't doubt the police believed her too.

'When did you find out?'

'Well,' Marcia crossed one banana leg over the other. 'I turned up for work that Monday morning at nine o'clock as usual.'

'That would be Monday the fifth of July?' suggested Helen, looking at her notes.

'If you say so,' shrugged Marcia. 'I should have noticed something was wrong straight away because usually Mr Kerney was already working in his office by the time I get in. But that morning the door was locked. I thought, that's strange. So I waited. And then eventually after an absolute age I heard Mr Churchill open up - he's the owner of the shoe shop downstairs.'

Helen nodded. 'I met him. Go on.'

'Well that's it really. I asked Mr Churchill to let me in with his key. I wouldn't normally only I could hear the phone ringing upstairs and Mr Kerney has a fit if the phones aren't answered.'

'Understandable,' Helen smiled encouragingly.

Marcia uncrossed her legs, sat upright and flipped the ash from her cigarette into the onyx ash-tray with a cherry-topped thumb-nail.

'Well, when I got in the office I couldn't believe it. All the filing cabinets were pulled open and empty. So were the drawers of Mr Kerney's and Mr Slaker's desks. Empty files all over the floor. It was chaos. My desk was about the only thing that hadn't been touched. Mr Churchill, I said, we've been ransacked. He said not to touch anything and he'd ring the police from his shop. Not that I could anyway because all our phones were all going at once. It was bloody mayhem I can tell you.' She took several quick puffs of her cigarette.

Helen was sitting on the edge of her seat leaning forwards. 'Well?'

Marcia flicked her ash again. 'You are Colin's sister aren't you,' she said hesitantly.

'Do you want to see my driving licence?' said Helen, exasperated.

Marcia lowered her voice. 'It was while Mr Churchill was downstairs that I did it.'

Helen frowned. 'Did what?'

'Took *certain items* from my desk.'

'What items?' said Helen barely able to control her irritation.

Frank could see Helen was about to explode. If she did Marcia would probably clam up so he quickly interrupted:

'Is that why you rang Helen? To tell her about them - these "certain items"?'

Marcia blinked her long ashes at Frank. 'I knew I shouldn't have done. The police didn't know. I hid them up my jumper.'

Not for the first time since he arrived Frank's eyes travelled to the skin-tight sweater Marcia was wearing - and wondered how on earth she managed to hide anything under there from the police's prying eyes.

'It was seeing it on the six o'clock news that made me think. And then when that notice appeared in the paper about Colin...'

'What did you take from your desk?' said Helen.

Marcia got up, walked over to a sideboard, open the cupboard and removed something. Without looking at it she held it out for Frank to take before returning to her seat.

'What is it?' asked Frank.

Helen and Frank looked at it together. It appeared to be a typed carbon copy list of names and addresses.

'Lifeplan clients,' Marcia explained. 'Former clients I should say. Colin asked me for them just before he disappeared.'

Helen was frowning trying to understand. 'What did he want them for?'

'What do you think? Some kind of scam.'

'Which you were involved in?' suggested Helen.

'Oh God, no,' said Marcia aggressively stubbing out her cigarette. 'I don't know what he was going to do with them. I just typed the bloody things.'

'How did Paul Kerney react when Colin went missing?' asked Frank.

Marcia lit another cigarette with a shaking hand. 'He was livid.'

'Kerney was angry?' said Frank. 'You're sure about that?'

'I'll say. What he wasn't going to do to him.'

'Can I keep these?' asked Helen holding up the types pages.

Marcia screwed up her nose. 'Sorry. I think I'd like to burn them. I shouldn't have kept them.'

'Well, can I copy out the names. No-one will know I got them from you.'

'I suppose so. Trouble is, Colin has the original. If he gets caught they'll know it's me anyway.'

'Then we'll just have to find him before that happens, won't we?' said Frank.

'Bloody female!' said Helen getting in the car and slamming the door. 'All she's bothered about is saving her own neck - which I bet she's in it right up to.'

'What?' said Frank, confused.

Helen flapped a dismissive hand. 'You know what I mean. She's not as innocent as she pretends.'

'I think she probably is. She's either incredibly thick or an exceptionally good actress. I know which my money's on.'

'Why were you so interested in whether Kerney was angry with Colin or not?'

'I was trying to gauge whether he was part of the fraud. But I'm not sure if I did.'

Helen frowned. 'I don't follow you.'

'If Colin was in on the fraud then Kerney might have been pissed off that he went his own way. On the other hand, he might just have been annoyed Colin did a bunk just when they were about to do the same. I don't know which is more likely'

'Do you think we should go to the police?' said Helen hesitantly.

'Probably. But until we know the extent of Colin's involvement maybe we should hold off.'

Helen smiled at him with relief. 'I was hoping you'd say that.'

'If you want my honest opinion, it sounds to me like Colin had nothing to do with this Kerney-Slaker business. I think he was doing something else, something of his own. He must have been up to something or he wouldn't have asked Marcia for those names.'

'Like what? Another fraud? I can't believe Colin would do that.'

For the first time Helen looked despondent. The whole business was beginning to get to her. 'Well if we can't go to the police what do we do?'

'I don't know. Visit some of the names on the list. Maybe we can get a clue from that.'

Helen flipped through the pages of her notepad. 'But there must be fifty names here.'

'We won't have to visit them all. Just enough to get an idea of what he was up to. We'll split them. You do half and I'll do the other half.'

Helen shook her head. 'No. You've done enough. I can't ask you to get any further involved.'

'Can't you?'

Helen squeezed his arm.

'Don't worry. It's probably all entirely innocent,' said Frank firing up the engine and selecting a gear. 'Let's hope it is.'

TWENTY-THREE

THEY drove back to the bus station in the centre of Norwich and over a coffee divided up the list that Marcia had given them. This proved more problematic than they originally thought. The addresses were spread all over East Anglia. Getting to them all would take an age not to mention the petrol. But there were some they could group together. One group was centred on Norwich which Helen gave to Frank. The other seemed to be in and around the market town of Caisterbury. Helen took these. She copied out the first batch of names and addresses on her pad. In alphabetical order Frank's read:

>Norman COTMAN
>Marion Frances HOLME
>Edna MONKSFIELD
>Florence Margaret Eleanor READ

And Helen's:
>Lilian FISHER
>Winifred JONAH
>Grace Ellen LEWIS
>James George SMITH

'What exactly do I ask them?' asked Helen, nervous now that it was coming to it.

'You'll have to play it by ear,' he said unsure himself. 'Most of them are old. Just get them to talk. Old people like to talk, especially when they've got something to moan about. But for God's sake don't mention my newspaper or there'll be hell to pay.'

'You know Frank, sometimes I wonder how you sleep at night.'

They finished their coffee and went their separate ways - Frank for his car and Helen for the bus home. They'd meet up later at his flat to compare notes. But before Frank got started on his group, there was something else he wanted to do first.

Frank hadn't been entirely honest with Helen when he told her he had never met Colin. The fact was that Frank had come across him once before. It dated from when he first started to work for the *Norwich and Ipswich Times*. His job then had been on the legal desk and he spent most of his days at the Norwich magistrates' courts reporting on petty criminal cases - shoplifting, vandalism. One day the manager of an electrical shop came up before their worships accused of stealing from his employer. It appeared the shop owner had suspected him of taking money from the till for some time but had never been able to prove it. So a sting had been set up to catch him. Posing as a customer, a plain-clothes policeman had rushed into the shop in a great hurry one afternoon, bought some items for cash and rushed out again without bothering to wait for a receipt. Ten minutes later the policeman returned with the owner and made the manager empty his pockets. Sure enough they found the ten-pound note the policeman had used to make his purchase, its number carefully recorded beforehand, along with a further forty pounds in various denominations tucked in the manager's shirt pocket. Still protesting his innocence, the manager had asked for seventeen similar offences to be taken into consideration. He was fined £50 plus costs and sacked from his job. Frank had reported the case which was printed in less than two hundred words on page seven. He'd recognized Colin immediately from the passport photograph Helen had shown him - something to do with the eyes - but declined to tell her in case she didn't know about the court case. But it posed the question of whether a petty criminal like Colin would be involved in a major operation like the Lifeplan fraud. On the other hand, Colin was up to something. Before he hared off on a possible wild goose chase Frank decided to do some digging of his own in the offices of the *Norwich and Ipswich Times*. He sought out the journalist who had written the original article about the Lifeplan scam for more of the background information.

'Fancy trading desks, do you Frank?' grinned the hack. 'Ballet not up your street?'

'I'm thinking of taking out life insurance,' said Frank. 'You know it makes sense.'

The hack had snorted his disbelief but filled him in on the details anyway. It seemed that Lifeplan had been in financial trouble for some time. It was all to do with the way the American parent company set up the business. Lifeplan had been what they called a "feeler company" - that is, testing the market to see how well they performed. Losses would be accepted for a while but if the business didn't make a return within a set period it would simply be wound up. Lifeplan had reached that point by December last year when the decision had been taken to pull the plug. All existing claims would be met but no new business was to be taken on after March. The company would then be wound up and all employees dismissed - managers, sales force, office staff, the lot. Naturally Giles Slaker as Lifeplan's managing director and Paul Kerney its sales director would be the first to know of the impending closure and had time to plan their next move, which turned out to be stripping the accounts and transferring the assets to numbered bank accounts in Switzerland.

All of which explained Slaker's and Kerney's disappearance, but not Colin's. Frank would be the first to admit he knew nothing about the insurance business, but it didn't take a financial genius to work out that one of the Lifeplan sales reps should have little input into what was essentially a back-office scam of major proportions. The only possible connection Colin might have was if he had somehow got wind of what was going on and tried to muscle-in. If so, that could be a very dangerous move indeed.

Meanwhile Helen was doing rather less well with her line of inquiry. Her plan had been to return to the house, hopefully avoiding Muriel, and borrow her mother's Morris Minor so she could get to the addresses on her list of Lifeplan clients. Fortunately Muriel seemed to be of a similar disinclination to see her daughter and had disappeared into her bedroom as soon as Helen's key went in the door. There then followed an exasperating twenty minutes while Helen hunted for the car keys which she eventually found in the pot of geraniums on the widow-ledge in the sitting room – for security reasons no doubt. Then she discovered the car was practically out of petrol and it wasn't until she found a self-service filling station that she realised she didn't have the first clue about how operate the pump or even where the petrol cap was. There was nothing else for it but to ditch her principles and act the dizzy female for the sake of getting the man in the Mercedes on the opposite side of the pump to help her. She even managed to crunch the gears and snarled in her rear-view mirror at the man's smug grin as she pulled away. By the time she got to the first address on her list it was late afternoon. She rang the doorbell of a terraced house. The door was opened by a harassed-looking mother of three who had never heard of Lilian Fisher, but on second thoughts maybe she was the old lady who owned the house before her and was now in a nursing home near Cambridge. Helen thanked her for her time and scratched the name off her list.

She barely fared better with her second address. She had great difficulty finding April Cottage, the name being blocked by a new-looking Ford Anglia parked on the drive. Eventually she found the sign. Yes, this was the place.

James, or as he insisted on being called, *George* Smith, seemed like a sad old man, a widow with no family living nearby who had quite obviously had some kind of stroke paralysing him down his right side. Despite his hemiparesis he insisted on making his visitor a pot of tea while Helen sat in his poky and rather smelly sitting-room. While he laboured with the tea caddy and kettle Helen explained her visit:

She was a journalist, she said, investigating the recent collapse of Lifeplan Assurance - he must have read about it or seen the report on the television. George said he didn't have a television and hadn't read a newspaper in years. Helen found that astonishing. Didn't have a television? In this day and age? How extraordinary. She filled him in with the barest details of the scandal as George hobbled from kitchen to sitting room with a tray of crockery and biscuits precariously balanced on his good left hand.

'I suppose as a former client you won't have been affected by the collapse?' she said accepting her cup with gratitude.

George seemed a little cagey. He said he'd had no problems with Lifeplan. When his wife died last year they'd paid out promptly and in full. He pointed out the Ford Anglia which he'd bought with some of the money, although since his stroke he hadn't been able to drive it much. No, it wasn't with the company he'd had problems.

'May I ask how you knew I was with Lifeplan?' he asked her sitting down in the armchair opposite. 'I thought that sort of information was restricted - client confidentiality and all that.'

Helen gave him her most obsequious smile. 'We journalists have our methods,' she said vaguely. 'Goodness, are they chocolate bourbons? Yummy.'

In the silence that followed Helen sat crunching her biscuit self-consciously loudly. So much for Frank's notion that old people like to talk. Trying to get George to say anything was like squeezing blood from a stone. It was almost as an afterthought that she mentioned Colin's name.

'Oops, careful. You've spilt your tea,' she said fumbling for a tissue.

George put down his cup with a trembling hand. 'Can't say the name rings any bells. Why, what's he done?'

'Nothing as far as we know,' said Helen quickly. 'He was one of the Lifeplan sales reps.'

The last thing she wanted to do was to put doubts in George's mind. She started mopping up the spilt tea with a tissue. As she did so she her notepad dropped from her lap onto the floor. Despite his paralysis George leaned forward quickly to pick it up.

'What's this?' he said turning the pad around.

'It's nothing. A list of other Lifeplan clients,' said Helen holding out her hand. 'Can I have it back please. It's confidential.'

George reluctantly handed back the notepad, but not before he'd had a good look at the top sheet. Then he stood up. 'I think I'd like you to leave now.'

Well that was short and sweet. Helen hadn't even finished her tea. Not that she was complaining. She'd already decided George Smith wasn't going to be any use to her and had been wondering what excuse she could give to escape without being rude. Seems he saved her the trouble.

'Well, thank you for your time,' she said taking her leave on the doorstep and adding with heavy irony: 'And for the tea.'

George said nothing. He waited until she had reversed off the drive and disappeared up the road before shutting the door. When he turned round again his face was still contorted but not so much from the effects of his stroke this time as from fear and anger. Before he handed Helen back her notepad he had read the names on her list and one name had jumped out at him as familiar: Winifred Jonah.

Helen's next call was no more productive. Grace Lewis was slightly hyper with some kind of nervous twitch that made her yelp at the slightest thing - a cat that hopped from a wall behind Helen's head or a light that went on in the toilet of the house opposite. Her husband had been in the navy and had died at sea. She wasn't even entirely sure he was dead since his body had never been recovered from the merchant vessel he had been washed overboard from in a gale. He was presumed dead although she was constantly expecting him to turn up at any moment. She thought Helen might have been him. As for the insurance company that paid out on his death, she wasn't even sure of the name.

Helen's final call of the day was to a woman who lived at the furthest end of a long winding road on one of the new housing estates. By the time Helen got there it was getting dark, the woman took an age to answer the door and when she did she seemed reluctant to turn on the hall light. Helen was even more nervous about driving at night as she was during the day and the woman seemed so vague that Helen thought she was on a hiding to nothing. When the woman closed the door while Helen was still in mid-sentence she didn't have the will to ring the bell again. She just turned on her heel and marched back to the car.

Winifred didn't know what to make of the young woman who had just rung her doorbell. Did she want to see Colin - or *Babe* as she had begun to think of him? She could have done if she had asked. He was in his box as always. He was so quiet these days that Winifred often forgot he was there. When she remembered she would go in and comfort him. She would sing him a lullaby she had learnt at school:

He smiles within his cradle,
A babe with eyes so bright.
He beams most like a mirror
Against a blaze of light:
This babe with eyes so bright.

Her babe with eyes so bright. That's what he was, her Babe, and he did have such bright, beautiful eyes, though not so much these days. Tilley didn't seem to like him much as she once did. In fact, whenever Winifred opened the door to put his food down she would run into the kitchen not even bothering to steal his food anymore. It had taken a while for Winifred to realise that Tilley was eating his food, and not until she noticed how fat Tilley was getting. Never mind. Winifred would cheer him up with a little jig. She'd dance it in the doorway hopping from one leg to the other and pulling out her skirts as she did a little twirl. He couldn't understand the joke about her poor old cripple knees. She would tell him that joke but he wouldn't laugh. He'd just sit there in his wheelchair staring back at her. Winifred would sing and do her little jig and then she'd skip out.

'Night night Babe,' she'd say and softly close the door.

TWENTY-FOUR

WHEN the police finally got around to speaking to Helen she no longer wanted to speak to them. She'd had a long and tortuous telephone conversation with Frank, mostly *sotto voce* so that Muriel couldn't hear what they were talking about, comparing notes about their respective interviews. None of the eight names had produced any results and yet these were the most likely on Marcia's list to do so. Frank had rung Marcia to see if she had any suggestions as to which they might try next but all she could do was to repeat that the shortlist she had made for Colin had been drawn up from the one in Frank's possession and she could no longer remember which they were. He got the impression she didn't want to remember. As far as she was concerned she had done enough to salve her conscience where Colin was concerned and didn't want any more involvement. She told Frank she had found another receptionist job with a firm of solicitors and just wanted to get on with her life and forget all about Lifeplan. Frank pressed her to try and she did come up with one or two names, but he guessed from the way she did it that all she was doing was picking names out of the air to keep him happy. He didn't want to press her too hard in case he should need her again at some stage. So he thanked her for her help, wished her luck with her new job and put the phone down.

That was that. Their best lead so far had come to nothing. All he could suggest to Helen they do was go through the rest of the names one by one and repeat the process already begun. They did try a few more, but by the time they started getting accounts dating back three years and more it was clear they were getting nowhere. To add to their woes, the weekly ad in the newspapers was bearing a similar lack of results. They had come to a dead end.

'What do you think we should do?' Helen whispered into the mouthpiece. 'Go to the police?'

'With what? A list of names? Vague suspicions? I'm beginning to wonder myself if we've dreamt all this up.'

'Oh, don't give up on me, Frank.'

'I'm not giving up. Maybe we should try the police, but it'd be better if I went alone. I am supposed to be a journalist, although after the way my editor has been looking at me I wonder if I still have a job. The police won't connect me with Colin. And I know a few of the uniform crowd at County Headquarters, at least I used to. Maybe I can get something – I don't know. But anyway, best you stay out of it for now.'

With Frank's words still ringing in her ears, Helen confronted the two CID officers now sitting in her lounge. She still wasn't sure quite how they managed that. It must be some technique they learn, she decided. They wouldn't be sitting there at all if Muriel hadn't started to come down the stairs on their third ring to answer the door. Helen guessed who they were as soon as she saw them in the front garden looking up at the first floor window. Just ignoring them was never going to work. They'd seen Muriel's car on the drive and had even gone over to inspect it, so they knew someone was in. Helen could have kicked herself for not putting it away in the garage. Helen opened the door apologising profusely for the delay and saying she had been on the loo. Funny how the most innocent statement to a policeman sounds suspicious. But now they were in the house Helen wasn't going to offer them any refreshments. She wanted them to leave as soon as possible.

The man looked a shifty character. His eyes never remained still but kept roving around the room while he was talking, alighting on nothing in particular and yet managing to make Helen feel she had secreted the stolen diamond tiara along with the gold cufflinks and silver cigarette case inside the Ming vase that was standing on the escritoire. He said his name was Dart and that he was a detective sergeant with Norfolk CID. Without being asked, he showed her his warrant card. The woman he introduced as WDC Jolliffe. She was younger than Dart and sat on the very edge of her seat clutching a shoulder-bag and staring unblinkingly at Helen. She didn't speak, but whenever their eyes met her face broadened into a radiant smile that was at once friendly and menacing.

Dart said they had come in connection with the Lifeplan insurance swindle, no doubt Helen had heard about it. As part of their routine enquiries they were interviewing all former employees of Lifeplan and wanted to speak to Colin. Helen said quickly - too quickly - that he wasn't in and she didn't know where he was. She added by way of explanation that she was a student at university in London down for the holidays and didn't really live here. That bit at least was true, as was the next about not having seen Colin for nearly a year. In that case, said Dart, was there anybody else living in the house who they might talk to?

'Only my mother, and she's out at the moment.' Helen smiled apologetically.

A squeak on the floorboards above their heads gave the lie to that one. Helen continued to smile while desperately fighting the urge to look up at the ceiling. Dart had no such qualms and stared pointedly at the overhead light-fitting and then at Helen who had the sudden urge to scream.

'Do you have any idea when your brother might be coming back?'

If she hadn't wanted to know the answer to that question so desperately herself she might have laughed at its irony.

'No idea. Sorry.'

'What about your mother? When is she due back?'

'Today probably – *possibly*. That is, she often visits her sister - my aunt. In St Albans. And stays over. Oh - for weeks. Often.' Helen nodded emphatically.

'Is that where she's gone? St Albans?'

Helen gave a heavily shrug of her shoulders. 'Who can tell?'

Convinced that the notebook Dart was writing in was the self-same one in which the desk sergeant in the park had taken down her missing persons report, she was certain, when the man stood up, that he was going to read her her rights or whatever it was they read to suspects, and accuse her of everything from perverting the course of justice to stealing the Crown Jewels. Given her present state of nervous disintegration, Helen would have admitted to anything. But all he did was thank her for her time and said he was sorry to have bothered her. WDC Jolliffe even shook her hand.

Still feeling faint, Helen closed the door as carefully as her trembling hand would let her and watched from the dining room window as the pair got back into their unmarked car and sat chatting for a few agonizing minutes before firing up and slowly driving away.

'Do you think they believed you?' asked Frank when Helen phoned him.

'Of course not.'

'Did they give you the impression Colin was someone they *especially* wanted to speak to or just another Lifeplan employee?'

'I don't know how you can tell. They don't give anything away. No, nobody they particularly wanted to speak to.'

'Maybe he isn't special to them,' mused Frank. 'Maybe it's just us who think he is.'

'I thought you were going to talk to the police?'

'I am – I *will*. But I have a job, too you know - just.'

Helen calmed down. 'Sorry. I'm still on edge. What can I do while you're doing that?'

'I don't know. Sit by the phone. Colin may yet turn up by himself and all this could be something of nothing. We could all be having a good laugh about it this time next week.' He paused. 'By the way, how's Muriel?'

'God knows. She's still not speaking to me.'

'Well, we can't worry about that now. Let's concentrate on finding your brother. Once that's done everything else will fall into place. Trust me.'

'I hope you're right,' said Helen.

*

Winifred was shaking her dusty at the door when the dark blue Ford Anglia drew up. It took her a moment to recognise George not having seen him for three months. Apart from being on the ambulance when it came to collect her he'd never been to the bungalow before. She couldn't think why he was here now but something about the way he slammed the car door and the expression on his face as he came up the garden path suggested this was not a social visit.

'We've got to talk, Winnie.'

'Oh yes?'

'Yes. I think you know what it's about.'

George pushed past her. As he did so she looked quickly up and down the street. It was deserted.

They sat facing each other in the sitting room. Winifred placed both hands on the arms and waited.

George looked about the room, wrinkling his nose like a rodent sniffing out danger. 'He's been here, hasn't he? I can smell him.'

'Who?' said Winifred, alarmed.

'There's no need to pretend with me, Winnie. I *know*. He came to see me, too.' George stared hard at her face. 'How much did you give him?'

Winifred didn't reply.

'Four thousand five hundred he got off me. *Four thousand five hundred pounds*, Winnie. Practically every penny I had.'

A slight sob escaped from his lips. It was the first time he had spoken to anyone about it and the relief was almost unbearable. But Winifred continued to look back impassively at George.

'I don't know what you're talking about.'

George leaned forward and put his hand on Winnie's. 'Can't we talk about this? You should talk about it, you know? You'll feel better if you do, believe me. You can talk to me, Winnie. I'm your friend. We're in this together.'

Winnie shrank from his touch. 'What do you want?'

George pulled back, frowning. 'Want? I don't want anything except to warn you. About the girl.'

Winifred took a sharp intake of breath.

'Has she been here already?' said George seeing her reaction. 'My God, they don't hang about. She's in it too. With Brearney.'

'Brearney?'

'Yes, Colin Brearney. He's the ringleader but she's as bad. She thought I didn't know, thought I was stupid. But that's how they work, see? First one and then the other. Blackmailers never give up. They always come back for more.'

'Get away from me. What is it you've come for? I can't help you.'

'Don't be a stupid cow. We have to fight them.'

'I want you to leave,' insisted Winifred, rising. 'Now!'

George was about to protest but stopped himself. Something had caught his eye. Tucked down beside the sideboard was a brown leather briefcase. George recognised it instantly. Ignoring Winifred's entreaties, he staggered over to the case dragging it from its hiding place.

'It's his!' he gasped rubbing the bag. 'The Brearney boy. 'I knew it,' he giggled. 'I *knew* he'd been here.'

He started fiddling frantically with his good left hand trying to force open the fastener but he couldn't quite manage it with one hand. Angry and frustrated, he went down on one knee in order to try to get a better purchase determined to get the lock open.

'Put it down!'

Shocked out of his reverie, George looked up to see Winifred standing over him holding the shotgun. She stood rock solid, legs apart pointing the gun at him.

'I said, put it down.'

'But it's got my money,' beseeched George. 'It's in here, I saw him put it in here.'

Winifred raised the gun and levelled it at George's head. 'Drop it or I'll kill you.'

But George was in too much pain to care. He set his features grimly and raised his chin.

'No!'

He staggered to his feet clutching the briefcase to his chest. Reason had left him. If Winifred was going to stop him she was going to have to shoot him. Turning his back to her he staggered towards the street door, opened it and went out into the night.

Winifred returned to the kitchen and flopped down wearily in the chair. She looked about her at the familiar objects that had followed her from home to home, from the farmhouse where she had been born and brought up to the flat she had shared with Albert and now to this bungalow. All she had ever wanted was a home and some security. And now it was too late. The world was closing in. She had retreated as far as she could until she had reached the place where no-one could threaten her ever again. That place was her mind. Within that strange world very little threatened her. Colin Brearney and all the rest did not exist. They were replaced by other creatures of her own invention. And now it was time for them to disappear too.

In resignation, she dropped the gun to her side, went to the bathroom door and, steeling herself, she opened it. Colin's eyes stared back at her.

'Sorry Babe. Time to go.'

*

After turning his flat upside down, Frank finally managed to find his Press Association card inside the lining of an old jacket where it had fallen through a hole in the pocket. Locating some of the officers he used to know at County Headquarters was proving rather more difficult. Those he did find didn't have a lot of time to talk to him beyond a friendly slap on the back and asking him what he'd been doing with himself since they last saw him.

'Oh, you know, the usual. Married, had a kid, widowed.'

'Yeah, yeah,' they joked.

He seemed to have chosen a bad moment to pay a social call. Something big was about to happen, some panic that no-one had time to tell him about.

'Is it the Lifeplan swindle?' he yelled after one passing sergeant.

'No flies on you are there, Frank?'

Frank fell in alongside him. 'Does that mean you've made an arrest?'

'Wait for the press release, Frank.'

'So it's true, you've arrested Slaker and Kerney?'

'Wait for the statement.'

'Well then, just tell me this: Was anyone else arrested other than Slaker and Kerney?'

The sergeant stopped and faced him. 'Who would you suggest?'

Frank shook his head and grinned. 'Just fishing. Where were they picked up? Johannesburg?'

'*Johannesburg?*' The sergeant looked at him as though he had lost his mind. 'Not unless it's now the capital of the Argentine. They were picked up at Heathrow Airport boarding a flight for Buenos Aires.' He walked off shaking his head in disbelief.

Frank didn't know if it was good news or bad. He hadn't found Colin, but it looked as though he wasn't with the two Lifeplan managers. Not that he ever thought he would but it was as well to make certain. It was something to tell Helen, at any rate. He'd learn more once the statement was released to the Press about the two managers' arrest.

On his way out of the station he passed the public notice board by the entrance. One fuzzy black-and-white photograph caught his eye and he read the description underneath. He went closer and read it again. Was it possible? He searched his pockets for the list Marcia had given him. Damn, he'd left it in his desk. The little hairs on the back of his neck prickled as he copied down the details from the notice board and hurried back to his office at the *Norwich and Ipswich Times*.

'What are you looking for?' asked a female colleague walking by his desk and carrying a mug of coffee.

'My street map of Norfolk towns,' said Frank frantically turning out drawers. 'Some sod's nicked it.'

The colleague went off, came back, and dropped a map on his desk. 'Here, borrow mine.'

Frank looked at the label. 'This *is* my copy.'

The colleague sipped her coffee and smiled apologetically.

Frank quickly located what he was looking for. He checked his note. He checked it again. He'd been right. This he had to tell Helen straight away. But as he reached for the phone on his desk, it rang.

TWENTY-FIVE
Friday 31st October - All Hallows Eve

'COO-EE! It's only me, dear. I'm not stopping, I only popped in to bring you this.'

Mrs Goffe held up a chromium-plated steel chain with the black leather loop at one end.

'Sorry I haven't brought it before now but Mr Goffe had it in his workshop. I wouldn't have found it at all if I hadn't gone in there looking for something else.'

Mrs Goffe put the dog lead down on the kitchen table. She looked at Winifred.

'Are you all right, dear? You don't look too well.'

'I'm fine,' insisted Winifred.

'If you say so.' Mrs Goffe sniffed and then cringed as a loud bang went off outside. 'Ooh, those blessed bangers! There ought to be a law! Bonfire Night isn't till next week and already the kids have started. I don't think my nerves are going to last till the fifth. I'd keep Tilley and Rover well indoors until it's over if I were you, Winnie. Have you thought of a name for him yet?'

'Babe,' smiled Winifred.

Mrs Goffe tested the name. 'It's different, I'll say that. Tell you what,' she tapped Winifred's arm. 'I'll make us a nice cup of tea, shall I? Cheer us both up.' And without waiting for an answer, she started filling the kettle.

She tossed her head in the direction of the bang. 'Mr Goffe blames the Americans for all this. They go in for Halloween in a big way over there. We learnt all about it when we were in

California last year. Do you know where that is, Winnie? California? Other side of the world. We went to see our Brenda. She's married to one of them.'

Mrs Goffe warmed the pot, put three spoonfuls of tea in and put the kettle on to boil again. Then she got two cups and saucers out of the cupboard.

'I suppose you can't really blame the kids what with Guy Fawkes and Halloween being so close together. It's all Trick-or-Treat round our way these days. Whatever happened to Penny-for-the-Guy that's what I want to know. Can't be bothered making them, that's the truth of it. And you try giving them a penny! You get a mouthful back, I can tell you.'

She paused from pouring the milk for a moment and thought.

'I did see one guy the other day, quite a good one, too. Two boys had it in a pram by the bus stop. Very life-like, it was. I thought it was so good I gave them five pee. But listen to this,' she set the cups and saucers down on the table. 'As I held the money out for them to take, guess who took it? The guy! It was another boy dressed up, see? Gave me quite a start I can tell you. But you'd never have known. Marvellous disguise!'

Mrs Goffe poured the tea then stood over Winifred, arms akimbo.

'Well, I suppose it's you we've got to get dressed up next. Are you still going to this fancy dress stomp tonight? I think you should make the effort, you know. Get you out a bit. Stuck here alone in the kitchen all day long, it's not healthy. Has anybody been in to see you? Like the warden, for instance? No, thought not.' She shook her head and then smiled. 'I tell you what: you have this.'

She produced from her bag an enormous orange pumpkin.

'I was going to give it to my Maureen to make a pumpkin head - you know, hollow it out, cut out the eyes and a mouth. I could do it while I'm here, if you like. Would you like that, Winnie? Hm? A Pumpkin head to put in the window? Have you ever made one before? They do it all the time in California.'

Winnie stared at the grotesque deformed fruit.

'It's easy enough to do.' assured Mrs Goffe. 'Here, I'll show you. Got a knife?'

Ten minutes later the head was finished.

'There,' said Mrs Goffe breathless from the effort but satisfied with the result.

Winifred eyed the hollowed-out head with its triangular eyes and grinning mouth.

'All you need is a candle and Bob's your uncle! Now, what are we going to use for your witch's costume?' She snapped her fingers. 'I know just the thing.'

She went out and came back with the heavy brown velour curtain that had been hanging in front of the bathroom door.

'I'll put it back when I come on Tuesday if you really want me to,' said Mrs Goffe holding the curtain up to examine it critically in the light. 'I see you've taken that lock off the bathroom door. Does that mean you want me to clean in there again now? I just popped my head round the door to have a look. I must say you've kept it well. Spotless, I'd say.'

Winifred grinned and continued to stare at the pumpkin head that grinned back at her.

'Yes, I cleaned it out.'

'Save me a job,' smiled Mrs Goffe. She gathered up the curtain material and threw it around Winifred's shoulders. It hung about her like a cape with just Winifred's round head poking out of the top. With her wild white hair and the light silhouetting through it, she looked not so much like a witch as a manic Buddha.

'There,' said Mrs Goffe. 'What do you think?'

Winifred touched the material then began to laugh, slowly at first, then her mouth spreading into a toothy grimace and her whole body quivered and wobbled beneath the cape.

'That's it!' exclaimed Mrs Goffe. 'Now you're getting the idea. You look like a real witch now!'

The two women laughed and laughed as a whole barrage of fireworks went off outside and a rocket screamed overhead.

*

Detective Sergeant Dart and Woman Detective Constable Jolliffe of the Norfolk Serious Crime Squad returned to the Brearney home shortly before five o'clock. This time Helen was determined not to let them in. She didn't know whether Muriel was in the house or not and she didn't much care even if she came waltzing up the garden path while they were standing at the door. She'd done nothing wrong and didn't see why she should be intimidated by them. Still, she was relieved that she'd had the foresight this time to have put Muriel's car away in the garage.

In the event the two officers didn't try to inveigle their way in as she had feared. They were content to stand on the path outside the door and exchange pleasantries. Unconvinced, Helen stood on the doorstep with the door pulled behind her and said if they were still looking for Colin he hadn't come back and she didn't know where he was. Perhaps it was because it was the truth that they thanked her for her help and added – almost indifferently - that in the light of recent developments they would not be returning. But they would like to speak to Colin should he eventually surface just to clear up one or two loose ends. That was all.

Helen was suspicious. 'Developments? What developments?'

'It's all in the paper,' smiled Constable Jolliffe who hitched her bag over her shoulder before walking off down the path with Sergeant Dart.

Helen hadn't seen a newspaper in days and had had to change channels whenever the news came on the television in order to conceal it from Muriel, which meant she was also kept in the dark. She wished with all her might that Frank would phone. And then, as if by magic, he did.

'Frank! Where are you? I've been going frantic here.'

'I'm in a phone box outside *The Garden House,*' he said. 'It's a pub on the Ipswich road just south of Caisterbury.'

'What are you doing in Caisterbury? I thought we'd finished with all that. Hang on a minute.'

She put the phone down in the hall and peered up the stairs. Muriel's door had been ajar but now it closed. Helen went back to the phone cupping her hand round the mouthpiece.

'Listen,' she hissed into the mouthpiece. 'The police were here again just now. They said something about developments. What's been going on?'

Frank explained about the arrests of the two Lifeplan managers and that Colin hadn't been with them.

'Well, that's good news - isn't it?'

'I'm not sure. But a couple of other things have happened since then that you ought to know about. First, you know the police found Colin's scooter?'

'That was weeks ago.'

'I know, but I've only just discovered where they found it. There was a picture of it on the notice board at the police station. I can't think why we didn't think of this before. It was in Caisterbury *two streets away* from one of the addresses on Marcia's list.'

Helen caught her breath. 'My God. The old woman, the batty one. Winifred something.'

'What?' said Frank irritably. 'I didn't hear that, a car went past.'

'I said can you remember the address? I don't have my list anymore.'

'Yes – wait a minute.' The pips went. She waited while Frank put some more money in the

279

coin box. 'You still there? I haven't much change left.'

'What was the other thing?' said Helen urgently. 'You said there were two things.'

'Oh yes,' said Frank. 'I had a phone call while I was at the office. The visa came through.'

Now Helen really was exasperated. 'What are you talking about, Frank? I thought we'd agreed Colin didn't have a visa.'

'Not Colin's visa. *My* visa. For Kenya. They're letting me back in.'

Helen caught her breath. 'Does that mean you're leaving?'

'Well, yes. But not yet. There's no urgency.'

She bit her lip. 'Yes, of course you must go. Your son...Charles.' Then she added in a rush, 'Can I come with you?'

There was a pause on the line. 'I suppose. In theory. If you were my wife. Will you marry me Helen?'

The pips went again. Frank out some more money in the box.

'That's my last.'

'Okay,' said Helen with resolution.

'What was that? Did you say yes you'd marry me?'

'No! Yes. Look, stay where you are, I'll come to you and we can go together. To see this old woman, I mean, Winifred Jonah - I've remembered her name. Give me the address again. Hang on.'

She ran into the kitchen and grabbed her pad and a pencil.

'Go ahead.'

She wrote down Winifred's address at 9 Ethel Smyth Close, Caisterbury.

'See you in half an hour.'

'Right,' said Frank.

'Right,' said Helen.

She waited holding the phone and hearing his breathing on the other end until the pips went again and then the line went dead.

Helen laid the pad and pencil down thoughtfully on the table next to the phone. What had she done? She thought she might just have got engaged to me married. Then suddenly galvanised, she went into the sitting room to find the keys for Muriel's car. But they weren't in the geranium pot. She hunted everywhere she could think of but she couldn't find them. She didn't hear Muriel come down the stairs or quietly close the street door after her. She did hear the garage doors open but by then it was too late. She rushed out into the street just as Muriel, deaf to Helen's pleas, was kangaroo-hopping the Morris along the road and disappeared round the corner.

Returning to the house Helen tried to go over in her mind what Muriel could have overheard of her conversation with Frank. Frank had said he was at the Garden House, but had Helen repeated the name for Muriel to hear? She couldn't remember. If she did, that was obviously where Muriel was going. Perhaps she had better ring the pub just in case and warn Frank that Muriel might be on her way to confront him. But instead of picking up the phone she picked up her pad lying next to it. The top page, with Winifred Jonah's address on it, had been torn off.

TWENTY-SIX

WINIFRED was preparing to go to the Halloween party. She did so mechanically not really understanding why she was doing it except that it seemed to be expected of her and that was somehow important.

About an hour ago, two small children had interrupted her preparations by knocking at the door. It was still light. She'd opened the door to two diminutive harridans dressed as ghouls. Winifred listened impassively to their chant of "Trick-or-treat, Trick-or-treat" for a few choruses before closing the door and going back to what she was doing. She didn't hear her empty milk-bottles being smashed on her doorstep.

Later, the phone rang. No-one phoned her anymore. She let it ring twenty times, thirty. They were persistent that was for sure. She didn't answer it. Eventually the caller had rung off.

Then there was another knock at the door. Who was it this time? By now it was dark outside and the light on the street silhouetted a slim figure against the glass panel standing very close to the door. Winifred wondered if it might be the little harridans again. Maybe it was that woman again, the one who came round before and who George had warned her about. In either case she didn't want to speak to them. But the knocking persisted. Whoever it was, Winifred would get rid of them. Gingerly, she unlocked the door and turned the handle.

The door fell in and Winifred tottered backwards under the force as Muriel stalked into the hallway holding a revolver in her outstretched hands.

'Where is he?' she demanded.

'Who?' gasped Winifred.

Muriel tossed her head and laughed. 'You know perfectly well who. I know he's here, so don't try to deny it.' She waved the gun about in what was meant to be an intimidating manner.

Winifred held her breath. Who *was* this woman? She wasn't the girl who came before. But she said she knew – she *knew* about the creature, her Babe.

'He's not here any more,' she panted desperately, her hands closing and opening involuntarily. 'He's gone.'

Muriel curled her lip. 'So, you admit he was here?'

'Yes.' Said Winifred.

'I thought so. Where is now?'

Winifred glanced involuntarily at the bathroom door.

Muriel caught the surreptitious look. 'Gone is he?' she snorted, and pointed the gun towards the bathroom.

It was then that Winifred made her move. She leapt at Muriel who with a cry fell to the floor. The two women grappled in the dark. There was a bang - and then all was still.

George was angry and frustrated. He had been cheated again, this time by someone who he thought was his friend, someone who was as much a victim of Colin Brearney as he was, someone he had tried to help.

Having managed to keep hold of the briefcase, George had waited until he got home to search its contents. But his money was not there. He ripped the thing apart as though by sheer anger he make the case spill out his money, to no avail. He threw the case across the room in disgust and cringed in despair. He had been so close once again. There was only one possible answer: Winifred had removed it herself. She had threatened him with a shotgun but she had let him go too easily. Yes, Winifred Jonah had his money. That was why she had let him leave. He'd brooded for two hours on what to but then finally made up his mind. He got into his car and drove back to Ethel Smyth Close.

George got there just as Muriel's gun went off. Almost immediately a series of fireworks exploded in the next street, but George was close enough to have heard the difference. He hurried up the path dragging his lame leg behind him.

The door to the bungalow was ajar but there was no light on. He stumbled blindly into the hall. The smell of cordite assaulted his nose. He called out Winifred's name but there was no reply, no sound at all. He fumbled for the light switch but couldn't find it. Putting out his hands like a blind man he stumbled on. Something lying in the hall tripped him making him cry out. Then from out of the gloom a figure slowly rose up. A hand reached towards him. George screamed. There was a click and light flooded the scene: Winifred was leaning against the wall, one hand still on the light-switch while the other held a revolver. On the floor at her feet was another figure: a woman.

George gasped when he saw her. 'Who is she?'

'I don't know,' said Winifred.

'Is she dead?' he whispered.

Winifred looked. Blood was seeping from beneath Muriel's pink cardigan and was slowly forming a shallow pool.

'I think so.'

George whimpered, sank to the floor and scrambled as far away from the body he could. But there was no time to do anything. Through the open door she saw the ambulance drawing up to take her to the Halloween dance.

'I must go,' she said.

'You can't leave me!' yelled the terrified George. 'Not with that!'

'Shut up!' barked Winifred.

She bent close to his ear. 'Now listen to me,' she hissed. 'This is your fault. If they find her they will blame you.'

'No,' George moaned shaking his head.

'Yes. But you'll be all right if you do what I say. Wait till I'm gone and then leave. Do you understand?'

George nodded. There was no time to say more. She could see Brian getting out of the cab. Grabbing her walking stick she switched off the hall light went out pulling the door to behind her just as Brian was coming up the path.

'Careful, Winnie,' said Brian putting out his hand. 'There's a load of broken glass on your doorstep.'

'Am I late?' said Winifred, breathless.

'No, you're all right,' said Brian. 'It's only just gone seven. You're the last. The others are on the back.' He opened the back door to the ambulance as the sky lit up with a flare of fireworks.

'Oh, Winnie!' said Martha Hodge when she saw her. 'Where's your costume? You haven't got a costume!'

Martha was dressed elaborately in a green flowing garment with a dozen bangles on each spindly arm and her nails painted black. A half-moon tiara sat on her grey curls, her lips green and black eye-shadow covered each lid. She looked suitably hideous. Crouching next to her was an even more horrible sight. Sadie Collins was draped head to foot in black gown with a classic pointed witch's hat on her head. Her face was painted completely white except for the wart on the very tip of her nose which had been picked out in green. Beneath the witch's hat her hair had been died red and was scooped up into two horns and lacquered severely into place. She, too, had painted her fingernails black.

When the two saw Winifred they cackled excitedly at her and at each other and practised their writhing technique. They really were quite accomplished hags.

'That's George Smith's Anglia, isn't it?' said Brian. 'Is he coming, too?'

'He's not feeling well,' said Winifred.

'Aow shame!' protested Sadie. 'I was looking forward to seeing 'im dressed up as Merlin.' She cackled again.

Brian settled Winnie in her place and strapped her in. Then he raised the steps of the ambulance and closed the back doors.

Inside the bungalow, George held his breath until he was sure the ambulance was gone. He did not know what to do. Was Winifred right? Could he be implicated in the death of this woman, whoever she was? Surely the thing to do was ring for the police, or an ambulance, or both. All other considerations were of secondary importance. Winifred said the woman was dead but George no longer trusted her. He needed to see for himself, but in the darkness he was disorientated. He didn't know where the phone was or even the light switch. He wasn't even sure where the woman was any longer. Oh, why had he come?

He managed to scramble onto to his knees and began to crawl in the direction he thought the door was, but all he did was come up against yet her wall. Now all he wanted to get out but he was disorientated and confused. His heart was thumping and his head pounded. He staggered to his feet and inched his way cautiously in the direction he thought the door was but whichever way he went the walls felt the same. Oh mother, he prayed, please help me. If only he could find the light switch. The pounding in his head was getting louder as blood throbbed behind his eyes. He thought he saw the glass panel in the street door but then it vanished again. A draught of night air. Surely he was near the door now?

Then his foot caught on something on the floor and he stumbled. The woman? He managed to suppress a scream. The thought filled him with in revulsion but forced himself to peer down through the darkness. He thought he heard a sigh. Then two green eyes peered back at him, he stumbled again and George could hold back his scream no longer.

'No!' he cried and fell backwards and then he screamed again as someone grabbed his arm. Light flooded the hall again blinding George for a moment as he turned in terror to come face to face, not with the dead woman as he thought, but with a man. George screamed a third time as unbelievable pain surged through his head and his right leg collapsed beneath him.

Drew caught him as he fell and laid him heavily onto the floor. The right side of George's face was distorted and he gurgled incomprehensibly and reached out with his left arm. Drew followed the gesture and gasped as he saw Muriel's body. Laying George gently down on the floor he went straight over and knelt next to Muriel's body but he could see he was too late.

'Who did this?' he demanded, but it was too late for George, too. The massive stroke that had taken away his power of speech finally broke the slender thread that held his life together.

All week as the story about Lifeplan had been unfolding in the newspapers and on television Drew had grown more and more troubled. He remembered the money Winifred had given him, money that the newspapers said she couldn't have because it had been embezzled by those two Lifeplan managers, money in any case she could not both have given him for his van and bought all those things - the curtains, the wallpaper, the new furniture - as well. Something was very wrong. Susan had told him not to look a gift horse in the mouth but to be thankful for small mercies, but that was not Drew's way. He had to know.

Earlier he had phoned Winifred. He let it ring and ring but got no reply. That was not like Winifred. Susan said he was making a fuss about nothing, that there was bound to be a simple explanation. Then she remembered. Didn't Winifred say she was going to a party? A Halloween party? But that wasn't until the evening, Drew said. He remembered the ambulanceman saying he would collect her at seven o'clock. Susan had just shrugged. But Drew could not let it rest. He brooded all afternoon until his wife finally lost patience with him and told him if it bothered him so much to go and see her himself if it was the only way he was going to be satisfied. And so Drew got into his van and drove the twenty-one miles to Caisterbury. But nothing could have prepared him for what he found when he got there.

The old man had had some kind of seizure, Drew guessed, but the woman had been killed by a single bullet through the heart. He found the gun beneath her body. It looked like an old wartime service revolver and he was surprised it even worked by the look of it. But whose revolver was it? Not Winifred's, that was for sure. The old man's, perhaps? But who had shot her, and why? Who *were* these people? He needed desperately to talk to Winifred.

But first things first. He had to ring the police - it was too late for an ambulance. He looked at his watch. Ten past seven. Winifred would be at the Halloween party. If he phoned the police now and explained what he had found and left straight away he could get to her and at least be with her when they arrived. He couldn't let her face them alone.

He stood up to use the phone in the sitting room. But as he went out into the hallway he noticed Tilley behaving oddly. He had been too preoccupied to notice her before, but now he realised that ever since he arrived she had been scratching at something in the corner of the hallway. It was just a door to a broom cupboard, and yet Tilley seemed determined to get inside. Curious, he stood watching her for a moment. Then he turned the handle of the door and opened it.

Drew had to cough and took step backwards. It was the same smell he remembered from last time he was here only this time it was much worse and he had to put his handkerchief over his face. What could possibly be causing such a stench? No dead rat, that was certain. Inside the cupboard were the usual paraphernalia of brooms and cleaning materials - but something else as well. Hanging from the bar was what looked like a tailor's dummy. It was suspended by its neck on a dog-chain, its body made of some kind of brown curtaining material and its head an enormous orange pumpkin. Drew snorted nervously. It was ludicrous enough to be almost comical. He was revolted by it and yet drawn to it. He touched the dummy's shoulder and it started to revolve slowly on its noose. As the pumpkin face came round Drew saw the two slits cut in the flesh for the eyes out of which stared two more eyes. Dead human eyes.

Drew spun round and held his mouth to stop himself from vomiting. He felt nauseous and it took several moments before he could stop retching. But as his breathing returned to normal he knew he could deceive himself no longer. He might be able to convince himself that Winifred had nothing to do with the death of that woman and the old man, but this was different. Only one person could have done this. And with that thought he was overcome with pity. Pity, of course, for that thing back there that had once been human. He didn't want to begin to speculate on who it was or why this terrible thing had happened. Winifred was still alive. What torments did she, did any human being have to go through to be driven to this? Whatever they were Winifred had borne them alone. With shame he remembered that even he had blamed her. He fell on his knees.

But there was no more time for pity. He could see what would happen next. Winifred would be arrested, tried and then incarcerated either in a prison or, more likely, a mental institution for the rest of her life. They could never let her out. He couldn't let that happen. He knew what he had to do.

Drew phoned his wife to say goodbye. Then he phoned the police and gave them the bare facts of where to come and what to find when they got there. Finally, picking up the shotgun he checked that both barrels were full. Then he laid the gun on the passenger seat of the van and slowly drove out of Ethel Smyth Close.

UNHOLY INNOCENCE

May 1199. Richard the Lionheart is dead and his brother John has just been crowned King of England.

John travels to St Edmund's abbey in Suffolk to give thanks for his accession. His visit coincides with the murder of a twelve-year-old boy whose mutilated body bears the marks of ritual sacrifice and martyrdom. This isn't the first time such a thing has happened. Eighteen years earlier another child was murdered in the town in similar circumstances.

Abbot Samson needs to find out if this is indeed another martyrdom or just an ordinary murder and appoints the abbey's physician, Master Walter, to investigate. Walter discovers a web of intrigue and corruption involving some of the highest in the land but unbeknown to him his own past holds a secret which will put his life in danger before the final terrible solution is revealed.

"Wheeler engages the reader's interest from page one and doesn't let go...A book which will appeal to historical novel fans..."
Eastern Daily Press

BLOOD MOON

November 1214. King John has returned to England having lost his empire to King Philip of France. Humiliated and desperate for support, he again travels to Bury St Edmunds where Abbot Samson has died and a battle is raging among the monks over who will be his successor.

In the midst of this there arrives in the town a seemingly inconsequential young couple and their maid. The wife is heavily pregnant and gives birth in the night to a baby daughter.

But then the maid is mysteriously murdered and it is soon apparent that the family is not all that it appears. With rebellion looming, abbey physician Walter of Ixworth is drawn once again into investigating a murder and a conspiracy that threatens to engulf the country in civil war and ultimately leads to the final nemesis that is Runnymede and Magna Carta.

DEVIL'S ACRE

January 1242. Brother Walter of Ixworth is dying. He is an old man but the prospect of death does not disturb him - indeed, he welcomes it to meet with old friends and see God in the face. But before he finally joins the heavenly host he is determined to solve one last mystery that has been plaguing him for decades.

But there are dark forces afoot that want to frustrate his efforts and are prepared to go any lengths to keep secret events that even now could disturb the government of England, even murder.

In his mind Walter returns to those far off times when Abbot Samson took him on a bizarre journey away from the comforting familiarity of Bury Abbey and into the wilds of barbaric Norfolk where the abbot's power is limited and met by a far greater one in the guise of the Warenne family of Castle Acre - or as some still choose to call it, the *Devil's Acre*.

CPSIA information can be obtained
at www.ICGtesting.com
Printed in the USA
LVOW04s1812111115
462088LV00031B/1199/P